"Buy it. Just do it. You'll feel so much better once you have."

SABRIEL

"The plot is so intriguing, I couldn't stop myself reading!"

ULTIMATE BOOKWORM

"I highly recommend this rollercoaster of a read!"

SEAN

"Loved it, basically read it all in one go."

LOUIS

"If you haven't read these books already—give them a go."

DAISY

D0259824

WELCOME TO THE
SHAPESHIFTER UNIVERSE

- - -

A NOTE FROM THE AUTHOR

When Dax Jones first showed up in my head, skinny, dark-eyed and restless, I had no idea how much he was going to mean to me. As a journalist I interviewed a lot of celebrities. They were fun—but the best stories I ever got were not from celebs. They came from normal people whose lives had been suddenly changed in some unexpected way. They were the *real* deal.

So Dax showed up kind of ordinary. And yet not. His name is a clue. Half ordinary, half extraordinary. I wanted to write about supernatural stuff but not in a wifty-wafty way. I wanted to imagine it as I believe it really would be. So I played the 'what if' game. What if you changed shape one day? Just shifted into something else? In this world—here, today. *Right now* while you're reading this. Look around you. How would people react if you were suddenly holding this page open with the claws and snout of a fox?

Ready to find out? Just sit back and enjoy the ride . . .

For my boys

OXFORD
UNIVERSITY PRESS

Great Clarendon Street, Oxford OX2 6DP

Oxford University Press is a department of the University of Oxford.
It furthers the University's objective of excellence in research, scholarship,
and education by publishing worldwide. Oxford is a registered trade mark of
Oxford University Press in the UK and in certain other countries

British Library Cataloguing in Publication Data
Data available
ISBN: 978-0-19-274608-5

1 3 5 7 9 10 8 6 4 2
Printed in Great Britain by Clays Ltd, St Ives plc
Paper used in the production of this book is a natural,
recyclable product made from wood grown in sustainable forests.
The manufacturing process conforms to the environmental
regulations of the country of origin.

THE SHAPESHIFTER

RUNNING THE RISK

ALI SPARKES

OXFORD
UNIVERSITY PRESS

1

The girl in grey fled across the forest—and the shapeshifter followed.

She had been running now for thirty minutes or more, and fine beads of sweat were forming on her upper lip. The creature was closing on her; she could tell. Beyond the faint chorus of birdsong she could hear only her own breathing and the thud of her expensive running shoes, but she knew without doubt that it *would* spring any time now. It would spring and she would be beaten. Suddenly, with a scream of surrender, she hopped up onto a fallen log and spun around to face it, hands on her hips, breathing hard. The creature leapt.

It landed softly on the log beside her without so much as a clip of its claws. It sat, curled its tail about its forepaws and regarded her with a grin which looked somewhat startling on the face of a young, red fox.

Lisa hurrumphed with annoyance. She sat down heavily and picked some leaf litter from the instep of her running shoe. 'You have a natural advantage, Dax!' she said grumpily. The shadow of the fox flickered and curled and now Dax was checking out his own shabby trainers. 'What, with a hundred and thirty quid running shoes against these old scruffs?' he teased. 'Don't beat yourself up. You really had my lungs working this time. You're definitely getting faster.'

'Hmm.' Lisa pursed her lips and folded her arms. He hoped she wasn't going to stay in this mood. Running normally made her feel good, even when he beat her, which he always did when he was DaxFox—as DaxBoy he wouldn't have a hope. Lisa was the fittest twelve year old he'd ever met.

'What's up?' he asked, knowing he probably wouldn't get an answer.

'Nothing,' she muttered, getting to her feet.

'More messages?' Dax peered at his friend. A well-turned-out blonde (babe in waiting, was what Gideon called her), she didn't look the type to be bothered by more than where her next new outfit was coming from, but, sadly, Lisa had had more to be bothered by in the past twelve months than most people get in a lifetime.

'Nothing!' she said, with that warning note in her voice.

'Come on—let's run back to the others now,' said Dax. 'I won't shift this time—so it'll be fair.'

She glanced at him. 'You're just humouring me!' she said, but with a flicker of interest. Lisa *loved* winning.

'Yep!' agreed Dax. 'But you've got to give me a head start!' He bounded off the log and away back through the trees and Lisa gave him precisely five seconds before giving chase. She passed ten seconds later. Good. He hoped the extra sprint might do the trick for her. When the messages came they could sometimes be very dark and unpleasant. Often they came with visions. Not that you'd ever know with Lisa. There was no airy-fairy stuff about the girl; no spooky voice and fluttering eyelids.

When Lisa got a trance the most you'd be likely to notice was a slight rubbing of her left shoulder while she stared hard at something. Sometimes she got a cold patch of pins and needles there. 'Like they're leaning on it, yakking in my ear!' she'd complained once.

Frankly, Lisa did not hold with the spirit world communicating with the earthly one—especially when the spirits chose to communicate through *her*, which they'd been pretty much queuing up to do since last summer. There was no question that her unwelcome gift was a useful one, though. Lisa could find lost things in a matter of seconds. You only had to ask and she'd raise her eyes to the heavens and mutter at you, close them briefly for a second, and then tell you exactly where your missing sock or key or bar of chocolate was. Sometimes she'd get fed up and say testily, 'Don't be so lazy. Have a *look* before you ask me!' She always knew when they hadn't.

Finding lost *people* was the less pleasant part of her ability. Usually they were *dead* lost people, or worse, people who were lined up for being dead fairly soon.

When he finally caught up with her, she was back with Gideon and Mia in the clearing. Gideon was still lying on the grass, half asleep in the warm spring sun, his freckled arm covering his eyes, a ladybird settled on his tufty fair hair, and Mia was sitting up, her arms around her knees, peering at Lisa closely. Going by Mia's expression, the extra sprint hadn't helped Lisa much. Lisa was flopped down on her knees, dragging the scrunchy band out of her hair and shaking her ponytail loose with a growl of frustration. 'Eeeesh! I *hate* these ones!' she cursed. She worked her fingers rapidly across her scalp and then down onto her left shoulder, as best she could reach. Mia moved across to her and touched her head gently with one hand. Within a second Lisa's face softened and the stressed lines across her brow eased away. Even two metres away, Dax could feel the soft cool pulse of Mia's healing.

'She all right?' he panted, skidding to his knees next to the two girls.

'She's fine,' muttered Lisa, grumpily, but not with much aggression. 'It's just this wifty-wafty, faffy, fluffy, blit-blat . . . ' she tailed off, but they all got it. The thing Lisa hated most about her ability was the vague bit; the sense of *something* about to happen, but no firm idea of what.

'Is it one of us?' asked Mia.

'Yes—no—I don't know!'

'Well, stop grinding your perfect little teeth—you know it won't help!' said Gideon from under his arm. 'The more manic you get about it the harder it'll be to work it out!'

Lisa's eyes flashed and Dax thought serious trouble was brewing for Gideon.

'Gideon! You could be a bit more sympathetic,' reproved Mia, narrowing her lovely violet eyes at him.

Gideon sat up and grinned. 'You know that doesn't help either,' he said. 'She's like a bad-tempered dog with nothing to bite. Let her get it out of her system—go on, girl!' He threw an apple from the remains of their picnic at her and Lisa caught it with an athlete's reflexes and hurled it hard back at him. Gideon let it get to within a centimetre of his face and then stopped it dead with a blink. But he gave an obliging yelp, as if the fruity missile had smacked his nose, instead of floating obediently in front of it.

'Again?' he said, scooping it out of its stasis and offering it up for another throw.

Lisa shook her head. 'No . . . it's no good if it doesn't actually *hit* you. It's much more satisfying when you squeak for real.' She got to her feet. 'Thanks anyway, though, Gid. Let's get back now. Dad'll wonder where we all are, and I expect Marguerite is doing a gigantic tea.'

Dax and Gideon exchanged pleased smiles. Marguerite's teas were fantastic. In fact, everything at Lisa's mansion was fantastic, from the mosaic-lined swimming pool in the beautiful seven acres of gardens to their huge guest bedroom with its own bathroom; Mia had one to herself! Marguerite was a fantastic cook and housekeeper. The butler was pretty cool, too. Lisa's dad was rich, and there was no hiding it. Lisa was oblivious to it; she'd been born into wealth—but the evidence still made Dax, Gideon, and Mia gasp.

'Imagine what it's like, living at Lisa's *all the time*!' marvelled Gideon as they walked along the winding woodland path back to the estate. In fact, the wood itself was on the estate and also belonged to Lisa's dad. 'No wonder she didn't want to come to Cola Club. She's got her own horse and everything!'

'Her dad's all right, too,' said Dax.

Maurice Hardman was an intelligent man who had made huge amounts of money in something to do with metal. He was delighted to have his daughter back for the holidays and found it hard to refuse her anything—even having a bunch of peculiar kids coming to stay.

'Well, *my* dad's all *right*,' muttered Gid. 'But he *never* gives me ponies and swimming pools! It's not fair!' He did a pretend pout.

In fact, he'd had a great time at home in his little house in Slough, telling his dad about their adventures and trying so hard to lift the television with his mind power, that in the end his dad gave up trying to watch the sport (telekinesis plays havoc with the reception) and went off to get the radio.

It made Dax feel a little bleak to think about the good times his friends were having with their fathers. As members of the Cola Club not one of them had a mother still living, which made their dads doubly precious. Dax had only seen *his* dad for a total of four days since last summer. All through his first term at Tregarren College in Cornwall, he'd been expecting his father to pay a visit. He'd had letters and postcards saying that Robert Jones *would* come—soon! Couldn't wait to come and see everything, and find out how a son of his had been selected by the education department of the *government*, no less, to go to this very special school.

Of course, he didn't know that the college was filled with something *other* than extra brainy students. These students were all Children of Limitless Ability, each with extraordinary powers, such as telekinesis, clairvoyance, healing, illusion and—in Dax's case only—shapeshifting. Across the course of eighteen months, one hundred and nine had been found and safely gathered in.

If Dax's dad *had* visited, he would have gone through a careful briefing procedure before being allowed on to the campus. Strictly speaking, no student should show off his or her powers outside the carefully controlled 'Development' classes, but it was impossible to keep it from spilling out from time to time. As you wandered down the crooked cliffside paths of Tregarren, towards the churning blue-green Cornish sea, you were apt to see at least one or two students floating tennis balls or *fading out* in front of your eyes or staging small fireworks displays from their open palms.

But Dax's dad, like only a handful of other dads and some stepmums, knew nothing about his child's ability. And he'd been at home for so short a time, sharing those precious hours with his wife, Gina, and their daughter Alice, that there had been no opportunity to say anything.

Gideon noticed Dax's expression and made a guess. 'Didn't get much time with your dad, then?'

Dax sighed. 'If you added up all the minutes we spent without Gina yakking in one of his ears, or Alice sticking to his back like a limpet in a pink dress—about half an hour, I reckon.'

'Half an hour should've been long enough!' chided Gideon. He couldn't believe that not one of Dax's small family knew about his ability. 'You've got to tell him, Dax! He should know!'

'Yeah—well—like I said, it was minutes at a time, and, Gid—how do you say it? By the time I'd nearly got to it, Alice was back in with another revolting doll to show him, or Gina was . . . *rubbing his shoulders*!' Dax made an expression of revulsion. He had no love for his stepmother, who had been given to slapping and poking and locking him outside in the garden for being 'ungrateful' or showing 'attitude'. Of course, as soon as Owen Hind had shown up, telling her that Dax was 'very special' and selected for education at a top college, at no expense, Gina's regard for him had magically changed.

He didn't know what was worse, when he'd first arrived home at Christmas. The Gina of old, who was spiteful and unloving—but at least honest about it (when his father wasn't looking)—or the shiny *new* Gina, who put extra chips on his plate and called him 'darling'. Of course, she couldn't hide her calculating expression from him *all* the time. She was trying to work out how she and her daughter might benefit from having a 'genius' in the family. She was also afraid. Afraid that Dax, now grown an inch taller and looking so well on the Cornish sea air and the good college food, might one day tell his father about his stepmother's nasty little ways back in the old days.

Of course, Gina didn't know that Dax sometimes *thanked* her for her mean nature. He often wondered if, without being locked out one autumn afternoon, he would ever have achieved his first *shift*. He'd got trapped and panic stricken in the hot garden shed and that was how it all began. At first it seemed that only extreme fear, panic, or anger could bring it about. An encounter with two bullies who'd beaten up his school friend Clive was the next occasion when Dax had shifted. Wild with fury, he'd sent them on their way bloodied and screaming. That same day, Owen had arrived.

Gideon was still pulling a face about the idea of Gina rubbing Robert Jones's shoulders. 'Yuck!' he said, sympathetically. 'But, Dax—hasn't he *asked* yet? Isn't he curious? I mean, mate, you're quite bright and all that, but anyone can see you're not a genius! You're not weird enough. Well—not in the *normal* way.'

Dax wondered how somebody could be *normally* weird, but he let it go. 'No—he's never asked. In fact, you know what? If I had to use one word to describe what my dad is like around me, it would be . . . *nervous*.'

'Nervous? You're kidding!'

'No.' Dax stepped carefully over an ivy-clad log, falling back from Mia and Lisa up ahead. His face was a mask of control, but Gideon could see the hurt and anger glimmering behind it.

'What does he have to be nervous about? Especially if he doesn't know!'

'He doesn't just *not* ask me. He *never* asks me. When I

talk about Cola Club, even about the football pitch or the lido, or Owen's woodsman lessons, he sort of grins and nods—and then ruffles my hair and changes the subject. It's . . . weird. Like he *does* know something, but doesn't want to admit it.'

'You should just say it!' declared Gideon. 'Just look him in the eye one day, and say, "Dad—I turn into a fox." That'd make him pay attention.'

Dax gave his friend a *look*.

'*Well!*' protested Gideon. '*Show* him then! That'd really make him stop in his tracks.'

Dax sighed. 'Maybe it's best that he doesn't know. I don't think he could handle it. All the time he was there he seemed, I don't know, so sort of . . . *brittle*. He didn't even look at me very much. And when he got called back to the rig early last week (just like—ha! ha!—he did at Christmas), he seemed happy to go.'

Up ahead, Lisa had stopped again, and Mia was looking at her with some concern.

'What is it?' said Gideon, as they caught up. Lisa was rubbing her shoulder again and looking very stressed.

'They just won't let *up* today!' she said, through gritted teeth. 'I'm going to have to run some more.' Lisa sometimes found that the only way to shake off the nagging of the spirit world was to outrun it. Dax felt a sudden shiver of concern. Whatever it was that was trying to get Lisa's attention was snagging at his too.

'You two go on back,' he said to Mia and Gideon. 'I'll run with Lisa some more.'

They nodded, understanding, and headed for the distant gates to the Hardman house.

'C'mon,' said Dax and shifted. He fled away fast, giving her something to chase and planning to let her catch up soon. It worked. She gave an indignant yelp and was after him in a second. After a few minutes he slowed down and waited for her to catch up and they settled into a companionable jog.

Any idea what it's about? he sent her, but she shook her head.

It's just too vague, she sent back. *I think . . . Uh-oh! Watch out, Dax—DOG!*

Dax cursed himself for not paying more attention to his fox senses. Dog had been *clearly* on his radar for at least two minutes, but he'd thought it was some way off. It was, in fact, but as the Labrador and its owners breached the top of a small hill they could see clearly down the track to where the twelve-year-old girl was running side-by-side, talking telepathically with a fox. To shapeshift back to a boy now would be a disaster; he would be seen. So Dax simply slid into the undergrowth like molten red metal and Lisa ran on up the hill, trying to look as if she'd never been in the company of wildlife.

I'll see you back! Lisa called in his head, and Dax moved swiftly away from the main path until he could no longer hear or smell the humans and the dog. He paused under the waxy green leaves of a rhododendron bush and considered whether to shift back into DaxBoy and rejoin Lisa on the path, further up, or whether to just run back as DaxFox. It would be laborious to run back with Lisa in boy form. Dax was quite fit as a boy, but always felt horribly heavy and lumbering compared to his fox state. Whenever he ran he would instinctively want to shift. Sometimes he felt more natural as a fox; a thought which worried him slightly.

As he pondered, a sudden hot burst of fox sense tore through him. Dax felt the fur on his back prickle and a pulse of *terror* suddenly hit his nose. The scent of another fox, in fear of its *life*, was so strong that Dax literally jumped into the air, catching his ears on the tangle of branch and leaf above him. At that moment a blur of copper streaked across the woodland in front of him. It was a vixen and as she shot past, he picked up one message in her terrified head, which she'd sent directly at him. 'GO!' Dax didn't hesitate. He leapt away after her, sensing that something truly terrible was in pursuit.

Dax was very fast, but the vixen was faster. He saw only the flash of white at the end of her tail before she was gone from his view. Behind him he could feel a rumbling force; the very ground was singing with it, as if a fast and deadly train were approaching on a track. He couldn't work out, at first, what it could be. The dog perhaps—but no, it had to be more than that. Most dogs were daft, lollopy things, standing almost no chance of outsmarting a fox and often only wanting to play.

Most dogs, said a cold voice inside his head, as he continued to pelt headlong through the springy branches, leaving a flurry of disturbed leaves in his wake.

But what about pack hounds? As soon as the thought formed Dax could smell them, perhaps half a mile away. Hounds. Horses. Humans. Three awful aitches. Now, with a cold, sick horror creeping around his throat and shoulders, he could hear the guttural baying of the dogs. Dogs who wanted no toy, no game, no choc drops. Dogs who wanted blood. *His* blood.

2

The sound of a horn drove the baying into more of a frenzy. There was no doubt the hounds had the scent. Dax froze for a second, wondering which way to run. After the vixen, or in another direction? In the end, simple fox instinct took him after her—perhaps she was heading for a good hiding place. He shot away through the undergrowth, her scent still warm on his snout, even though she was nowhere in sight.

Dax fled down a steep embankment of ash and elder, his paws barely making contact with the earth, he moved so fast. He remembered that hounds found it hard to follow a scent through water, and he could smell a stream not far away, coursing through the lowest part of this woodland. He ducked under some brambles, feeling the jagged thorns catch at the points of his ears and sending several smaller creatures scattering in terror as a predator thundered through their world.

He had to flatten almost to his belly to clear the underside of the brambles, which knotted themselves along the woodland floor for several yards, but a glint of white and brown movement caught his eye as he scrambled out from under the thorns—the water! Dax plunged into it, sending a small tidal wave across the shallow pebbly bed of the stream. Too noisy! He could *feel* the hounds respond and veer in his direction; he could smell the excitement in them. Dax turned west and ran along the stream, one second up to his ankles, and the next almost to his haunches and swimming when the silt and pebbles sank suddenly downwards. The swimming was agonizingly slow.

Shift! Shift! urged a voice inside his head, which he recognized as Owen's. It made perfect sense, but Dax was terrified of stopping, and although he tried to push the shift, it wouldn't come. He needed to stop—breathe evenly—make it so—and he wasn't sure that he had time. He could clearly hear the dogs crashing through the brambles now, and the excited shouts of the hunt not far behind them. The fear that pulsed through him was unlike anything he'd ever experienced. It made his insides feel like water and his head cloud with confusion. One strand of his strength seemed to buckle and fall away from him, giving in. If another strand—and then another—followed, he realized he would sink into the stream and prepare to die.

This awful weakness might have been his end, if he hadn't spotted a hole in the bank. It was a foxhole, no doubt about it. A tight one, which maybe the hounds could not get through; he didn't know. The vixen had not gone into it; there was no recent scent. Dax didn't pause. He hurled himself from the water, straight into the hole. The smooth darkness of the earth wrapped around him and he scrambled deep, deep, and deeper into it. Small roots brushed his snout and ears and gave him a clawhold, as he pushed further into the ground. Gone to ground. That was what they called it. Dax's fear chased him, snapping at his tail, but the earth, its feel, its smell, and the dull echo of it in his ears, called to him, held him, was more comforting than any bed.

In a few seconds the narrow tunnel opened into a small chamber, just large enough for Dax to turn around in. There was old grass bedding on the floor and a few small animal bones. It was a fox's home, no question— but thankfully not currently occupied. A fight with a territorial dog-fox was the last thing Dax needed. He scanned the hole, using all of his senses in the gloom, to work out if there was another exit. There wasn't. It was a dead end. If the hounds could make it in, it would be *his* dead end.

Dax turned his tail to the earth, backing into its curve, and trained his eyes on the pale light seeping into the foxhole from the winding tunnel he'd charged through. He guessed he was perhaps seven metres into the ground. He panted hard, almost silently, but in his head his heartbeat thundered. The hounds were in the stream now—and horses too. He could hear hooves making heavy, metallic contact with the submerged stones, and before them, the splashing of dozens of paws. Men were shouting. Dax froze. They were approaching the entrance to his hiding place, and if they'd made it this far along the stream, the hounds would surely snatch his terrified scent as he'd bounded into the hole in the bank.

His only hope now rested on the size of the hole, and the size of the hounds.

In all his life, Dax had never heard anything as petrifying as the noise the hounds made at the entrance to the foxhole. Their baleful barks began to lift in register and urgency. They knew he was here. They knew he was trapped. Their throats filled with howls of joy and they began to scrabble and tear at the earth with their paws and then one of the huntsmen gave a shout of triumph. 'Got 'im!' Still, no hound had breached the entrance. Perhaps there was a chance. How long would they keep trying? How long would he have to exist in this state of awful, awful, dark fear?

Suddenly there was a metallic, grinding clunk. The huntsman had evidently pulled back the hounds and was digging in towards him. Dax frenziedly tried to work out whether the tunnel widened out past the mouth, or if it remained the same dimensions right down to the chamber. A cold ache in his belly told him that his whiskers had recorded a widening, not far inside. His first few seconds had been a scramble—and then he had run more freely. He knew it was so. The huntsman need only dig for a minute or two, and then the hounds would be able to course inside, and drag him out for a thirty second exhibition of how a fox dies.

God alive, Dax! Shift! bellowed the voice in his head again. Dax didn't know if it was his subconscious, taking on the voice of Owen—or whether it really was Owen, in touch telepathically. He hadn't been in touch telepathically before, but it wasn't impossible, particularly if he was with Paulina Sartre.

It was beside the point. Dax couldn't shift. The hole around him was simply too small. If he tried he would crush himself to death. His blood coursed urgently in his ears, as if making the very most of its last few circulations. Soon it would ebb out of his throat, a final outgoing tide. Already Dax felt his life force spiralling down, spent. He couldn't move, although, caught in that defeated downward spiral, his spirit still beat and bawled and fluttered like a moth against glass, hopelessly crushed down by impossible odds. This was not how it was meant to end. He had been meant to *do* something. Why escape the murderous intent of his old Cola Club principal, only to die, dragged from a hole in the ground, torn and screaming?

The digging stopped. There was a shout and the pent-up fury from the hounds swelled to a cry of united delight as they were released back towards the hole. They would come one by one and the first would have the prize of dragging him out; he'd be borne out into the day, to be sent back into unending darkness in a few bloody seconds, while his fellow humans watched and cheered and leant down to touch the mess to smear on the foreheads of the younger ones.

He could hear the slobbering of the lead hound as it squeezed itself along the dark tunnel. He could smell the residue of old meat on its teeth and salty sweat on its neck. Dax closed his eyes and sent a final message, in case Lisa could pick it up.

Gone to ground. Not coming back. So sorry.

There was a thud on the back of his neck. Now the canines would puncture his skin. This did not happen. Dax snapped his eyes open, and saw that the hound had not yet reached him. It was still some feet away, wriggling and slavering towards its prey. What? There was another thud, and Dax realized it was a hard clod of earth that had hit him. The metallic sound was back—but this time above him. The hunt must have worked out how far back he was, and decided to dig down, to be sure of getting him. Even as this thought struck him, so did the force of more earth, piling down over his head and neck. With it came a sudden flash of light, and the glitter of small pebbles tumbling past him.

The hole widened and widened. *I could shift now! I could shift!* thought Dax. But could he? He leapt towards the hole, understanding that his last hope was a slim one. The huntsman would almost certainly be upon him with the edge of his spade before he had managed to shift. But as he sprang upwards, he felt the hot breath of the lead hound on his hind paw, and realized there was no better option.

As soon as he was clear of the earth he was seized. A fist brutally grabbed the back of his neck and a man hauled him in towards his chest, pinning the fox's writhing body to it and forcing his other forearm tight across its throat. Dax kicked and fought and turned his snout to catch a final bite of his attacker. Any moment a dozen hounds would be tearing him apart—he could at least make a final impression.

But three things occurred to him at once as his teeth sank into the man's hand in the scramble that followed. One was that there were no hounds—they were all still underground, or trying to get there. The second was that there were no other humans. They, too, were some distance away, impatiently stirring up the water of the stream as they waited for the gory cabaret to start.

The third thing was that the blood on his tongue was familiar.

Owen didn't shout when he was bitten. He was too busy running. He was a well-built man and the fox was light. He thundered up the steep bank and pounded through the woodland faster than Dax had ever known him move. After perhaps two minutes of hard sprinting, during which Dax was so shaken he thought his teeth might fall out, Owen dropped him unceremoniously on a pile of leaves and bellowed: 'DAX! SHIFT! And get a BLOODY MOVE ON!'

In an instant Dax sank under the weight of his human body. He saw Owen's shocked face flood with relief. He tried to get up but instead slumped into the leaves. He tried to speak, but his teeth were chattering so hard, he couldn't. His throat felt like petrified wood and his whole body shook. Death had not come and, for a few seconds, Dax had forgotten how to live.

Owen knelt down in front of him and began to roughly check him over for wounds. Apart from a few scratches from his dash through the brambles, there were no signs of what he'd just narrowly survived. Dax felt his eyes roll up. He wanted to sleep.

'No, Dax! You can't!' said Owen, trying to pull him up. 'We have to go. The hunt is coming.'

He was right. Dax's ears had become muffled with shock and exhaustion, but he could still hear the hunt moving in their direction. He tried to get up again and managed to get to his knees this time, before sinking back. Owen made a sharp noise of frustration and hauled him up on to his shoulder. Dax dangled awkwardly, and then managed to hang on around Owen's neck. Owen walked a few yards to a sturdy oak tree and then leaned Dax up against it. 'Try to stand,' he said. 'You need to be as human as you can be. We can't outrun them. Dax!' He grabbed Dax's face, which had been lolling sleepily to one side. 'Dax! Focus! Don't drift off. You're not out of danger—you reek of fox! Now—wake up and *climb*!'

Dazedly, Dax looked up and saw that there were branches within easy climbing reach. At any other time he would have been up them in seconds, but now he felt as if his limbs were encased in concrete. Owen gave him a hard shove. Dax opened his chattering teeth to explain, and then the hunting horn sounded again. It shot some hot urgency into his veins, and immediately, instinctively, he turned and scrambled into the tree. 'Up! Up!' urged Owen, through his teeth.

He was only just in time. As he reached the fourth branch, three metres off the ground, a river of brown and white dogs flowed along the path and curled into the clearing beneath the oak. They made straight for Owen, but ignored him, leaping instantly at the tree. Owen turned and looked angrily at the chief huntsman, who was approaching on a chestnut mare, holding a small whip and dressed in a red coat.

'I thought you lot were banned,' growled Owen. 'Get your dogs off me.'

'Special licence, my good man. We're drag hunting—and sometimes a fox stumbles accidentally in the path of our dogs,' shouted the hunt leader, over the baying, as more mounted hunters cantered up behind him followed by some on foot. 'Now, be a good chap and move over. It must be in that tree. It's injured. Kinder to finish it off.'

'There's nothing up that tree except my nephew,' said Owen stonily. 'Foxes can't climb trees.'

'Wouldn't put it past them—they're clever little curs,' said the hunt leader, leaning forward in his seat and favouring Owen with a tight smile. 'Or more likely, your nephew's got a soft spot for vermin and has it stuffed inside his shirt.'

'Dax! Can you see a fox up there?' called Owen, and Dax leaned down from the branches and yelled, 'No. Nothing up here except me!' The hunt leader looked up, startled.

'You're hiding him! You little mongrel! Get down from there!'

'Don't speak to my nephew that way,' said Owen. The hunt leader gave him a mutinous look, but he could hear the steel and the command in his adversary's voice. His horse stamped uneasily.

'Get the dogs off!' he suddenly snapped, and several

of the hunters on foot ran across and hauled the frustrated hounds away from the foot of the tree. The hunt leader pushed his horse forward and turned it in a tight arc at the foot of the oak. 'You, boy!' he called, his voice flat with distaste. 'Drop that fox! It's vermin! It's already killed half the henhouse at Cooper's farm. We've been asked to do a cull.'

Dax leaned down towards him and stretched out his arms, anchoring himself with his legs. 'Look!' he said. 'No fox!' It was plain to see, and the hunter cursed.

There was a shout, some way behind him, and everyone turned, excitedly. The hounds streamed away as fast as they had arrived, leaving the foot hunters in their wake. The hunt leader curled his lip at Owen, then turned his mount and thundered away after them. The foot hunters stood for a moment, and then began to follow as Dax slid down from the tree and into a sitting position at its roots. Only one, briefly, held back. He was staring hard in the direction of the others, but then he turned and looked from Dax to Owen. His face was familiar to Dax—and the hint of a sneer in his smug smile was *very* familiar. The last time he'd seen his old enemy was at college the previous term. Owen shook his head slowly and the boy pursed his lips, but nodded and then turned to follow the hunt.

In the madness of the last half hour, Dax realized the weirdest thing had to be meeting Spook Williams.

3

Owen half carried, half dragged Dax back to the house. Dax kept insisting he could walk—and then his knees would crumple and he'd be sinking down into the earth again. The last of his energy had deserted him along with the hunt. Now he couldn't seem to get his heartbeat under control and wave after wave of coldness broke across his neck and shoulders, making his hair prickle and his jaw tremble. More than anything, he longed to sleep. The effort of getting back to the house was almost more than he could stand.

Owen kept pulling him up, talking to him, checking him, and Dax kept nodding and getting up again and saying he was fine. In fact he thought he'd never been less fine. Just saying the words was almost beyond him, and each laboured syllable came out with a gasp. Finally he stumbled into some bushes on the edge of the Hardman estate and was violently sick.

Afterwards, covered in a cold sheen of sweat, he curled into a ball at the foot of the nearest tree, until Owen hauled him up again. 'C'mon, Dax. We're nearly there,' he said. 'You can make it.' Dax had stared at him dully and finally Owen had sighed and just picked him up. Steady and determined, he carried the stupefied boy up the long gravel drive to the Hardman house, until Evans, the butler, and Marguerite came running out to help. They swiftly got him up to his room and Marguerite ran a warm bath while Evans helped him out of his filthy, spattered clothes. After Dax had shakily got himself into the warm water, Owen sent Gideon in to sit with him.

'He's in shock,' he heard Owen say to his friend. 'He needs warming up, then he needs some sugar water, which Marguerite is getting; then he needs to sleep.'

Gideon came in, looking scared. He sat down on the cork-topped chest beside the opulent roll-top bath and peered at Dax. 'You all right, Daxy boy?' he said, with a wan smile. Dax nodded vaguely. He was feeling better in the warm water, but all right was still some way off. 'What happened?' asked Gideon, leaning on the curved enamel and biting his lip.

Dax said, 'Fox hunt.' It came out raspy and thin. Gideon looked appalled.

'You mean—you mean they—?' But then Marguerite came bustling in.

'Enough of this!' she said, shooing Gideon out. 'You're meant to be keeping an eye on him to see he doesn't drown, not bombarding him with questions!' She was a strong woman, and had Dax out of the bath, dried, and in bed in less than two minutes. He lay back against the crisp, smooth linen and drank the tepid sugar water through a straw, as he was bidden, and, just as soon as he could, pushed the cup onto the bedside table, closed his eyes, and sank gratefully away into the soft grey of sleep.

* * *

He slept for twelve hours, waking along with the others before breakfast the next day. Sitting up in bed, his mind fumbled for something *big* which had happened yesterday. He ached, as if he'd been in a fight.

'How you doing, Dax?' came a yawny voice and he glanced across to where Gideon was stretching luxuriously under his quilt. His fair hair was sticking up in all directions. 'Owen said you were in shock, yesterday. You still in shock, or can we get breakfast now?'

Dax laughed at his friend's tender enquiry. 'No—I'm not in shock now.' He wrinkled his brow as the events of yesterday drifted back to him. 'Is Owen still here? What was he doing coming here anyway? He was the last person I expected to see.'

'Dunno,' said Gideon. 'He wants to talk to us both after breakfast apparently. Good job he did show up, though, eh? You were about to be a dog's dinner!'

Dax grinned, but a shiver ran through him. Gideon sat up in bed and fixed him with an eager look. 'Come on! I've waited all night to find out what happened.'

Dax told him about leaving Lisa on the path, and seeing the vixen shoot past—and then the whole unlovely episode of his frantic chase, ending in the fox hole.

'Why didn't you shift?' demanded Gideon.

'At first it just happened too quickly,' explained Dax, rubbing his head as he tried to remember. 'It was just fox instinct to run. And, you know, it's always harder to come back to being DaxBoy than it is to shift to DaxFox. I would have had to concentrate—and there was no time. Then, in the fox hole, there was no space. I would've buried myself alive.' The shiver passed through him again and he clenched his fists to keep it in check. The flashes of memory that were returning to him were not at all pleasant.

'So then what?' asked Gideon, bouncing slightly. He loved a good story.

'Well, I thought I'd had it. I tried to send Lisa a sort of goodbye message.' He paused, gulped, feeling even now the residue of despair. 'But I didn't get anything back.'

'Nah—she couldn't send to you,' said Gideon, unexpectedly. 'She was working too hard sending to Owen.'

'What? What was happening? Tell me.'

Gideon bounced a little more, clearly pleased to get involved with the story. 'Well, Lisa was running up the drive when Owen arrived and just then she got one of her funny moments—you know—all whooo and whaaa.' Gideon made weird wavy movements with his hands and rolled his eyes about. 'So Owen asks what's up and then she starts screaming about you and trying to run back into the woods.

'So then Owen makes her stand still and tell him what she's getting, and she says you're going to be ripped into bite-sized pieces by a pack of dogs and that you're jammed in a tiny hole and can't move. So then Owen makes her shut up (which takes some doing!) and sit down and *send* the location to him, while he grabs a spade from the gardener and runs into the woods.'

'Send? To Owen?' broke in Dax. Lisa could send telepathically to *him*, but he didn't know anyone else who could 'receive' her.

'Yup!' said Gideon. 'Owen can pick it up! I never knew either! Anyway, she sits and sends—while Owen runs into the woods to dig you out, finds the spot, hopes for the best and whacks the spade in. Lisa gets this "last goodbye" from you and sits here in hysterics (we'd all come along by then, and all we knew was that she was kneeling on the lawn with her head in her hands, bawling her eyes out) and then—bam!—Owen gets lucky and digs up a fox! Mate—you should've seen the state of you when he got you back!'

Dax grinned, ruefully. 'Come on,' he said, getting out of bed. 'I'm starving.'

Down in the conservatory, breakfast was being served. Marguerite was delivering bacon, eggs, and fried bread to Lisa's father while Mia tackled some fresh fruit salad and muesli and Lisa toyed with a boiled egg.

'Ooh! Bacon for me, please!' beamed Gideon. 'And two eggs, fried bread, baked beans, mushrooms, and tomato. And tea! Same again for Dax!' Marguerite beamed her approval at them both and hurried back to the kitchen.

'Where's Owen?' asked Dax.

'Oh, he was up ages ago,' said Lisa. 'You know what he's like. He wants to see you and Gideon in the library when you've had breakfast.' Lisa was concentrating hard on her egg, but now she looked up at Dax. Her face was serious and Dax realized that he was not the only one having aftershocks from yesterday's events. He smiled at her sympathetically and sent *I know. Are you OK?* She nodded and sent back *You?*

'I could eat *three* breakfasts this morning, I reckon!' said Dax, by way of reply, and she smiled, with some relief.

Mia, sitting next to him, reached across and touched his shoulder, and at once a wave of relaxation broke across him. 'You look a lot better now,' she said. 'What a scare that was! No harm done, though.' Dax nodded and reached for the teapot and a cup. The healing was great, but he still wished they would stop talking about it.

'I'll have that damned hunt arrested if they come on to my land again,' commented Maurice Hardman from behind his newspaper. 'They're not licensed on *my* estate!' It was reassuring the way he took the Colas' adventures in his stride. After the initial confounded stare when Gideon first floated his small suitcase along the hall—and the cocoa choking fit he'd suffered when Dax unexpectedly shifted one evening—Maurice had remained remarkably calm.

'He does a great underwhelmed,' Gideon had observed.

Mia, of course, had a more understated gift, but she had already vanquished one of Maurice's migraine headaches during their stay and he was in deep awe of this. 'Saved me from two days in a darkened room,' he had muttered, gratefully. 'You're a wonder!'

Breakfast was excellent. Bacon, fried to perfect crispiness, and freshly seared mushrooms began to revive Dax considerably. He felt the horror of yesterday ebb further from him and happily shoved the memory into the darkest recesses of his mind. It was just another Cola adventure. Time to move on. Lisa seemed to be of the same mind, because she had pulled out of her reflections of yesterday already, and was once again haranguing her father about getting her pony down to Cornwall.

'You could organize it, Daddy! You *could* make them agree, if you really wanted to, you know it!' Lisa stabbed her spoon sulkily into her soft-boiled egg, and it made a squelching sound, like something nastily injured.

'Sweetheart, for the last time, you *cannot* have Chrysler stabled at Tregarren,' said her father, with far more patience than she deserved, thought Dax.

Lisa lifted her stubborn chin and narrowed her eyes across the table, challenging her father. Maurice Hardman simply shook his newspaper and began studying the financial pages.

'Look—I don't mean he has to be *on* the college grounds!' insisted his daughter. 'Couldn't we find a stables in Polgammon and have him kept there? Then I could get out to him every weekend—or at least every *other* weekend. It's not fair that I don't get to see him since my head went wonky. It's not my fault!' Lisa's mouth actually began to pout at this point, but her friends knew better than to get involved. They went on earnestly seeing to their breakfast.

Her father sighed. 'Darling—your head did not go *wonky*. You were blessed with an extraordinary gift, that's all.' He rested the paper on one knee and slid a slice of buttered toast into his mouth, before giving Lisa a tight smile which said 'Enough!'

Lisa's expression suddenly changed to one of concentration and then to a faint smugness. 'Daddy,' she said, 'Grandma tells me you were *always* like this as a child, too! Unbearably calm and always *right*!'

Maurice Hardman choked slightly, and Gideon leaned around and helpfully thumped him on the back. Lisa smirked.

'That's out of order!' her father complained, as soon as he'd swallowed. 'You tell *her* that ganging up on me is unbecoming for a dead woman. I get no peace!' Once again he picked up his paper, shook it, and stared determinedly at the financial section.

'Give him a rest, you brat!' said Gideon, pouring himself a second cup of tea. Fortunately Lisa was giggling now, evidently being entertained by some story about her dad as a little boy, delivered by her late grandmother, so she didn't round on Gideon.

'Do you ride cross country, then, Lisa?' he asked. 'Jumping over all the fences and stuff, like that girl in *Black Beauty*.'

'Sometimes,' said Lisa, coming back to the living. 'Of course, I *used* to go out riding a lot *more*,' she added waspishly, but her father did not react. 'With some of the girls from other families.'

'Did you ever go hunting?' asked Dax. He felt Mia stiffen beside him. He knew it was an unfair question, but he had to know. Lisa stared at him and then back at her plate. She waited until they'd all begun to look at each other uncomfortably. Dax eyed her carefully, trying to read her thoughts, but she wasn't sending any.

'I might have done, once,' she said. 'There is a very strong hunt fraternity around here, and I knew quite a lot of other girls who were going to join. But that was *before*. Before Cola Club and before you, Dax. Anyway, they wouldn't let me join now if I tried. I'm a thief, remember.'

When Lisa had first begun to get her powers, nearly two years ago, it had started with the 'finding'. She had been able to tell her school friends where things they had lost were hidden. She didn't know *how* she knew—but she was always right. Eventually, her classmates decided that Lisa was stealing their things and then revealing where to find them. It was the only explanation they could find. Lisa's popularity plummeted. If that wasn't bad enough, she then 'saw' the death of one of those former friends. When it came true in every detail she had spiralled into despair.

A top psychiatrist was called in to find out why Maurice Hardman's little girl, who wanted for nothing, was in a state of such abject fear and misery. By now the spirits had got in touch, clamouring for her help in contacting the living, showing her unhappy scenes of how they met their death. Endlessly they nagged her to warn, to reveal, to explain—to inform of hidden wills or treasures; even to send search parties out for their bodies.

Even though Lisa had kept her mouth firmly shut in the psychiatrist's sessions, *something* must have got through. Paulina Sartre had known where to find her, and had collected her only a week later. Her friends, her expensive school, her fantastic home, her pony— everything was to be left behind since her head had gone wonky.

'I'm glad hunting has been made illegal, at least,' said Mia. She was a committed vegetarian. 'Even if people are still trying to get away with it, at least it's sending the right message. All animals should be protected from stupid human beings.'

'My heart agrees,' sighed Gideon. 'But my stomach can't.' He stuffed another slice of bacon into his mouth and munched it, favouring Mia with a meaty, unsympathetic grin.

As soon as they'd eaten, Dax and Gideon went to the library, where they found Owen sitting on the shiny leather sofa, leafing through an old book on natural history. Owen smiled at them and looked Dax up and down. 'You look a lot more human today!'

Dax felt embarrassed. 'Thanks for digging me out,' he said. 'Sorry I was such a wuss on the way back.'

Owen shook his head. 'I was amazed you could walk at all. You were in deep shock, you know. I would've been, too.'

'Did I dream it, or was Spook Williams there?' asked

Dax, and Gideon looked startled. Clearly, this was the first he'd heard about their old adversary.

'He was there,' said Owen. 'Forget about it, though. It's over.'

'What?' spluttered Gideon. 'Spook Williams—in the hunt?!'

'He was on foot,' said Dax.

'In the hunt?' demanded Gideon, again, and Owen sighed.

'Yes—he was there! He lives near here, don't you know? Now—please—we have to get going so will you forget about yesterday and pay attention? I came to take you back to Tregarren, Gideon.'

Gideon swung around from staring at Dax, to stare at Owen instead.

'Me? I thought you'd come for Dax. What do you want me for?'

'Well, I think it would help if Dax came too,' said Owen, folding the book shut and returning it to its shelf. 'I'm sorry to deprive you of your last couple of days here, but I wanted to get you back before the term started properly.'

'But why?' asked Gideon.

'There's someone you need to meet.'

'Who?'

Owen regarded Gideon for a moment. 'You'll find out when we get there—now don't,' he raised his hand, 'go on about it. You'll find out soon enough. Just go up and get packed, both of you. We leave in half an hour.'

4

Of course, Gideon kept badgering Owen on the way back to Tregarren College, from the back seat of Owen's jeep, where Gideon and Dax sprawled throughout the three hour journey. Owen, though, drove on and resolutely refused to say anything more. Eventually Gideon gave up, although he was excited, and slightly worried, Dax suspected, about the mystery visitor. It wasn't his dad, or anyone he knew; that much he'd managed to work out.

He lolled across the back seat and then started worrying Dax about the situation at home again.

'I reckon you should just do it one day—in front of them all!' he said, grinning at the idea of it. 'I'd *love* to watch Gina's face! And Alice's.'

Dax sighed, but had to laugh. Gina would probably set the garden hose on him.

'Did she keep her promise about getting all those dolls out of your room?' asked Gideon.

'Nah, of course not. It's not my room any more. It's the Dolls' Annexe.' As soon as Dax had left for Cornwall the previous autumn, Gina had swept into his dank old room, repainted it lilac and given it to her daughter. Now, whenever Dax went home, Alice *would* take the dolls off his bed (which now wore a frilly pink quilt), but they remained everywhere else; a vast crowd of pink-cheeked, dimpled, wide-eyed, ever-smiling statues. Whatever Dax did, he had a silent, eerily happy audience. He had been very glad to leave it behind when the invitation to Lisa's had arrived. He'd be happier still to get back to his own bed at Tregarren—the only one that had really felt like home.

Once they'd crossed into Cornwall, the unique scent of the county began to work on Dax. Since shortly before he'd first begun to shapeshift into a fox, his sense of smell had been acute. He could usually tell precisely who'd come into a room, without looking. He also scented *moods* on people—fear, anger, violent intent— also happiness and good intent. It was a useful tool at Tregarren College, with so many strange and often conflicted children. Most of the students there had now come to terms with the earthquake effect their powers had had on their lives—each of the one hundred and nine Colas there had developed their extraordinary gifts within the last two years, and all were aged eleven or twelve when the 'changes' began—but a handful were still troubled and displaced. It helped to have some extra sense of these children, and Dax had sometimes been able, in subtle ways, to help. When Darren Tyler had appeared to be as chirpy as the rest of his class of illusionists, Dax alone had smelt the misery wafting from the boy. He had been able to talk to Darren until the boy opened up about his terrible homesickness, and then Owen had arranged special leave for Darren's gran to come and stay in Polgammon for a weekend. Darren had perked up amazingly, and now smelt as happy as the other Colas.

The other benefit of his fox sense of smell was that Dax could tell how close they were drawing to Tregarren, and with every mile that passed the tide of his happiness rose a little higher. His first term at the college had concluded in a terrifying struggle over 150 fathoms of mineshaft—and ended in the death of the college's first principal—but Dax still loved it, even though charming Patrick Wood had turned out to be a killer, ready to dispose of anyone who threatened his career. Dax had nearly been disposed of.

Once the fuss had died down and the steady and gifted Paulina Sartre had taken over as principal, nobody had seemed to miss Patrick Wood. Their 'liking' for him had turned out to be nine-tenths hypnotism. Dax's happiest moments had occurred beneath the granite cliffs which protected the small campus and its students from the outside world. At Tregarren, Dax felt hope and confidence grow in him—and his time there with Gideon, Lisa, Mia, and Owen meant everything to him.

'Oh! Oh! Can we stop at the Chocolate Parlour?' begged Gideon, as they drove through the small, pretty village of Polgammon, where the students spent their pocket money on weekend visits. Owen laughed and, unexpectedly, pulled over. Dax and Gideon spilled out of the jeep, their legs stiff and achey, and ran into the sweetshop. It was wonderfully quiet inside, not teeming with other Colas as it would usually be, and Gideon went into an almost trance-like state at the array of chocolate goodies under the glass display. Mrs Whitlock, the shop owner—a middle-aged lady who knew him well—smiled indulgently. 'You know, I got in extra supplies of the almond crunch with you in mind, Gideon!' she said and Gideon beamed.

They stocked up on supplies. Gideon was famed for his love of chocolate—and should have been twice his size going by the amount of it he ate. Dax bought a couple of bars and some mints and a bottle-shaped whisky liqueur for Owen. His allowance was now gone. He would get more 'Cola money'—a small amount every student got each week—but he never received money from Gina.

Back in the jeep, Dax's excitement was making him feel fizzy and light-headed. As they turned another tight bend, the high mossy stone walls on either side of the narrow road dropped away and the lane widened into a large, curved, gravelled turning place in front of a tall stone chimney. It looked like an old tin mine steeple—and that's what it once was. Now, though, it was the gateway to Tregarren College and golden light spilled from the narrow low windows on either side of its sturdy oak door.

Mr Pengalleon, the gatekeeper, flung open the door and Barber, his big, brown, shaggy dog, came lolloping out to greet them in the evening light. Owen gave him a fond pat on the head and Dax and Gideon dropped to their knees to give him a much more thorough fussing.

Barber, as always, sniffed hard at Dax and threw him a dog thought. *Fox*, commented Barber, in Dax's head. *Boyfox*. *Chocolate*, he added, and Dax knew his attention had switched to Gideon, who must pretty much always smell of chocolate.

'Welcome back, lads,' said Mr Pengalleon. His accent was Cornish and his voice was roughened by sea air. He looked and sounded much like a sea captain, with his grey-white beard and his thick dark greatcoat. In fact he had been quite high up in the Royal Navy, Owen had once told them, and had done several years' duty as a lifeboatman based in Helston.

Mr Pengalleon led them into his sitting room, which was also the entrance to Tregarren College. The room was the interior of the chimney, and perfectly round, with brick walls, painted white, into which were set three more oak doors. The floors were also dark oak and an old cast-iron fireplace held a modest blaze (it could get very cold on this part of the coast, even in April). Mr Pengalleon's desk, chair, a couch, and a high-backed, winged leather armchair were the only furniture in the room. The door which swung shut behind them was fitted with a complicated electronic lock, which only Mr Pengalleon and a few of the staff knew the code to. If a student was on weekend leave, they would be given a signed slip which they had to show before Mr Pengalleon would allow them out. If you forgot or lost it, you were stuck. Mr P was absolutely, and quite cheerfully, unmovable.

'Here—I've made these for you, before you go in,' he

said, and handed each of them a blue china mug, filled with hot, foamy cocoa. They received them gratefully after their long journey.

'Well done, Ted,' murmured Owen, from behind the curls of aromatic chocolate steam. 'You have many hidden talents.'

'Well, the kitchen staff aren't all in yet—you might've struggled to get anything decent from the cook,' said Mr Pengalleon. 'I gave some to the other—' Suddenly he broke off, looking flustered. 'I . . . er . . . gave—'

'Don't worry, Ted,' said Owen. 'It'll be sorted out soon.'

Dax and Gideon exchanged glances as they drained the last of the cocoa. What was up? Dax sensed keen embarrassment from the gatekeeper, and a slight concern within Owen. It was something to do with Gideon, and why they'd been brought back early.

At length Owen put down his empty mug. 'Come on, you two. Let's get going.' They shouldered their heavy bags, stuffed with their holiday clothes, and followed Owen through the door which led out opposite the main entrance. Stepping through it was as dramatic as ever. Dax felt the hairs rise up on his arms and the back of his neck, and a deep thrill passed through him as they gazed at the sea, energetically hurling itself onto ragged black rocks way below them. The door opened onto a narrow walkway, with a high stone wall to stop them from plunging to a nasty death. The view always took Dax's breath away. A fine sea mist was rising across the small forked peninsular that jutted out on two levels from below the steep granite cliff. Tregarren College had been recently built here, on the site of a disused tin mine. Made with local stone, it was a long, low, graceful building, turning on three sides around a neat quadrangle, with a lawn and a fountain in a square pond at the centre. Its windows were tall and wide and reflected the moody Cornish sky.

As they navigated the steep and winding paths, cut roughly into the cliff, the wonderful smell engulfed Dax's senses. The air was damp and the horizon blotted out by the white sea mist, but he could hear the pulse of the ocean, eternally pushing into the land. On the lower part of the 'fork' which made up the campus, was a sports field, and in the V-shaped gap between this and the higher part where the main college building stood, was a natural lido. Here the sea was captured and becalmed behind a ring of rocks, and students could swim in good weather.

As the day darkened, the little white orbs which were strung at head height all the way down the zigzagging paths and steps suddenly glowed. It was a beautiful sight.

'Wait,' said Owen, stopping at one of the small curved cottages which were built into the cliff face beside them. These were where most of the staff lived and they looked as if they had simply grown from the rock and soil and grass that surrounded them. There were chimneys in their conical, dark grey slate roofs and thick, eddied glass in their high windows. Like something from a fairy tale, they were half caves, literally stretching deep into the granite cliff, with a sitting room at the front and kitchen, bedroom, and bathroom underground.

Owen unlocked his door and threw his bags inside, onto the stone floor. 'I'll take you both down to the dorm first, then come and light the fire,' he muttered. Dax and Gideon looked at each other again. They knew the way to their dorm. And how to light the fire.

They descended more steep cliff path and ducked under a rocky outcrop, fringed with damp fern, before crossing the stone bridge that spanned a busy, shallow stream, cutting urgently across a plateau of rock in a shallow bed, intent on throwing itself abruptly over a precipice. Beyond that was the dormitory; another low, slate roofed building, built of the same stone as the college. They shoved open the door and stepped inside, where the stone floor and golden wood were so familiar. They dragged their bags along the corridor to the sitting room which was dark and had no fire lit yet. It was odd, being back before everyone else. A spiral staircase led them to their room. They shared it with Barry, a 'glamourist' who could disappear at will (usually), but he wouldn't be here yet. Each room off the long upstairs corridor had four beds, four trunks, and four wardrobes, but only Dax, Gideon, and Barry slept in theirs, their beds set beneath slanting windows in the ceiling, which framed the ever-changing sky.

As soon as they stepped into the room, they stopped. The neatly made-up beds were the same as ever, but on the furthest one sat a boy. He was reading a book, and as they came in he looked up, taking off round-rimmed spectacles. Dax felt the air abruptly *push* around his best friend in a shockwave. The boy standing beside him—and the boy on the bed—were *both* Gideon.

5

There was a crash, and Dax realized Gideon—*his* Gideon—had dropped his bag on the wooden floor. Dax glanced quickly at Owen, but their teacher just shook his head, very slightly, and said nothing.

The boy on the bed stared at them, and then frowned and put his spectacles back on. He stood up, laying his book aside, and regarded Gideon, pushing his hands into his jeans' pockets. Then he nodded, and murmured: 'They said you looked like me.'

Gideon walked slowly towards him, pausing once or twice, as if the boy were a wild animal and possibly dangerous. Dax could not see his friend's face, but the slow movement was strange enough. Gideon reached the boy's bed and then circled it, turning to study from all angles. To Dax's immense surprise, his first words to the stranger were, 'Stillborn. They said you were stillborn.'

The boy looked back over his shoulder and then sat down on the bed again. 'So they did,' he said. 'And did *you* believe it?'

Gideon sank down at the other end of the bed. He was very pale and his green eyes glittered wetly. 'Actually,' he said, in almost a whisper, 'no.'

The silence that followed was thick. The twins stared

at each other without self-consciousness. It was like a mirror for each. The same tufty fair hair, the same eyes, same freckles, same square jaw. The other boy was perhaps a little thinner, and the glasses made a small difference. Also the way he sat, with rounder shoulders and less confidence, set him apart from Dax's best friend.

Finally Owen spoke. 'This is Luke, Gideon,' he said. 'Sorry if it was a bit of a shock. I think maybe you two should have time to talk. Dax and I will go and get the fire lit downstairs.' Neither boy spoke, nor broke off from his appraisal of the other, as Owen propelled Dax back out of the dormitory.

'All right?' he said, as they walked back down the upper corridor.

'Where did you find him?' asked Dax, his head feeling light with surprise and confusion.

'On the Isle of Wight,' said Owen. 'Mrs Sartre picked him up a few days ago.'

'Is he a Cola, too?' said Dax, as they wound their way back down the spiral staircase. Owen said nothing for a while, but stepped across to the fireplace and bent to light the kindling and coals which had been laid there. As a small blue-yellow flame began to take hold, he sat back on his heels and said, 'We don't know. Luke says not.'

Dax curled himself up into one of the armchairs closest to the fire. 'But I thought you told me you never bring anyone here unless you're absolutely certain they are!' he said. 'Didn't you use Triple Eight on him, or something?'

Owen shot Dax a *look*. He was not proud that when

he had first met Dax, it had been necessary to imprison him in a moving truck and use a nasty vapour to trigger a panic attack. At the time, before Dax had been able to shift at will, it was the only way to be sure he really *could* turn into another form. Dax had forgiven Owen long ago, but wasn't above the odd dig.

'No, Dax,' Owen said, steepling some sticks onto the growing fire. 'I only have to use Triple Eight for shapeshifters. Now stop grinning like that, or I'll put some in your tea!'

Dax laughed, and felt a little more grounded.

'Luke says he has no powers,' went on Owen. 'And as far as we can tell, he's not lying. But he's a special case. We've had no twins up to this point. Brothers, yes— there's Jake and Alex Teller, the mimics—but no twins. It's a great opportunity for study.'

'Who has he been living with?' asked Dax.

'He was adopted as a baby, by a childless couple. The father died some years ago, and the mother is not in the best of health. She was willing to let him come here, when she heard he had a brother. She'd had no idea. Nobody had.'

'Gideon had.'

Owen sat back in his own armchair, the fire now growing steadily. 'Yes,' he mused. 'That wasn't the reaction I expected. He couldn't possibly have known; even his father didn't know. Although he does now, of course. We've been in touch and he's coming to meet Luke next week. Very shocked. These things happen, though. Records go astray and babies actually *do* get mixed up and lost.'

'But wasn't he *there* at the birth?' asked Dax. 'Surely he knew he had *two* sons!'

'No—look, Dax, this is kind of private stuff, and I think Gideon will have to fill you in on it—but his mum and dad were not together when he was born. It's complicated and not really our business. Gideon will tell you when he wants to.'

They sat in silence, gazing into the fire. Dax wondered what was happening back up in the dorm. Owen was probably wondering the same, he thought. After his five hour drive though, he was tired, and before long Owen was breathing evenly, his eyes closed and his head resting into the wing of his armchair. Within minutes Dax, too, fell asleep.

'Oi! Stop snoring, the pair of you! We're hungry!'

Dax and Owen both jerked awake. Blearily Dax took in the low state of the fire and checked his watch. He and Owen had been snoozing for more than an hour. Gideon patted Dax's cheek. Luke stood a little way behind him. 'C'mon! Wake up! We need to get some food!'

Owen yawned, stretched, and grinned. He was clearly relieved that both the twins weren't in such a state of shock that they couldn't eat. The small party trooped across the eerily silent campus, ducking under the rocky outcrop and turning down the stone path to the main college building. In the refectory, a long, high-ceilinged room filled with many round oak tables and leather-padded oak chairs, four places had been laid out for their evening meal.

'Glad to see you all at last!' said Mrs Polruth, the head chef and catering manager. She alone, it seemed, had come in to feed them that evening. 'Do you know what time it is?' she added, with a reproving smile.

'Sorry, Mrs P,' said Owen. 'We promise to scoff up quick, so you can get away home.'

'You'll do nothing of the sort!' said Mrs Polruth, bringing a tray of covered dishes. 'When I cook Launceston Pie, I expect it to be savoured, not stuffed!'

She placed a deep, hot, earthenware dish in front of each of them. Each dish was filled to the brim with chopped beef, vegetables, and rich brown gravy, topped with sliced potatoes and encircled with a kind of pastry halo. They all groaned with pleasure and got started as Mrs Polruth returned with lemonade for the boys and a mug of cider for Owen.

It was some minutes before anyone spoke. Finally, with a sigh of satisfaction, Owen paused between forkfuls and regarded Luke and Gideon, both tucking into their food in almost perfect rhythm; a strange double image in the light of their table lamp.

'How goes it with you two?' he asked.

Luke and Gideon exchanged glances and then grinned back at Owen and Dax. 'We're all right now,' enthused Gideon, and Luke nodded.

'He showed me his telekinetic thing,' said Luke, looking slightly dazed at the memory. 'I didn't really believe it until then. All that stuff you told me, Owen—I mean—is it all for real? I thought maybe this was a—I don't know—a kind of New Age place, with, you know, chanting and candles and stuff, and people talking about visions and whatnot. Like in those shops you get, with the tarot cards 'n' all. I didn't think you could actually *see* stuff.'

Owen smiled and nodded. 'It is pretty hard to take in at first. It took *me* a while. But you get used to it. It's fantastic. A bit scary at times, but really fantastic.'

Luke looked at Dax. 'Is it true?' he asked. 'Can you really turn into a fox?'

Dax nodded and swallowed his mouthful of beef and potato. 'I'll show you later,' he said. 'I'd show you now but Mrs P would object—at the dinner table!'

Luke laughed, slightly nervously, and went back to his supper. He glanced at Dax a couple of times, as if unsure whether to believe him.

'So—what do you reckon?' Dax prodded. 'Can you do any stuff, Luke? Have you tried?'

'Nah!' sighed Luke, shaking his head. 'I can't even wiggle my ears. I'm the dud twin.'

'Don't be daft,' said Gideon, and already there was a protectiveness in his tone. Dax felt an instant twinge. He didn't like the feeling. Of course Gideon was going to be protective of Luke. He was his long-lost brother. Dax tried to bury any further twinges as they finished their Launceston Pie and Mrs Polruth brought dishes of hot spiced apples and clotted cream.

By the time their meal was over it was past ten o'clock. Dax was nearly asleep in the last of his apples and cream. Owen prodded him. 'Wake up, Dax—it's time to go to sleep.'

As they made their way back along the orb-lit paths to the dorm, Owen kept step with them, when he could just as easily have left them to head straight back to his cottage higher up the cliff path. He walked close to Dax as the new twins moved slightly ahead. 'You OK, Dax?' he asked, quietly, and Dax was struck, again, with the thought that Owen was almost an empath. In truth, he was feeling tired, and slightly upset. It was just too weird, seeing Gideon in double and not knowing how he fitted in with his best friend's life now.

Dax smiled and said, 'I'm OK. Just whacked.'

'Yup. Me too,' Owen smiled back. 'You'll be fine, Dax—you and Gideon. You know that, don't you?'

'I reckon,' said Dax. The twins had gone into the dorm ahead of them, and Owen stopped at the door.

'He's going to need you,' he said. 'Just to be you. OK? To be Dax.'

Dax nodded, although he wasn't really sure what Owen meant.

'Now—go and get a decent night's sleep,' said Owen, giving his shoulder a heavy pat. 'You've had an extraordinary forty-eight hours. No bell in the morning— sleep as late as you need. G'night.' And he turned and made his way back up the path.

In their dorm room Gideon and Luke were already getting into bed. Dax said little as they chatted from pillow to pillow. Their voices were very alike, although Gideon's was quicker, more confident, and Luke had a slightly more rounded southern burr from his life on the Isle of Wight. Dax padded across to the white tiled bathroom to wash and brush his teeth. When he returned and slipped between the cool white, lavender-scented sheets, the twins were still talking sleepily. Settling his head back on the pillow and watching a few stars glint through the misty sky in the slanted window over his head, Dax sighed. Even with the strangeness here right now, it was still wonderful to be back at Tregarren, breathing in rhythm with the sea. 'Shut up, you two,' he said, at length. 'I need some sleep.'

'Sorry, mate,' said Gideon, and they lowered their voices for a while. Dax screwed his eyes shut, and pulled the quilt high around his ears, to muffle the sound. Happily, in a few minutes the twins had fallen asleep. He relaxed his shoulders and slept also.

When he woke up the following morning, the bedroom was silent. It was past ten. Pale spring sunshine was shafting through the slightly open window above him and a light breeze stole in. A bit of paper fluttered up and down, pinned under the clock on his bedside table. It was a scrawled note from Gideon. 'You looked so lovely, all asleep!' it quipped. 'It didn't seem right to wake you! Gone to show Luke around. Catch us up!'

Dax got out of bed, washed and dressed quickly. He felt much better after a long night's sleep. He didn't like being left behind, but he was no longer feeling as strange and displaced as he had last night. Outside, he sniffed the air and recognized Gideon's scent in the direction of the lido. He shifted fluidly into DaxFox and ran lightly down the path and across the school playing field. He found them climbing among the rock pools. Gideon was holding a small crab and occasionally floating the poor creature above his cupped hands, while it scrabbled its orange legs in a sideways scuttle to nowhere.

Luke looked up first and his mouth fell open when he saw Dax. He sat down on a rock and stared. Gideon glanced across and the crab plopped wetly back into his hands. 'Hi, Dax,' he said. 'Sleep well?' Dax nodded, settling himself on a flat-topped rock and curling his tail about his forepaws.

Luke was still staring at him in disbelief. 'Is that . . . ? Is that really . . . ?' he murmured. Dax shifted again and Luke fell over backwards into the rock pool. They hauled him out.

'I just—I—I mean!' spluttered Luke, his spectacles wonky and seaweed on his shoulder.

'Sorry,' said Dax. 'I should have warned you!'

'How do you do it?' gasped Luke. 'It's—it's weird. One second you're . . . fox . . . and the next, you're . . . boy. I didn't see the joins!'

'No—it's not like in the films, is it?' said Gideon. 'I kept hoping it was going to be like one of those werewolf films, and he was going to go all stretchy and howly and sprout hairs and fangs and writhe about in agony!'

'Yeah—sorry to disappoint you,' said Dax.

'But it's just a bit of wavy stuff—like glamour. And there he is, all furry and cute!'

Dax snorted.

'Sorry, Dax,' said Gideon, with a grin. 'Of course, you're cute even when you're not furry.'

Dax scooped up a handful of seawater and threw it at his friend and within seconds they were all spattered, salty, and spread with seaweed. They had to go back to the dorm to wash and find fresh clothes. Gideon showed Luke the Tregarren College uniform, which was left, neatly pressed, for each of them, in the large, four-part wardrobe at one end of their dorm room. It was standard charcoal-grey trousers, white polo shirt, with TG stitched on to the breast pocket in turquoise, and a turquoise sweatshirt to wear over it in cooler weather.

'You get to wear what you want at weekends—but you have to wear the sweatshirt or polo shirt if you go into Polgammon,' explained Gideon. 'You get Cola money every week, in case you don't get any from home, like Dax.' He nodded in Dax's direction. 'I've told him about your lovely stepmum,' he explained.

'Mum gave me some money,' said Luke, and it seemed strange. Of course, it wasn't his birth mother, but so few of the Colas spoke of 'Mum', even when they had a stepmother or an adoptive mother.

'Good—Cola money's not much,' said Gideon.

Over breakfast—again, just a single table laid out for

them in the large, empty refectory—Gideon continued with his tutorial on Cola Club.

'It stands for "Children of Limitless Ability",' he told Luke, with relish. 'It means that they don't know *what* we're all capable of!' he added, dramatically. 'I think that's really why we're here! Because they daren't set us loose on society, because of what we might do!'

'But they let us home for holidays,' added Dax, drily.

'Yeah—well,' Gideon shrugged. 'For all we know, they could be *watching* us the whole time! We have to promise never to do our stuff when anyone is looking. And if we ever did . . . ' He trailed off and then drew his finger abruptly across his throat, making a guttural slashing noise.

Luke looked at Dax and said, 'Is he always like this?'

Dax grinned, happy to be included. 'It's sad, but true,' he said.

'So what do you do here?' asked Luke. 'Do you all, like, do spells and things?'

Gideon snorted. 'Get off it! We're not bloomin' witches and wizards, if that's what you mean! That's just a load of made-up cobblers from normal people who are *trying* to be like us! You don't need a wand to be a Cola. You either are—' he shot his porridge spoon high into the air, coasted it around the table twice, and caught it deftly—'or you aren't.'

Luke grinned, impressed. Gideon was having a fantastic time, and no doubt about it.

Dax stirred his porridge and added, 'Some of the

healers and clairvoyants use bits of chanting and stuff to help focus their minds. It's nothing from any dusty old leather books, though. They can chant anything they like—*Manchester United* or *She sells seashells on the seashore.* Doesn't matter. It's whatever works. They like a smelly candle as well, but they manage well enough without them. You wait till you meet Lisa! Someone more totally *un*like a clairvoyant you can't imagine.'

'Lisa's a spoilt brat!' said Gideon, cheerfully. 'But we like her. Mia's a bit wifty-wafty, though. She really can't help it.'

'What does she do?' asked Luke, buttering his toast liberally.

'She's a healer,' said Gideon. 'The best! Fantastic! She actually healed a broken ankle right in front of us last year.'

'Will I like her?' asked Luke, and Dax and Gideon laughed.

'You can bet on it, mate!' said Gideon.

The first few students were due to arrive at teatime that day, with the rest coming in the following morning. As the trio of boys wandered round the college grounds, Gideon chatting excitedly to Luke about their adventures over the past few months, Dax noticed a quickening around him. Staff were arriving. Mrs Dann gave them a wave when they passed one of the classrooms and the sinister Mr Eades, in his grey suit, nodded curtly at them from his office next to Paulina Sartre's.

The principal also called to them as they sat by the

fountain in the quad. She stepped onto the grass and walked across with her customary grace and elegance. Paulina Sartre had pale auburn hair, usually knotted into a soft chignon at the base of her neck. She wore gold-rimmed spectacles through which her silver-grey eyes regarded the world calmly, and was invariably dressed in something dark and flowing.

'Dax! Gideon! Luke! How glad I am to see you,' she said, her French accent lending extra charm to her words. They smiled at her, warmly. She was a woman who commanded immense respect, and was responsible for 'finding' the Colas, with her mind power of 'seeing'—sometimes even before their talents emerged—and sending Owen to collect them. The unsettling thing was when Mrs Sartre got a 'prescience' as she called it, of something to come, regarding her students. She was always worrying about them, and not very good at hiding it.

Now she approached them and touched each boy lightly on the head. It could have been an 'aunt-like' gesture of affection but Gideon and Dax knew better. At her touch, the hair on their scalp would rise to her fingers, as if statically charged.

'Good—good,' she said softly, almost to herself, as she patted Gideon's and Luke's heads in tandem. Turning to Dax she rested her fingers on his head slightly longer, and he felt a light pulse pass through his skin. She blinked and caught her breath and he knew she was 'reading' him. 'Dax Jones,' she murmured, 'you are lucky to be alive.' He nodded quickly and looked away. He didn't want to be reminded.

'Well—I must go,' she said, brightly, detaching herself from them so quickly that Dax could almost hear the air around them snap. As she strode back across the quad she looked over her shoulder and called, 'Luke—Gideon—I am glad you are together. You feel wholeness now, yes?' And then she disappeared back into the college.

There was silence. Dax glanced at Gideon and saw he was looking at Luke. Luke returned his look with something Dax couldn't measure in his eyes.

'C'mon, you two—stop feeling wholeness now!' said Dax. His voice sounded too shrill.

'Yeah, right,' said Gideon, breaking away from his brother's stare. 'Let's go and see Barber.'

Luke also blinked and seemed to collect himself. Dax could not shake off the feeling, as they walked up towards the gatehouse, that Luke and Gideon knew something that nobody else did.

You're just being jealous, he told himself. But that didn't take the feeling away.

6

'Dax! Is it true?' Lisa came bounding along the playing field in her new running shoes to the stout wooden fence-post where Dax was sitting.

'Is what true?' asked Dax. He knew what she meant but he wasn't in the mood to help.

'About Gideon's twin, of course!' Lisa skidded to a halt and looked at him, breathlessly.

'Oh—yeah. Yeah, Gid has a twin. His name's Luke.'

'Where is he?' demanded Lisa. 'I've got to see this!'

Dax jumped down off his post and began to walk back across the field. Lisa followed. 'He's in the post room, I think,' he said. 'Gideon's been showing him around and stuff.' He tried hard to keep the heaviness out of his voice, but it still came out flat and grey and as enthusiastic as wet cardboard. Gideon and Luke had gone off while he was still finishing his lunch. He'd hurried through his pudding to catch up with them, and then suddenly thought that perhaps he wasn't wanted. The idea made him feel more dejected than he wanted to admit, so he'd ended up just wandering off on his own.

'You're jealous, aren't you?' Tact was not one of Lisa's strong points.

'Of course I'm not.' Dax walked faster.

'Aren't you? I would be. Three's a crowd and all that.'

Dax said nothing. Sometimes Lisa really annoyed him. Especially when she was right.

'Everyone's talking about it,' she went on. 'We all thought there were no more Colas.'

'Well, there aren't,' said Dax. 'Luke isn't a Cola.'

'What—no powers? Nothing at all?'

'Nope.'

Lisa shrugged. 'That *is* weird! A normal kid! What's he like?'

'He's OK. Wears glasses. Comes from the Isle of Wight.'

Lisa paused for a bit in her interrogation and he could feel her trying to pick something up from him, telepathically.

'Do you mind?' he snapped, and shifted into DaxFox before she had time to answer. As soon as he was fox, he sped away at top speed, slipping under the fence and beneath some low, windswept bushes before working his way along the stone paths and up the steep steps towards Owen's cottage. Once there, he leapt lightly up onto the deep sill of the cottage window. Through the old, eddied glass he could see light, but he couldn't make out the teacher's shape. He turned his back to the glass, curled his tail about him, and sat down, lifting his snout and gazing out to sea. The sea breeze played with the fine fan of white whiskers around his snout and ruffled the fur in his ears. His dainty black claws scraped finely against the stone sill as he sat. He still remembered the day when he had first shifted—and the amazement of discovering he was a fox. He'd been accidentally trapped in the shed in the garden, after Gina had locked him out, and it had become so hot that he'd had a panic attack and passed out. Then he had awoken to discover he'd changed. He'd changed a lot.

His first journey outside, to get food off a tip and water from an old tyre, was still bright in his memory. Being a fox had meant freedom for Dax. He shuddered to think about how his life might still be had he not developed his shapeshifting powers. He'd still be back living with Gina and Alice, sleeping in his tiny, damp room and enduring the daily drought of love and attention he had got used to since he was four, when his mother died.

Coming to Tregarren had totally transformed his life, turning him from a puny, cold, sad boy into a healthy, bright, and happy boy. And fox, of course. Above all, it had brought him Gideon. His best friend. Even though the first day they'd met Gideon had dropped a football on his face and given him a Chinese burn, their friendship had brought Dax out of himself; made him laugh at himself.

Now everything was different. Gideon was no longer the other half of 'Dax and Gideon'; he was now a third of 'Dax and Gideon and Luke'. *You're being stupid about this!* Dax told himself. *Luke's only just got here! Of course Gideon's spending time with him. Wouldn't* you, *if you'd just discovered your long-lost brother?* It wasn't as if Luke wasn't a nice enough kid, either. He was perfectly all right. Dax would just have to get used to him. He'd have a hard enough time here, anyway, having no powers at all. Dax made up his mind that Gideon would *never* know about his jealousy.

'Well, well, well! Still backing into corners then, Dax?' came a light voice, dripping with sarcasm. Dax jumped and realized that Spook Williams was descending the stone steps. He'd been so lost in his thoughts that he'd ignored the boy's scent. Dax shot him a look, but did not shift. He did not feel like talking to his arch enemy. Spook sauntered on down the steps towards him. A tall boy, with dark red hair and a pale complexion, Spook moved languidly, like a lizard. He wore jeans and T-shirt, but, preposterously, over this, a long flowing black cloak, with hand-stitched crescent moons on it. Spook seriously fancied himself as a world famous magician, and was intent on developing his persona even at the age of twelve. In fact, the cloak looked quite good on him, because it echoed his slightly slithery way of walking.

It was common knowledge that Spook had written to several television production companies to suggest ideas for a magic show featuring a talented twelve year old. As yet, he'd had no replies. Or perhaps the people who ran Tregarren College had seen to it that his letters had never reached the television companies. Dax guessed that Spook knew better than to reveal that he was a *real* illusionist, capable of making almost anyone see the most incredible things with the power of his mind. Last year the whole school had been treated to a spectacular firework display, created entirely by Spook and his illusionist classmates. What Spook hadn't yet worked out, was that Dax, and Dax alone, had not seen a thing.

One of the side effects, it seemed, of being a shapeshifter was that Dax was resistant to this kind of glamour. He could only be minutely affected by illusion. All he ever saw was a slight waviness in the air, like the heat haze over tarmac on a very hot day. He had discovered this the previous term and it had proved to be very useful. Only his close friends knew and, so far, had managed to keep it a secret. Perhaps Spook had *some* idea, because his dislike of Dax had been evident from the moment they'd met.

'Sorry I couldn't stop and chat the other day,' sneered Spook, as he reached the step beneath the windowsill. Dax stared on out to sea as if he had not noticed the boy at all, but the fur on the back of his neck was beginning to rise up.

'Looked to me like you'd had a bit of an adventure, Dax! Had you been digging for worms?'

Dax felt his tail flick involuntarily across his feet. He steadied it.

'Owen looked like he'd been digging too. You must both have had a great time,' persisted Spook and then let out a high pitched chortle. 'I heard that you cried like a girl when he got you out!'

Dax ran his fox tongue over his fox teeth and seriously considered biting Spook. How good it would be to sink his needle-sharp canines into the boy's throat and hear him shriek. At that moment the cottage door flew open and Owen stood there, glowering at them both.

'Spook, you say *one* more word about this—to *anyone*—and I will slap you into detention with Mr Eades every day for the next four weeks.'

Spook jumped, but he shot Owen a mutinous look. 'I haven't said anything to anyone! Of course I haven't! I was just winding up Dax, that's all.'

'Do you think,' Owen glared back at him, 'that any winding up is really necessary? Have you any idea . . . ?'

At this point Dax leapt down from the sill and shifted back into boy form. He was horribly embarrassed to have Owen talking to Spook about his misadventure.

'Look—can we just forget it?' he urged and Spook shot him a look of contempt.

'Yeah, Dax,' he said, 'forget it. No trouble at all. Any time!' And he flounced off down the path, his absurd cloak rising behind him in the sea breeze.

Dax looked at Owen. 'What did he mean? That I should thank him for not spreading it all round the school?'

Owen studied him for a while. 'You haven't worked it out, then?'

Dax screwed up his face. 'What?'

'No—well, you were probably too out of it to notice. Why do you think the hunt suddenly turned and left us? The hounds were all over your scent and even the leader was still convinced you'd got a fox up your jumper.'

Dax didn't like the turn of this conversation. 'Go on,' he said.

'Spook threw an illusion, that's all. He realized who I was pretty quickly, obviously, and then caught sight of you—put two and two together—and conjured up a convenient little vixen, due west. The humans all got to see it, and they hauled the hounds on after them.'

Dax felt slightly sick. 'You're telling me I owe one—to Spook?'

'Well, don't let's get out of hand!' Owen laughed. 'He didn't save your life—he just got us out of an uncomfortable situation. In quite a stylish way.'

'Spook? Stylish? Give me a break!' Owen said nothing and Dax was forced to shrug. 'OK. Fair enough. I guess it's quite a cool thing to do. He probably wouldn't have bothered, though, if you hadn't been there.'

At this point, two fair-haired boys emerged on the steps below them. 'Dax!' hailed Gideon. 'Where have you been? Come on! I want to take Luke up to the woods and Mrs Sartre has given us a pass!'

Dax gladly ran down to join the twins. It was good to get away from Owen's revelation about Spook.

They climbed back up to the gatehouse where Barber jumped all over Gideon and Luke—and reserved his usual, more respectful head-push for Dax. Barber knew that this boy was also a fox and this seemed to make it inappropriate for him to jump up and try to lick his face. Mr Pengalleon punched in the code and allowed them outside into the late afternoon sun and they trekked up to the ancient wood which sprawled along the top of the cliffs above Tregarren. From their vantage point, sitting in the gnarled roots of elderly trees which clung to the edge of the land, they could see more and more students arriving in the campus below, moving around like ants.

'What are they going to make of me, then?' asked Luke, skittering some pebbles over the cliff edge, which Gideon then seized with his mind and circled back upwards into his brother's palm.

'You don't have to say,' said Gideon. 'Nobody has to tell anyone about what powers they've got—or haven't got. Of course, it all gets out eventually, but in your case, if you just go all broody and mysterious every time someone asks, they'll probably think you're hiding something really immense and amazing.'

'That's what I'll do then,' said Luke. He didn't sound convinced.

'Are you sure that you really can't do anything?' asked Dax.

'Oh yeah,' said Luke. 'They did Development with me for a week before you got here, trying to work out my psychic stuff. I had to look at symbols and then try and *send* them through to Mr Hind with my head. I just sat there with my eyes screwed up, holding my breath and going pink in the face—nothing! They did it the other way around, with Mrs Sartre sending to me. I drew stuff, but I was only guessing. Dud! Nothing going on there. Then I had to sit in a chair and stare at a pencil until my eyeballs fell out, trying to get the stupid thing to move. Nothing.'

Gideon let out a low whistle. 'Must be something! How about spirit communication?'

'You what?'

'You know—do you hear voices in your head—from the beyond?'

Luke gave Gideon a sceptical look. 'Yeah, right!' he said.

'Blimey!' said Gideon. 'You've got a lot of surprises coming.'

'We've got quite a few psychics and clairvoyants,' explained Dax, eyeing a shiny beetle running across his shoes, and feeling a bit peckish. 'They have to fill out little pink slips of paper whenever they get messages from people's dead friends and relatives. Then Mr Eades or someone has to sign them before they're allowed to be passed on. Gideon's always getting them from his—from *your*—Auntie Pam.'

'We have an Auntie Pam?' asked Luke.

'*Had*,' corrected Gideon. 'She's been dead for donkey's years. Not that she lets that stand in her way.' He dug a scrap of pink paper out of his jeans. 'She's already been at it, and the term hasn't even started. Jessica Moorland gave me this as soon as she got here.'

Luke and Dax peered at the slip. Printed at the top was SPIRIT COMMUNICATION NOTICE. Jessica had neatly written her name, the date and time, and the name of the recipient of the message—*Gideon Reader*. Underneath *from Auntie Pam* was written '*Don't forget your fish. Don't touch number three. Get your hair cut.*'

'Mad as a jar of gerbils,' sighed Gideon. 'Never makes any sense.'

They all laughed and Dax felt a little less tense. Auntie Pam was good for that.

At teatime the refectory was once again teeming with students. Colas from all over the country had now arrived and there was a bright and excited atmosphere in the room as friends got back together at their usual tables and talked about their Easter break. Although it was technically forbidden for students to flex their strange powers outside their 'Development' classes, little displays of ability couldn't help but leak out, and there were free-floating bowls of soup in the air; shrieks, as illusionists masked their classmates' food as live mice or a wriggling squid; and the occasional annoyed 'Oof!' as someone walked into someone else who was invisible.

Barry, their glamourist friend, had joined Dax, Gideon, Luke, and Lisa at their customary table. He was switching himself on and off with great glee, snapping in and out of their vision. 'See! I can do it really quick now!' he declared. 'I've been practising all Easter break!' After about a minute of their friend blinking in and out of view, Gideon got weary and tipped his chocolate milkshake through the air above Barry's seat. Immediately the robust form of their friend appeared, his annoyed gasp outlined in dripping brown liquid. 'Gideon! You little worm!' he shouted.

'Sorry,' laughed Gideon. 'But we think you're lovely and we want to see you all the time!'

'I can't do it now, anyway!' muttered Barry, coming

completely back into view and wiping his dripping hands in Gideon's hair. 'You've really put me off!'

Dax handed Barry a napkin, laughing. He liked Barry—and was not totally resistant to *this* kind of glamour, for some reason. Although his fox sense revealed the usual wavy lines in the air and that, combined with his sharp nose and the adenoidal whistle that Barry always made while he breathed, meant he was rarely caught out.

Luke was staring in amazement at all these goings on, and as Dax watched him he saw the boy's face abruptly soften and his eyes haze slightly as his mouth fell open. Dax didn't need to turn round to know that Mia was heading for their table. Luke put down the knife and fork on either side of his egg, ham, and chips tea, and stared. Gideon grinned and watched. Mia sat down next to Dax, opposite Luke, placing a bowl of pasta and a glass of apple juice on the table. She lifted her eyes to Luke and gave him a smile. Luke smiled back weakly.

'Hello, you must be Luke,' said Mia. Her voice was cool and soothing, like springwater over pebbles. Luke nodded and gazed on.

'It's lovely to meet you,' went on Mia. 'We couldn't believe it when we heard Gideon had a twin brother. But there's no doubting it now. You're almost totally identical, aren't you?'

Luke nodded, his eyes still hazy and his mouth still open. Gideon reached across and snapped his brother's mouth shut, as he had done for Dax two terms before.

' 'S all right, Luke. You'll snap out of it eventually. You can't help it, mate. That's the Mia Effect.'

Mia blushed and concentrated on her food and Luke managed to refocus his eyes on his brother, as Gideon went on, 'She's the healer I told you about. She's brilliant! I'll kick you in the shin if you like, so you can find out!'

'No, Gideon!' said Dax and Lisa, in unison. They had all learned in the last year that although Mia was incredibly gifted at healing, she had not initially known how to release the pain that she absorbed from the people she healed. For weeks she had carried an immense load of other people's pain, unable to offload it. If Owen Hind hadn't realized what was going on just in time, Mia might very well have died. Now she'd had many sessions learning the various ways of releasing the pain, and was getting better at it all the time, but her friends were still very protective of her and anxious that she never took an injury or a headache from them if she couldn't immediately get rid of it.

'How are *you*, Dax?' asked Mia, quietly.

'I'm fine,' said Dax, shovelling in a huge forkful of hot cottage pie and carrots.

'Really?'

'Mmm!' Dax beamed at her, rolling his eyes for emphasis, but she didn't look convinced.

'Lisa told me a bit more about what happened in the woods on Friday.' She shivered. 'Dax, you must, *must* take care!'

Dax swallowed and coughed quietly. 'I just wish

everyone would forget it!' he said. 'I'm fine! Thanks—but really, I'm all better now!' He beamed at Mia and she smiled gently back, sending him her usual wave of warmth and kindness, so he felt a little ashamed of lying to her. *All better now* was a bit of an exaggeration. The fact was, ever since he'd woken up on Saturday morning, after his long and exhausted sleep, he had been trying to completely block out the events in the woods. The few flashes of memory that had managed to sidle into his mind had left him cold and sick and shaking, and there was *no way* he was going to have that! So he had—as efficiently as any wild animal—put the experience in its place; a warning against running into dark holes when in danger. And that was it. No more thought was required. If only people would shut *up* about it!

7

Throughout the evening at Tregarren, Dax made a supreme effort to be relaxed and friendly around Luke. The quartet of friends had become a quintet, and Mia and Lisa were fascinated by the new twin. Luke, too, seemed more relaxed, as they sprawled across one of the old leather sofas near the fire in the joint common room. He clearly, and unsurprisingly, adored Mia and kept glancing across at her, as if unsure that she was real. Lisa, meanwhile, was keen to find out about his life before Cola Club.

'So how did it all happen, then?' she asked, leaning on to the knees of her white designer jeans and peering at him. 'Oi! Over here!' She snapped her fingers and Luke pulled his gaze away from Mia, looking embarrassed.

'Don't worry,' said Lisa. 'In a day or two you'll be more or less normal again. Then you'll realize that *I'm* incredibly gorgeous and Mia's really boring!' Mia laughed. She found the 'Mia Effect' very embarrassing, and was grateful whenever her friends made fun of it.

'Sorry,' said Luke. 'What did you say?'

'How did you get here? What was happening beforehand? Did you want to come? Did you put up a fight? I did! I went mental! Well—*actually*— they *did* think I was mental . . . ' concluded Lisa, with a sigh.

'No—I didn't put up a fight. I wanted to know what it was all about,' said Luke. 'Nothing much happened before, really. I was just at school, doing all right. Had a couple of mates, but nobody like—not like Gideon,' he added.

Dax squashed down hard on the jealous pang he felt at these words. He would *not* give in to it! 'Go on,' he urged.

'Well, you know, it was just me and Mum . . . '

'What's your mum like?' interrupted Lisa. 'Most of us haven't got one!'

'Yeah—I heard about that. Weird. Well, Mum's . . . Mum's great. She's lovely. I mean, to me, she just *is* my mum, because I've never not had her. But she's a bit disabled now, and I think it was hard on her, because Dad died when I was six and she's had to look after me, and work and stuff.'

'Do you miss her?' asked Lisa.

'Well . . . yeah . . . a bit. But I'm allowed to phone her, and she's got her sister living with her now, and they seem quite happy, so that makes me feel OK. She said I should take the opportunity, you know, when Owen came.'

'So did Owen just show up out of the blue?' asked Dax. He remembered vividly his first meeting with Owen, in the sitting room with Gina. Owen had worn a suit, and looked very odd in it, with his long curly hair and outdoorsy skin. Dax had been quite suspicious of him at the start, but still preferred to take his chances with the stranger sent by the government, than stay with Gina and Alice. And Gina was delighted to get rid of him at no cost, so everyone was happy.

'I came home from school one day, and he was there, having tea with Mum,' said Luke. 'Told her I had been traced as being the twin brother of one of the pupils at a school for gifted kids, and they thought I probably had the same potential.'

'And so your mum said "Wow!" and sent you off with him,' concluded Dax.

'Well—no!' said Luke, looking at Dax as if he was mad. 'She did a bit of checking, first! She wasn't just going to sign a form and hand me over, was she?'

Dax said nothing. Gideon shot him a sympathetic look.

'Anyway, I came here a week before you all got back, and then Gid and Dax showed up—and now you're here and we're all up to date,' said Luke.

'And you really can't do anything?' said Lisa, quietly, leaning in to him, so the other Colas nearby couldn't hear.

Luke sighed. 'No,' he said patiently. 'I really can't!'

Lisa leaned back again and surveyed him with fascination. 'Wow!' she said.

Dax was relieved to get to bed that night, even though Barry, Gideon, and Luke were vaulting from bed to bed and throwing pillows around. Well, Gideon was half throwing, half floating—and Barry was doing more of the on and off switch disappearing act which was still having a big effect on Luke. Of course, they were hugely enjoying having a new audience; especially one with no powers, who would be completely in awe of them, thought Dax. He pulled the covers over his head and barely even noticed that he'd shifted, curled up in a comma in the dark centre of the bed. After another five minutes of looning about from his dorm-mates, Dax let out a low growl. Silence fell.

'Oops!' giggled Gideon. 'Daxy-boy's all furry and fed up! We're being too noisy! Sorry, mate! Fox needs his sleep.'

They quietened down and got into bed, and after a few more minutes of occasional low chatter, finally fell asleep. Dax slept too, for a while, but not well. He drifted awake repeatedly, finding he was back as a boy and watching the luminous hands on his bedside clock at 11 p.m. then 12.09 a.m., then 2.15 a.m. At 2.35 a.m. he sighed, sat up, shifted to fox and slid out of bed. There was no earthly point in trying to sleep when he was like this. Better to get out.

Dax took his own private path, up the cliffside, to the wood above the college. It was impossible to climb up or down in human form, but as a light, nimble fox, with four agile paws, Dax could be among the trees on the clifftop in seconds. A half moon gave him enough light, and his fox eyes were as keen as his other fox senses. As usual, as he entered the comforting cloak of the trees and trotted lightly along on the soft woodland floor, he was aware of myriad other creatures. Small rodents, roosting birds, even insects, were bristling with the threat of an approaching predator. A nearby badger foraged on for beetles, unbothered by the scent of dog-fox; a tawny owl swooped low over his head, calm and focused, seeking a vole or a mouse, and its mate, in a tree nearby, gave out regular high-pitched squeaks of encouragement. The smell of the wood at night relaxed Dax; it was like stepping into a cool bath after a day of heat. Once again, the velvet darkness enfolded him lovingly; one of its children.

Dax stopped to lick up a couple of large, nutty beetles; he was almost always hungry when he was a fox. At first, he'd struggled hard *not* to eat disgusting things, but the truth was that the very first thing he'd eaten as a fox, way back in that over-heated shed, was a dead spider. He'd not done a dead spider again, but yes . . . beetles, worms, a few live spiders—just dainty, wriggling snacks to keep him going. So far, he *had* resisted killing and eating small mammals or birds. It was quite difficult to contain the hunting urge, but the boy inside the fox was soft on furry or feathery things and always overruled the instinct, even though DaxFox was certain he *could* catch small prey. His reflexes were as fast as any other animal, even if he was only a part-timer.

He had reached an arrangement with the kitchen staff, that they would keep fresh meat leftovers for him in an agreed place in the dining room every night. When the urge to eat got very strong, he would turn tail and bolt for the refectory and wolf down some cold pork, bacon, or chicken. But for now, the little protein snacks of insects and worms would do.

Whenever Dax felt out of kilter as a boy he found that the feeling rarely followed him when he was in fox form. In the half-moonlit woods, he certainly felt much, much better, but he knew he was not OK. He guessed it had to be the Luke situation. He would get used to it. He *would*. He liked Luke—he really did. If he had met Luke back in his life before Cola Club, he was sure they would have got on. Luke was quiet and bookish, but shared Gideon's sense of fun. He seemed open enough, and certainly had to be possessed of courage, to be able to uproot himself from his mother and his whole life. To be the only child at Tregarren without a supernatural power was also going to be hard for him, and yet he was here, and ready to deal with it. Yes, Dax decided, he liked *and* respected Luke. He was just going to have to adjust to sharing Gideon.

There was a push of air around him and Dax realized, with a thud of shock, that he was no longer walking alone. Grey and insubstantial though it was, there was no mistaking his otherworldly protector. Its muzzle was dark grey, with flecks of white, and its eyes were white discs in the night. Dark grey paws stepped silently on the dead leaves and roots beneath them, leaving no indentation.

You're here! You're here! I can see you! Dax stopped and turned to look the wolf in the eye and the creature stopped and reflected his movement, as though it was his mirror image. It regarded him calmly, and sent no thoughts back.

Dax was thrilled. The wolf had come to him before, but only ever in dreams, in the halfway place between awake and asleep. *I'm so glad to see you! I owe you so much!* Dax babbled in his head. The wolf dipped its snout as if to say, 'No problem.'

Dax waited, and watched awhile, and then asked, *Is there something you need to tell me?* The wolf dipped its snout again, but still gave no message to him. Dax tried to work out what it meant. *Can you still speak to me—when I can see you?* The creature shook its handsome, shaggy head and sighed—a small pearly fog of outward breath rising in the air between them. Dax realized that making itself seen was an immense effort for the creature and that perhaps it couldn't *talk* as well.

After a few seconds the wolf turned and walked through the trees, glancing back once at Dax to make sure he was following. Dax did, and the wolf took him towards the edge of the woods, where more light was wandering through the sparser branches. The soft wind sighed in the leaves of an ancient apple tree, its boughs sprinkled with insubstantial blossom. The wolf stopped here and looked back at Dax. Then it lifted a paw and, very deliberately, ran its claws three times along the base of the old tree's trunk. It sat down and looked back at Dax. Dax nodded, uncertainly. *OK—got that*, he sent, *sort of*. The wolf gave him another brisk snout-dip and then looked up steadily into the branches until Dax followed his gaze. He couldn't make anything out. No message lay in the tangle of bark and leaf and dim night sky. *I can't see anything! What do you mean?* The wolf turned back to him, but it was looking more and more see-through. Dax realized its energy was fading. *I'm sorry!* he sent, desperately. *I just don't understand!* He had a sudden idea. *Will you try Lisa? Try Lisa!* He just caught the slightest nod from the wolf as it faded completely away.

Dax slumped to the floor, disappointed. What was he supposed to have found out? Was it another warning? When he had first come to Tregarren College, in fact, even *before* he'd come, the wolf had been warning him. In dreams. Even while he was still sleeping in his cramped, damp room back with Gina and Alice. He wished the creature could be a bit more direct! All the warnings made perfect sense *after* Principal Wood had tried to kill him! It would have helped to have had a bit more *before*hand. But it seemed his friend in the spirit world, or wherever he now existed, could only ever get brief statements across to him, and these were clouded by the confusion of sleep, or interpreted by another medium, like Lisa or Jessica, and so not always pure.

The wolf had been the first shapeshifter, found by Owen and Patrick Wood months before they discovered Dax. A tough, streetwise boy, brought up in a succession of children's homes, the first shapeshifter had instinctively known that Patrick was a fake, interested only in his own power and need to control. He saw through Patrick's immense charm almost immediately—like Dax, he was immune to that kind of glamour—and the principal, realizing the threat, had manoeuvred him into a road accident and then left him dead, still in the form of the wolf. A shapeshifter will revert to its true form if it knows it's dying, but one killed instantly will remain whatever it has become.

Dax had, unintentionally, evened the score. Patrick Wood's body now lay 150 fathoms beneath the college after falling through a trapdoor in his own study floor. It was meant to be Dax's exit from this world, but Patrick miscalculated and took the plunge himself. There was no practical way of recovering his remains. The study had been converted into a book store. Dax never went in. Few people did.

Frustrated though he was, Dax was also now getting very hungry. Something warm-blooded and packed with protein and fat shrank away from him in the undergrowth. Dax's snout snapped round towards it and DaxBoy overruled very quickly, before he was beyond stopping himself. *Get down to the refectory! Now!* He leapt to his feet and fled back through the woods and down the cliff path, hunger now obliterating nearly every other sense. He was at the refectory window in less than a minute, leaping onto the large metal bins beneath it and up under the top window which was left ajar for him. He padded across to the plastic tub beside the cutlery drawer, knocked the lid off it with his snout and devoured two cold pork sausages, three gloriously fatty, crispy rashers of bacon, and a hunk of cider-roasted gammon. He *could* have shifted back to a boy for this process, but his sense of taste as a fox outstripped his boy sense so wildly that eating anything this tasty in fox form was amazing. When he'd emptied the tub, with a blessing on the kindly kitchen staff, he drank a pint of cold water from the bowl thoughtfully laid next to it.

In a minute he was back at the dormitory and padding silently back to his bed. He checked his paws, quickly, for mud (the laundry staff got fed up with muddy fox prints on their sheets) and then crept back under the quilt, turned round once, wrapped his tail about him, and fell into a warm, food-fuelled, dreamless sleep.

8

Classes began the next morning and they were much like classes in any other school. In geography, Mrs Dann talked them through the geological make-up of the British Isles and explained the knock-on effects it had on the country's industries. She was a good teacher and used to holding the class's attention, so she was frustrated to note that Dax Jones was sitting at the back, staring into the middle distance.

'So, Dax,' she called out, at length, 'what geological feature is known as the Backbone of Britain?' Dax jumped in his seat and his eyes refocused guiltily on his teacher.

'Um . . .' he began. She sighed and put her hands on her hips. Gideon and Luke turned round and looked at him sympathetically, while Spook sniggered at a desk to his right.

'Don't strain yourself, Mr Jones,' said Mrs Dann, waspishly. 'The Pennines are known as the Backbone of Britain—forming, as they do, a ridge roughly along the middle part of the country. That'll be a first for you, obviously, although everyone else heard it ten minutes ago!'

'Sorry, miss,' mumbled Dax. 'I didn't sleep that well last night.'

'Well, put more effort into sleeping tonight!' snapped Mrs Dann, illogically, and turned back to the whiteboard. 'Don't even *think* about it, Gideon,' she added, without looking, as Gideon abstractedly scooted his pencil rubber in a small whirlwind formation over his desk ready to pelt Dax cheerily on the nose. The rubber fell back onto his desk with a small thud and Gideon studied his textbook diligently. Sometimes they wondered if Mrs Dann didn't have some powers herself. Her ability to pick up illicit class-time power flexing without even looking was uncanny.

As far as they knew, none of the teachers at Tregarren had any supernatural powers, apart from Principal Sartre, although Dax was growing more and more sure that Owen had some level of ability—a kind of intuition, at least; and he was certainly able to pick up Lisa's telepathy, if she sent it to him with enough concentration. She had told Dax that the only reason she hadn't come hurtling into the woods after him during the hunt incident, was that reading him *and* getting her information through to Owen had taken all of her concentration. 'There could've been fifteen firemen in tutus performing *Swan Lake* all around me and I wouldn't have noticed,' she'd said.

Dax shivered, shoved the memory of that day firmly into the darkest corners of his mind, and determinedly focused on Mrs Dann. The lesson moved on. They were drawing maps and adding geological details when the next interruption came. Dax picked it up seconds before— and so did Lisa. For Dax it came as a scent. Gideon and

Luke, although they hadn't stopped their work, were both suddenly very excited. Adrenalin abruptly began to pulse through them. At that moment, Lisa, two desks away from Dax, suddenly sat bolt upright. Dax turned to look at her and saw her frowning with concentration.

'Do you need an SCN slip now, Miss Hardman? Or can it wait?' sighed Mrs Dann. She knew that sometimes the mediums could be so nagged by a spirit that any attempt at concentrating in class was hopeless.

Lisa shook her head. 'No,' she said. 'I'm fine.' She glanced at Dax and sent him two words. *She's coming.*

Who? Dax sent back, but Lisa just shook her head again and bent it back over her work. A second later the door was lightly knocked and opened. At that moment both Gideon and Luke rose to their feet in unison and dropped their pencils on their desks at precisely the same time.

Mrs Dann sat back in her chair and muttered, 'Oh, I give up! Barton Park Comprehensive, take me back!'

Owen stood in the doorway, looking quizzically at Gideon and Luke. 'You know, then?' he asked and both boys nodded in such perfect symmetry that they were beginning to look like an optical illusion.

'Sorry, Mrs Dann, I have to borrow Gideon and Luke,' said Owen and Mrs Dann waved them out.

'Go on! Go on!' she said, wearily and Owen grinned an apology at her. The twins quickly followed him out into the corridor and they walked away quickly.

Dax felt horribly excluded. Something important was happening with his best friend—and Gideon hadn't even glanced at him. *What is it?* he sent Lisa, irritably, but she just shook her head again and went on with her work. *Oh, thanks a bunch!* he snapped but she merely changed pencils and carried on. For a friend she could be extremely annoying.

As soon as the lesson ended, Dax caught up with Lisa outside in the quad. 'What?' he demanded. 'What's happening!'

'*I* don't know!' snapped Lisa, scooping her long blonde hair up into a sparkly hair band.

'But you *sent* me that message! You said, *She's here*! What was that supposed to mean?'

'Oh, do keep your hair on, Dax! I don't know what it meant. I just had a quick message come through and before I could stop myself I just, kind of, broadcast it! I can't help it if you pick these things up.'

'But *who's* here? Is it to do with Gideon? *Stop* checking your stupid fingernails and just concentrate, will you!'

Lisa resolutely carried on inspecting her perfectly manicured nails and the temperature around her dropped. 'I am not some kind of information service for jealous mates,' she said, icily and Dax ground his teeth. 'If I say I don't know, it's because I *don't know*! You, of all people, should understand. You know I get endless messages and half of them are complete nonsense. It might be about Gideon or it might be about Barber the dog! Now, if you don't mind, I've got stuff to do.' She stalked away angrily, leaving Dax as clueless and frustrated as ever.

He decided to try to find Gideon, but there was no sign of him, or Luke, as Dax traipsed disconsolately around the campus. He guessed that the boys were deep below the ground, in one of the Development rooms. Perhaps Owen had discovered a way to bring out Luke's hidden talents. That was another thing, it occurred to Dax, suddenly. If Luke had no talents at all, how come he'd done that standing up in unison thing? There must be some kind of link between them. But then, he reasoned, that was not uncommon, even in ordinary twins.

Sitting on the fence at the end of the playing fields, Dax watched a few of the other students kicking a ball about. Gideon would find *him* soon, wouldn't he? He'd find him and tell him what was up. You didn't leave your best mate out of things for long. There was a faint whistle behind him. 'Hi, Barry,' said Dax and Barry gave a sigh of annoyance.

'You're not supposed to know I'm *here*!' he complained and bloomed into sight a few feet away.

'You'll have to hold your breath, then!' laughed Dax, cheered to find a friend.

'Bloomin' adenoids!' muttered Barry, hauling himself heavily up onto the stout fence next to Dax. 'I'm having 'em taken out next year!'

'That'll help,' agreed Dax. Barry's nasal passages were obstructed by enlarged adenoidal glands, which was what gave him his familiar whistle. They'd all got used to it, and actually found it quite endearing now.

'Won't really make any difference with you, though, will it?' sighed Barry. 'You'll still know I'm there!'

'Not if I've got a bad cold,' pointed out Dax. 'Mess up my sense of smell, stop whistling, don't bump into anything, and make me squint a bit, and I definitely won't know you're there.'

'Yeah—well, I'll look forward to that day.' Barry knew about Dax's acute fox senses; he also knew about his resistance to glamour. Dax had also told him that although he couldn't see him when he was properly invisible, he *could* make out the strange waving around of the air. So, certainly close up, even with just sight he could tell that *someone* was using an invisibility power nearby.

'What's up with Gideon, then?' asked Barry.

'I don't know,' admitted Dax.

Barry looked surprised but didn't say anything. They sat in silence on the fence, the sea breeze buffeting the backs of their heads. At length Barry said, 'Who's that? Is that Spook? I didn't know he was allowed to have a dog.'

Later, Dax realized it was the strong sea breeze which had deprived him of his early warning. It wasn't until Spook was a few feet away that he picked up the scent.

'Hi, Dax!' called Spook, with a fake cheeriness. There was a look of mean anticipation on his grinning face, and a woven leather lead wound tightly around his hand. Straining and whining on the end of it was a wild-eyed foxhound. 'Thought you might like to meet an old friend!' shouted Spook and dropped the lead. Immediately the hound let out a deep, guttural bay and bounded across to Dax, who sat frozen on the fence.

The effect was horrible. In his rational head, Dax *knew* there was no real threat. It was just one dog—and he was not a fox at that moment. But a more primeval part of him reared up in terror. His throat seemed to swell with fear and he couldn't swallow; his hands gripped the fence like twin vices while his legs seemed to liquefy and drip away from under him. The hound jumped up at him, baying and sniffing, and he could see the spit dripping off its teeth, the quivering pink tongue snagging over its sharp canines. The world around him seemed to buckle and go dark as a panic of terrible power washed over him. He thought he might scream, but no sound could escape from his solid throat. He could feel his eyes widen and a cold sweat now prickled through his hair, down his spine, and across his chest. The hound was getting more and more excited and had grabbed a jawful of his trousers at the knee, rocking his useless puppet legs. He could feel its hot breath and teeth against his skin.

If Barry hadn't been with him, Dax later thought, he might well have just somersaulted backwards over the fence, rolled down the steep drop, senseless, and fallen into the sea. It seemed all he was capable of was winking out of existence—and, more terrifying still, part of him *wanted* that. To be gone. To be away, at any cost, from that horrific, searing panic.

But Barry jumped down off the fence, and kneed the dog in the ribs. 'Oi!' he said. 'Get off, you ugly mongrel!'

The hound whined and let go of Dax's trousers, but it circled, still, in a frenzy of excitement, panting and hungrily eyeing the boy who smelt of fox. It made to come at him again, and this time Dax really thought he *would* faint. He had not moved from his position on the fence, but he was as scrambled inside as someone who'd just done a dozen cartwheels and vaulted over a moving train. Barry shoved the dog away again, and then Dax became aware of laughter; helpless, gurgling laughter. Spook Williams was literally doubled up on the playing field, and some distance behind him the football players had stopped their game and were standing around, watching. Some of them were laughing, too, although one or two looked at each other uncertainly and one— Darren Tyler—was walking over to Spook, looking angry.

'Chip! Chip! C'm'ere!' gasped Spook, through his laughter. 'C'mon, boy!' Reluctantly, looking again and again back over its squat furry shoulders, the hound returned to Spook.

'Cut it out, Spook, you git. It's not funny,' said Barry, far away in Dax's ears. He had dropped his head, in exhaustion, and was staring at his knees, one of which was revealed through a toothy tear in his school trousers. Dax could feel his jaw shaking, and clamped it shut. He said nothing and did nothing. Barry had more of a go at Spook and eventually Spook got to his feet, still laughing, and took the dog away. The footballers waited a while and then returned to their game. Dax was still looking at his knee. A little blood seeped across the ragged tear of the cloth.

'Dax! Oi! Jonesy!' Barry was back at his side. 'You all right, mate?'

Dax took in a shaky breath.

'Shall I go and get Mr Hind? You don't look too good.'

'No!' Dax snapped out of his stupor. The idea of Owen knowing what had just happened was appalling to him. 'Don't tell anyone!'

'OK,' said Barry, uneasily, helping Dax down from the fence. 'But you know that Spook's going to tell everyone anyway. What was up with you, mate? I mean, it was a nasty mutt and all that, but . . . '

'Nothing,' mumbled Dax, walking back towards the dorm. 'Thanks for getting it off me, Barry.'

Barry trailed behind him for a while and he could smell the boy's confusion. Dax felt deeply ashamed. He'd never felt more stupid and feeble. He didn't even want to look Barry in the eye. What he wanted was his best friend. He needed to find Gideon; Gideon always straightened the world out with one daft comment, whenever it went off kilter.

As if he had picked up Dax's signal, there was a sudden shout and Gideon was standing way off, over at the edge of the quad, waving and motioning for him to come across. Dax broke into a run and reached the quad a minute later, panting, and hoping the remains of his panic attack were no longer evident. If they had been, perhaps Gideon wouldn't have noticed anyway. He was looking excited and strange, and grabbed Dax by the arm as soon as he was close.

'Come with me! Come with me!' he gasped and hared

across to the other side of the grassy quadrangle, skirting the pond and fountain and dragging Dax through the glass door on the far side. He hauled him along the corridor and then straight into Paulina Sartre's office, without knocking.

Inside, the principal was sitting at her desk, Owen was leaning against the windowsill, and Luke was sitting on the leather sofa beside the fireplace. Next to him was someone else.

It was a girl, about their own age. She was small and very pretty, with thick dark hair, cut into a shiny bob, a dusting of freckles over her nose, and sparkling green eyes. She smiled at Dax winningly. 'Hi,' she said. 'You must be Dax. I've heard a lot about you.'

Dax looked, confused, at Owen and then at Gideon. She was a complete stranger, but she seemed weirdly familiar. The girl remained seated, her slender hands folded in her lap, beaming at him with an expression he knew oddly well.

For a few seconds, nobody spoke. Then Owen stood up. 'Gideon,' he prompted, and Gideon glanced at Luke and then across to Dax.

'Dax,' he said, an excited and strange edge to his voice, 'meet Catherine. She's our sister.'

9

Dax was speechless. The air just went out of his throat in a gasp. He stared at the girl and she smiled back, while Luke and Gideon grinned.

'Sorry to weird you out, mate!' said Gideon, at last.

'You—you *knew*? You knew you had a sister?' spluttered Dax, finally finding his voice.

'Well, kind of,' said Gideon, shifting on his feet and looking faintly embarrassed. 'Ever since Luke got here we've both felt that something else was coming. Some*one* else.'

'And here I am,' said Catherine and got to her feet. She was dressed in fashionable sportswear and expensive trainers, with a glittery silver clip in one side of her shiny dark hair. She stepped across to Dax and held out her hand. Like Lisa's, it was perfectly manicured. She made him think of a successful saleswoman, polished and slick. He took her hand and shook it, dumbly. It was warm, and she squeezed his hand firmly, exactly as the successful saleswoman would have done.

'I'm really pleased to meet you, Dax,' she said, with another winning smile and Dax suddenly realized that she was American.

Tiredness struck him—it must be the shock. 'Can I sit down for a bit?' he asked.

'Of course, Dax. Here.' Mrs Sartre touched his shoulder and guided him to an oak and leather chair to one side of her desk.

'So—you found her even in America?' Dax asked the principal, and she nodded.

'We really think Catherine is the last,' she said, sitting back down beside her desk, while Catherine, Luke, and Gideon all settled back into their seats around the book-lined room. 'For a while, as you know, Dax, we thought *you* were the last. One hundred and nine Colas. But now we know it is one hundred and eleven. One, one, one. It is a strong number.'

'Is she a Cola?' he asked, and noticed Catherine pull a small, amused face at being spoken about as if she weren't present. He knew it was rude, but he was too thrown to care.

'We think so. Although we don't know exactly how. She's registering lots of different abilities, in different ways, is that not so, Catherine?'

Catherine was holding Gideon's hand. 'Yes, Mrs Sartre,' she beamed, and a pencil on Principal Sartre's desk rose shakily into the air before dropping back with a small click and a roll.

'You seem really . . . relaxed!' said Dax, staring at the girl. He was trying hard to get her measure through his senses, but found it difficult. Probably because she was from another country, and because he himself felt so strange.

'Oh—I may seem it, but I'm actually *so* excited!' she

exclaimed, sounding incredibly like a character in one of the American teenage dramas that some of the girls watched in the TV room. 'I was like—hey! This can*not* be happening to *me*! For a while I was totally freaked out, but now—y'know . . . ' she smiled at her brothers and her green eyes sparkled, 'I can't think of anywhere I'd rather be!'

'Well, I think it's time your brothers gave you a tour of Tregarren,' said Principal Sartre. She stood, and so did everyone else. 'Be sure to explain all our rules,' she added. 'And don't be tempted to show off, Gideon.'

Gideon grinned and said, 'Who, me?'

Dax fell in behind the triplets as they left, but Paulina Sartre touched his shoulder again and made him stay. There was a strong charge in her fingers, and he knew she wanted to ask him something.

'I'll catch up with you,' he called after them, but they were already chatting and laughing and heading out into the quad. They didn't look back.

'What is it?' he asked, as the principal's study door closed behind him again. Owen had remained in his place by the window.

'This is difficult for you, yes?' said the principal, turning him to face her and still touching his shoulder. Her soft grey eyes rested on him and he knew she was reading him. He made no attempt to block her.

'Well . . . it's pretty weird, don't you think?' he said.

'Pretty weird? Yes. But then, that's what we all are, no?'

She released him and ushered him back to the sofa. Dax sat. It was only as his tail curled around his paws that he realized he'd shifted, without giving it a thought, into a fox. He coughed in embarrassment and shifted quickly back. 'Sorry,' he said.

'Not at all,' she murmured, and he noticed Owen smiling sympathetically. 'It is your instinct. You feel a little threatened.'

'No, I don't,' protested Dax. 'I'm fine.'

'Yes, yes, I know. You are fine. What I mean is, you feel unsure. It *is*, as you say, pretty weird.'

'What I feel most is *tired*,' mumbled Dax.

Paulina Sartre sat down again too and took off her spectacles to rub her eyes briefly. 'Yes, well, it's all been quite exciting. We found Catherine only six days ago, in California. We had no idea that there were Colas outside the United Kingdom. We hadn't even found any in other parts of Europe.'

'But how—how could she have gone so far away? And how could they have all been split *up*?' demanded Dax. 'It doesn't make sense. How can you *lose* triplets? They're really rare. You can't just mix them up and send them all off in different directions!'

Owen shifted by the window and said, 'Gideon's mum, like I told you, wasn't with his dad when she gave birth. They had split up before he even knew she was pregnant. It seems that when she had the babies she made the decision to have two of them adopted—not an uncommon situation for a single mother with no means of support. She chose to keep Gideon and then Luke and Catherine were put up for adoption. When she and Gideon's dad got back together, he only knew she'd had one child—his son. We would have found out about this much sooner, but the records office where the information was kept was flooded eight years ago and many of the relevant documents were lost. The fact is, we would never have known, never have gone looking for Luke, if Mrs Sartre hadn't had a number of episodes, convincing her there was a sibling. Two siblings, as it turned out.'

'So what about Catherine's family in America? Did they just say yes and let her cross the world in less than a week?' asked Dax. 'I can't believe that!'

'Catherine was with foster parents,' said the principal, lightly. 'They were willing to let her go when they realized she would get an excellent education. She had only been with them a few months, so she was fairly happy to move on.'

'Foster parents? I thought she was adopted, like Luke?'

'Not so lucky,' said Owen. 'She *was* adopted at first. Healthy, pretty babies are always adopted. But her adoptive parents were killed in a car crash when she was four. Then she went into care for a while, and then there was a second adoption, but it ended badly. The mother turned out to have mental health problems, and couldn't cope. She was discovered trying to have Catherine exorcized by the local priest. It was the priest who contacted the social services.'

'Exorcized?' gasped Dax. 'You're joking!'

Owen shook his head. 'We wondered if Catherine was showing up some early Cola patterns. A handful of our Colas here did experience weird happenings when they were much younger, on a more minor scale. To someone with mental health problems, that could be very frightening. Anyway, needless to say, Catherine ended up back in care, and she's been with a succession of foster families ever since. Not unusual by the time a child gets to five or six. It's very difficult to find families willing to adopt permanently when children get bigger.'

Dax wondered, briefly, why he was being told all of this. Mrs Sartre seemed to read this.

'What do you make of her, Dax?' she asked.

He stared at her, surprised. 'You want to know what *I* think?'

'Yes. You have an interesting slant on these things,' she said. 'You are not affected by glamour, I think.'

He stared at her. She knew! And Owen must know too.

'Not much,' he mumbled, wondering how many other people knew his secret.

'So?'

'I—I don't know,' he said, frowning and trying to trace his own thoughts on the sister from America. 'She's . . . she's very bright. Sparkly. I think she'll get on well. People will like her.'

'And you, Dax? Will you like her?' The principal leaned across her desk and looked at him closely.

Dax looked back at her levelly. 'You know I'm jealous enough of Luke as it is.' She nodded and smiled at him, approving of his honesty. Dax sighed. 'I don't know how I feel about another one—I don't know what's going on inside *me* yet.'

He found them all again at teatime. Catherine was sitting with them at their usual table, and two other Colas— Jessica Moorland and Claire Farmer, a telekinetic from Gideon's development group—had also drawn up chairs to sit next to the new girl and chat. Dax could hardly squeeze into his usual seat, next to Lisa.

'No problems settling in then,' he murmured to Lisa, trying to find space for his plate of spaghetti Bolognese.

'None at all,' said Lisa, watching the new arrival intently. 'She's been fighting them all off! I think she may be a bit like Mia—they're all very charmed.'

'Are you?'

'Don't know. Haven't had a look in yet. What do you know about her?'

Dax briefly related some of what he'd heard from Owen and Principal Sartre. 'She's not had it easy,' he concluded and Lisa pulled a face.

'Who has?' she said, which Dax felt was hardly fair. Lisa had always had the best of everything from her adoring father; Gideon had had love and support and the same parent throughout his life—and Luke, too, had managed to end up with excellent adoptive parents. There was no question that Catherine had come off worst when the triplets were split up.

'Still, she seems to have overcome it all,' said Lisa, brightly. 'I like her top.'

Dax shook his head in exasperation. 'Sometimes you're so shallow, Hardman!' he said and she flicked a pea at him from her plate.

Catherine was engaging, there was no doubt about it. Her accent, her fluid, pretty movements and gestures, and her intensely friendly manner were all intriguing. Luke and Gideon seemed to be enjoying showing her off. Gideon kept doing little bits of power, heedless of the rules, spinning cutlery around and interfering with the vegetables on their plates—and Luke was grinning and excited, sitting on Gideon's left and peering round at his new sister. Catherine was constantly squeezing and touching people, too, Dax noticed. He knew that Americans were generally meant to be much more outgoing and 'touchy-feely' than the British, so he supposed this was normal. All the while Catherine talked to Gideon, Jessica, and Claire, there were little touches to an arm, a shoulder, even a cheek—and she kept squeezing Gideon's hand. It was something which would have been odd in the extreme from anyone else, but with Catherine it seemed completely natural.

Dax leaned his chair back and reached behind Lisa to touch Mia on the back. 'What do you think?' he asked, and she scraped her chair back to answer him.

'She seems lovely,' she said, with her usual warm

smile. 'Gideon and Luke are lucky to have found her. I'd love to have a sister.' That was another thing, of course. Colas were almost always lone children. They might have step- or half-brothers or sisters, but only a handful had true siblings. There was a brother and sister among the telekinetics, Dax knew, and also the two brothers, Jacob and Alex Teller, who were telepathic and also uncanny mimics. They'd had him in stitches last term with their impressions of Spook and the sinister Mr Eades.

'Ow! You horror!' Catherine had just let out a girlish yelp and Dax saw that Gideon was up to his usual tricks. He'd just given her a Chinese burn on the wrist, so he could demonstrate Mia's healing power. He'd done the same when he'd met Dax. Catherine was trotted round to Mia who told Gideon off, as usual, and then took Catherine's suntanned wrist in her hands. Catherine's mouth opened in a small 'O' of astonishment. 'Wow!' she said. 'Are you for real? That is *so* amazing!' She held up her wrist which now bore no sign of the red mark Gideon had inflicted upon it. She picked up both Mia's hands and stared into the girl's face. Mia blushed. 'How do you *do* that?' gasped Catherine. 'That is just an awesome power! I wish I could do that. What a gift to the world!'

Mia was now looking acutely embarrassed. At last Catherine let go of her hands, and she quickly picked up her soup spoon and concentrated hard on her minestrone. Lisa was giggling helplessly beside Dax. 'Wow!' she mimicked, in a low voice. 'Mia—you are *so awesome*!'

'Shut up!' muttered Mia. She finished her soup quickly, and then got up. 'I'm going back to the dorm,' she said. 'I'm whacked.'

As she left, Catherine called out, 'Hey—wait up, Mia! I'm in your dorm! Can I come back with you?' Mia smiled and nodded and Catherine bounced up out of her seat, planted a kiss on each of her brothers' foreheads, and skipped off after Mia.

In the moments after she had gone, nobody spoke. It was as if all their energy had left the room with her. At length, Gideon looked across at Dax. 'Big shock, eh?' he grinned, and rubbed his hair with a yawn. 'Freaky enough getting Luke, I reckon!' Luke grinned too, almost the double of his brother. 'But now—blimey—three for the price of two. How lucky can this college get?'

'Has your dad been told?' asked Dax.

'Yeah—they called him last night. He's coming down tomorrow, for a family reunion,' said Gideon. 'We're all going up to Polgammon for a big dinner and hugs and crying and stuff. Catherine'll do all the hugs and me and Luke will take it in turns to cry. Dad'll probably join in too.'

Dax wondered how Gideon could take it all so lightly—but he reasoned that perhaps the only way Gideon *could* take it was lightly. His whole life must have been pitched over in the last week. Dax badly wanted to get him alone and find out how he was really feeling. There had just been no chance. He made up his mind to wake his friend and take him out on a little midnight foxwalk—if they could manage it without waking Luke too.

After tea, while there was still a little light left, Dax told Gideon he'd see him back in the common room. He had a quick journey to make. Shifting swiftly, he shot up the fox path to the woods above the college and made his way back through the trees to the spot where he'd met the wolf, the night before. Pausing, he sniffed the air, tried to remember precisely where the wolf had led him, and then moved purposefully east until he arrived at the edge of the woodland and found the old apple tree. He stared up into it and tried to work out what the wolf had been trying to tell him. It had scraped its claws on the old trunk of the tree and stared up into its branches.

But Dax could see nothing significant in the tree—just leaves and a few blossoms. No clues at all. With a sigh he turned about and headed back to the cliff path.

Back at the common room he hoped he might be able to talk to Gideon about the night before, ask what his friend thought, but he found only Luke on their usual sofa near the fire, talking to Barry and dealing out some playing cards.

'Where's Gid?' he asked and Luke glanced up from his swift dealing.

'He's gone to bed, already! Says he's done in, what with all this long-lost stuff.'

Dax went up to find Gideon but there was no chance to talk to him. His friend was buried in his quilt, only a tuft or two of yellow hair showing on his pillow. It was only eight o'clock and Gideon was sleeping like the dead.

10

The door to Development 12 opened and Gideon staggered out, looking slightly grey.

'How was it?' asked Dax, anxiously. He was glad now that he hadn't bothered to wake up his friend for a fox-trot last night. Clearly Gideon had needed his sleep—and a whole lot more of it by the look of him. 'Was it that bad? Do they put probes into your skull or something?' Dax was beginning to feel more and more nervous. Gideon slumped down next to him and shook his head.

'Nah . . . no probes. You go into this long metal coffin-like thing—you slide in on a shelf, like a pizza going into an oven.'

Dax nodded, feeling no better. When the principal had told them in assembly that morning that they would be asked to take part in some tests, he had no idea they'd shipped in a Magnetic Resonance Imaging scanner. The incredibly expensive machinery, used to spot tumours and other ailments inside patients, was there to examine their brains and bodies in fine slices; taking myriads of cross-section pictures.

'It bangs and thuds, you know?' Gideon was going on, rubbing his eyes and yawning. 'Like road works. The noise is how it takes your X-ray thingies. It's how the noise bounces back off your squishy insides that makes the map of what you look like under your skin and bone. You have to keep really still so it doesn't go blurry.'

'Doesn't sound *that* bad,' said Dax.

'It *wasn't*. That bit was *fine*.'

'So why are you looking all weirded out, then?'

'Well, they offer to play music into these little headphones for you, while you're in there—because it takes about fifteen minutes.'

'Yeah?'

'I asked for chart stuff and . . . I—I can hardly stand to think about it . . . ' Gideon shuddered and grinned and started to laugh.

'What?'

'I was trapped in a metal box, unable to move a muscle—and they played non-stop Celine Dion.' Gideon began to shake out several pent-up shudders and horrified cackles as Dax laughed himself nearly off his seat. If there was one kind of music Gideon couldn't stand it was syrupy pop rock.

'I did shout out,' snorted Gideon, his face now returning to its normal pinkness. 'But nobody could hear me above all the bashing and crashing. I tell you—I should sue them for emotional injury.'

They were still laughing when Mr Eades opened the door to Development 12 and peered at them both darkly. They composed themselves. Mr Eades hardly ever spoke a word; he was a grey man in a grey suit, with grey hair and a greyer manner. He was really quite scary.

'Please step inside, Mr Jones,' he said, in his dull, flat voice. Dax did as he was told.

'Now—you will need to put your signature here,' said Mr Eades, once the door was closed behind them. D12 was a square room, lit with fluorescent strip lights. Its floor was thinly carpeted and its walls had white-painted cork tiles; to soak up noise, Dax imagined. To one side of the room a second area was sectioned off behind glass, and two white-coated women were attending to a desk of switches and monitors. It was very high tech and made Dax think of a recording studio. Which it was, in a way, he supposed.

Mr Eades was holding out a form on a clipboard. Attached to it with a piece of string and a knot of sticky tape was a pen, which he put into Dax's right hand. Dax scanned the piece of paper and noticed that Gina's signature was already at the bottom. She'd given consent for him to have these strange inside-out tests, as he thought of them. He read a paragraph or two but most of it was in some kind of medical or legal gobbledegook. He didn't trust Gina to have checked it out properly; she wouldn't care if they wanted to stick hot rods up his nostrils and fry his brain, but he did trust Owen, and he knew that Owen was aware of the programme of tests. If Owen thought it was OK, so did Dax. He signed.

'Now, Mr Jones,' said Mr Eades, guiding him across to the scanner. 'You will need to lie down and relax for fifteen minutes or so, but keep absolutely still. Do you need to go to the toilet? Now would be the time.'

Dax shook his head and looked at the MRI scanner. It was large enough to accommodate an adult, and rose up from the floor in an arch-topped oblong of white painted metal, connected to the studio walls with tubes and wires and metal struts. Reaching into it was some kind of conveyor belt and there was a special resting place for your head. It was softly lit inside and there was, indeed, a set of headphones, lying on the headrest.

'It gets very noisy,' said Mr Eades, guiding Dax to sit up and then lie down on the conveyor belt. One of the women in white coats came out and positioned his head correctly, placing a couple of sticky pads with wires attached on each of his temples. She smiled at him. 'You can have some music on,' went on Mr Eades and Dax grinned to himself.

'Classical, jazz, or chart music?' intoned Mr Eades flatly; the most unlikely DJ in the world.

'Classical,' said Dax, quickly.

The woman in the white coat smiled again and put the headphones over his ears. 'Just relax and stay really still,' she said, and then reached up and pushed a button. At once the conveyor belt started to move and Dax began to slide into the metal tube. He didn't enjoy the sensation. It was a tight fit and the metal interior seemed to skim barely above his nose. Once inside he found there was a strange mirror arrangement above his eyes, which allowed him to see across the room, even though he was encased in thick metal. Dax gulped. Several times. He felt his heart rate increase. He didn't like this. Mr Eades had retreated to the booth behind the glass and shut the door and the women were attending to the various buttons and monitors on the other side. There was nothing to hear but his own ragged breathing, amplified by the metal that curved tightly around him.

Dax struggled to be calm. He was to be here for a quarter of an hour. He had to relax. He closed his eyes. He tried some of the self-hypnosis thing that Owen had taught him, but no sooner had he imagined himself in his usual woody glade than a tinny rendition of 'Greensleeves' started up in his headphones. It wasn't as bad as Celine Dion, but it was pretty dreadful, played on a cheap keyboard with a lurching rhythm and incorrect chords. It distracted him, briefly, from his surroundings.

Then the *real* noise started. It sounded as if someone had just hit the scanner with a spade and Dax jumped violently and then anchored himself again, remembering that he must be still. The crashing and thudding went on and on and Dax began to feel a cold, sick shake in the pit of his stomach. There was something horribly familiar about the sounds around him, coupled with not being able to move in a tiny, tiny space.

For a few seconds, he fought his mind valiantly, trying again and again to self-hypnotize, taking deep breaths, digging his fingernails hard into his palms to distract himself from the thoughts that wanted to rush into his head like water over a broken dam. He bit on his tongue and tasted the salty rush between his teeth and prayed the metallic sting would hold off the thoughts but it was no good. No good at all. He was paralysed and the darkness in his mind was taking over. He felt the protective shield of his common sense flex and crumple like tin foil in a flame and with a truly horrible belt of terror, Dax was back inside the earth.

He was deep in the foxhole with the noise of huntsmen and their spades hacking away at the only way out, and the guttural death-call of the hounds curling coldly around the dank passages and into his terrified ears. Dax lay frozen inside the metal tube, but his heart was beating so fast he could hear it and a cold sweat ran across his skin. A thunderous wave of nausea began to build inside him, marching up across his chest and to his throat while at the same time that awful, black, sinking feeling of defeat began to wash over him as it had done in the foxhole: a feeling that it would be better to give up and feel no more, no more—that any kind of nothingness would be welcome after this hideous, tearing, shrieking, nameless fear . . .

There was a tugging feeling on either side of his head and Dax realized in a flash of shock that he had shifted. The sticky pads on his temples ripped lightly against his fox fur and were gone. Lost in wild instinct, Dax had shot out of the scanner and was cowering in the corner of D12, shaking so hard he couldn't see properly.

The door to the booth crashed open and Mr Eades stalked out angrily. 'What on earth are you doing, Jones?' he demanded and then stopped when he saw the fox crouching beneath a chair in the corner, trembling and staring fixedly at the floor. Dax couldn't move or respond in any way. He couldn't even see Mr Eades. All he could see was the scene in the foxhole, just before his rescue, playing over again and again, like a DVD set on a loop. The lead hound's teeth; the dark, oppressive earth with its fine network of roots; the terrible howls and thuds of the spades; the warmth of the hound's excited breath on his face; the sick resignation to death. Somehow the scene just would not move on to the part where Owen broke open the soil above him and hauled him out.

'Yeow! Bloody hell, Dax! Cut it out!'

At last he was snapped back into reality. Dax realized he was biting someone. It was Owen. His vision swam and refocused and he saw Owen nursing his left hand, which was lightly bleeding from a track of sharp teeth marks. Dax tried to say sorry, but only let out a yelp. He was still in fox form. Owen seemed to realize he was 'back' and picked him up bodily and took him out into the corridor. 'Stay there,' he said firmly to Mr Eades, who had been about to follow. The grey man pursed his lips, but let the door to D12 fall closed, leaving them both in the empty corridor outside. Owen put Dax down and sat on one of the chairs.

There was a pause. Dax wanted to curl up and go to sleep. He also wanted to apologize, though, so he pulled together his remaining energy and shifted back into a boy. His shirt stuck to his back and when he uncurled his fists he saw four crescent-shaped wounds in each palm. His fingernails had broken the skin.

'Sorry about biting you.' His voice sounded raspy, like dry leaves. 'How long was I . . . like that?'

'About five minutes, I think,' said Owen, still inspecting his left hand. 'It took me that long to get there. Don't worry—it was only a little dig. Although it's the second chunk you've had out of me this month! You've had your rabies shots, yeah?'

Dax smiled weakly.

'That's better,' said Owen. He looked up at Dax and sighed. 'What happened to you in there?'

Dax shook his head and wrapped his arms around his knees, balling himself tightly together. He hated, *hated* having to explain to Owen just how much fright had got hold of him.

'Dax,' persisted Owen. 'You had a panic attack. Do you have any idea why?'

Still, Dax struggled. He so badly needed Owen's respect, and since this term started—since *before* it started—he'd been nothing but a pathetic heap of nerves.

'OK—let me take an educated guess. You got a flashback. To the day of the fox hunt. Am I right?'

Dax nodded bleakly. Well, he should have known Owen would guess.

'I wish I had thought about it,' muttered Owen. 'It was pretty stupid that I didn't. Dax, a lot of people get panicky inside an MRI scanner. They should have given you the panic button to hold.'

'Panic button?'

'Yep—there's one on a flex that runs into the scanner

with you, which you hold in one hand. It communicates with the booth. Usually just having it in your hand is enough to keep you calm. They obviously, in all their excitement, forgot to give it to you. I will have words,' he added, grimly.

'Oh,' said Dax. He couldn't think of anything else to add.

Owen regarded him for a moment. 'I know about the dog, too, Dax,' he said. Dax glanced up, fresh mortification assaulting him. 'Spook's allowance has been stopped for a month,' added Owen. 'Sorry, Dax, but of course he couldn't resist telling all his mates about it, so it got back to me. One of his friends, Darren Tyler, thought it was pretty poor. Didn't know much about your recent history, but could see that it was really bad for you—had quite a go at Spook. And then told me. Apparently Spook got one of his drag-hunting fraternity pals to recommend him as a helper and walker with a local pack and he managed to get a dog out for a walk. We've also been in touch with *them*, and that's the end of *that* little alliance.'

Dax felt another wave of tiredness. Owen stood and yanked him up by the elbow. 'You need to go to bed for a while. Have a bath, have a sleep, and then get a good tea down you. We'll talk some more about the panic attacks, but really, Dax, you don't need to be ashamed about them. Loads of people get them at some point and after what happened to you I'd be amazed if you *didn't* have a few aftershocks. We'll tackle it in Development.'

'What about the scan?' asked Dax, looking uneasily back at D12.

'We'll have another go at a later time—when you're up to it.'

They climbed the stairs out of the subterranean Development corridors and Owen sent Dax straight back to the dorm. As he walked up the steps to the door, Catherine emerged, looking very pretty in the Tregarren College uniform.

'Does it suit me, Dax?' she laughed, spinning on the spot and holding her hands out like a dancer. He smiled and nodded—she was like a blaze of energy.

'I'm so, so excited to be here!' she said, grabbing hold of his hands and beaming at him, her green eyes sparkling. 'You really must tell me about being a fox! That's just so *out* of here! Can you do it? Can you show me now? I *love* animals!'

Dax was so tired now he could barely talk. 'Sorry, Catherine,' he mumbled. 'I will show you, but right now I've got to get some sleep.'

Catherine immediately looked stricken and squeezed his hands extra hard. 'Oh, Dax—I'm so sorry! I'm such a goofball! Always thinking everyone's on hyperdrive, like me! My last mom said I was like St Elmo's Fire! You go get some rest! I'll catch you later!' She dropped his hands and bounded away.

Dax trudged upstairs and went to run a bath, but felt so tired that in the end he just took off his shoes and clambered into bed fully clothed. He was asleep in seconds.

11

He began to spend almost more time as a fox than as a boy, slipping into vulpine form more easily than he could remain human, and he didn't really know why, except that perhaps Paulina Sartre was right. He felt lost and vulnerable. Gideon had not been in his company for even five minutes without either Luke or Catherine or both in tow. The triplets had had their emotional meeting with Gideon's dad in Polgammon, eating dinner at the big hotel and spending several hours catching up. Before the evening was halfway through Michael Reader was talking openly to Catherine about coming to England for good and Catherine had announced she was changing her surname to Reader. Gideon had filled Dax in on the details while they were brushing their teeth the next morning.

'He doesn't know where to put himself!' said Gideon, foaming at the mouth and staring at Dax through the mirror. He spat some pale blue froth into the sink and then took a palm full of water and gargled enthusiastically. 'I cink he awways quanted ga gorter!'

Dax translated this and then shook his head wonderingly at his friend. 'Doesn't any of this bother you, Gid?'

Gideon shrugged. 'Why should it? I mean, I know it's weird—but weird is normal these days, isn't it? She is my sister. And Luke's my brother. I don't know them—but I *do* know them. It seems . . . like it was meant to happen . . . Three of one. One of three.'

Dax screwed up his face. 'You sound like a medium!'

Gideon winced, which was reassuring. 'Yeah—I do a bit, don't I?'

Dax glanced at the bathroom doorway, knowing that Luke or Barry would arrive at any time and then this precious bit of one to one conversation with Gideon would be over. He persisted. 'I mean—won't it bother you to have to share your dad with a sister—and maybe a brother, too?'

'Nah—he can't adopt Luke. Luke's taken already. Though he'll come and stay, I expect . . . '

'But . . . the sharing?'

Gideon shrugged again. 'Things change,' he said. He didn't ask Dax what *he* thought. He just chucked his toothbrush in the glass and left.

After classes that day, Owen was taking a small party of interested Colas up to the woods, to give them some more tuition on bushlore. Dax, Lisa, and Mia met him at the gatehouse and at first it seemed that Gideon would not be coming. Dax felt his shoulders sag as he leaned into the thick stone sill and stared out of the gatehouse window, down the winding cliff path, seeing nothing of his best friend. Gid had *always* done bushlore with them! Owen checked his watch and made to go.

'Triplets gone AWOL then?' asked Lisa, giving Dax a searching look. 'Oh, will you *stop* that, Dax!'

He realized, once again, that he'd shifted, and swiftly returned himself to boy form, still pink with embarrassment. Paulina Sartre had been spot on. Now all it took for him to feel threatened was a throw-away remark from Lisa and—bang! He was a fox. It was like a nervous twitch.

'No—they're coming,' said Mia, peering past Dax's head. The triplets were heading up the steep path, Catherine bounding ahead like a mountain goat, her shiny hair swinging in the wind. Dax gritted his teeth. Triplets. They. It seemed Gideon was now only available in a pack of three.

'Sorry we kept you all!' grinned Catherine as she swept into the room with a gust of sea breeze behind her. 'Hey, Dax!' she beamed at him. 'Go on! Do it for me!'

Dax sighed and shook his head. 'No, I'm annoying Lisa,' he said, testily. 'Anyway—you'll see it sooner or later.'

Catherine had been pestering him to shift in front of her all week. Strangely, considering how often he was doing the fox thing these days, she seemed to keep missing all the action. Catherine's smile didn't fade for a second. As Gideon and Luke stepped in behind her she skipped across the room and slipped her arm through Dax's.

'Well then—you can walk me to the woods and when Lisa's not looking, you can do it then!' She smiled archly at Lisa, who was narrowing her eyes at Dax.

'Come on, you lot! We'll be losing the light soon,' said Owen, and they all trooped out of the gatehouse and up the path into the woods. Catherine hung on to Dax and chattered away about the college and the staff and the Colas and how she was doing in Development.

'They say I'm really coming on!' she breathed, excitedly. 'You have no idea just how *cool* this is! I can lift a notebook! It's true!' Dax had to laugh at her enthusiasm. He pulled his own notebook, for scribbling down Owen's bushlore information, out of his pocket and handed it to her.

'Go on then! Show me!'

Catherine let go of his arm and fell back a little, weighing the book in her palm. She bit her lower lip and looked suddenly lost. 'I'm not sure if I can do it *here*,' she murmured and Dax felt guilty. He knew very well how hard it was to call on Cola powers to order in the early days.

'Don't worry,' he said, but Catherine was trying. The notebook was rising, very slightly, at one end. It hovered at an angle, its spiral binding an inch above the girl's fingers. Then it dropped. Catherine pouted.

'That's it!' she said, flatly.

'No—that's really great!' Dax encouraged. 'You have to keep practising.'

'I'll never be as good as the rest of you!' she sighed. Then she seemed to flick her brightness switch up again. Immediately her 400-watt smile was back on and she was running ahead to catch up with her brothers. As she reached Gideon and Luke she jumped into the air and thumped them both on their shoulders. Dax noticed that as she linked arms with them she leaned more towards Gideon. Gideon definitely seemed to be her favourite.

'Fire time,' said Owen, when they reached a small clearing. 'Sticks, please—plenty of them!'

'But we've done fires!' protested Gideon. 'We've done loads of fires!'

Owen looked at him sagely. 'Yes, Gideon, but not *this* kind of fire. And it's an important kind. Smokeless.'

Gideon shrugged. 'But I *like* smoke,' he muttered and let out a yawn.

'Great. I'm glad you're enjoying it. You'll be less keen on it when you're trying to warm up and eat *and* keep yourself hidden,' said Owen, kneeling on the wood floor and breaking some twigs.

'Aah,' said Gideon, nodding. Luke grinned next to him.

'I like this stuff,' he said. 'We used to do it in Scouts.'

Owen nodded, approvingly. 'Good—so what do we need then, Luke?'

'Um . . . well . . . not damp wood. That smokes like mad.'

'True,' said Owen. 'Young green sticks will smoke too. And old bark. Get your twigs and small branches from the top of the pile if you can, or cut them off deadfalls. As dry as you can find. Then you'll need to get rid of any bark. Dax—hand these round. Catherine—come and watch me before you try this. Luke—have you used these?'

116

Dax gave out Owen's stash of woodsman knives as Luke nodded. The short, sturdy blades with a gentle curve to one side were bound with waxed string along the handle and sheathed in leather. They had all been taught how to work with these essential tools, taking care always to cut away from the body and *never* to work wood on their thighs and risk severing an artery. After many weeks of Owen's expert guidance, Dax, Gideon, Lisa, and Mia were quite adept at safely working twigs, roots, and branches into the shapes they needed for camping.

Owen showed Catherine how to hold the knife and shear off the thin bark from a small branch. She was awkward with it, and kept pulling the wood down onto her knees. 'No,' said Owen, firmly, holding her wrist as she was about to strike her blade down again. 'If you miss you'll carve through your femoral artery and probably bleed to death before we can get you back to the college.'

Catherine looked up at him with wide eyes. 'Truly?'

Owen couldn't help grinning at her stricken face. 'Truly!' he confirmed. 'Although, fortunately, we do have the world's best healer with us.'

'Isn't she amazing?' marvelled Catherine, reaching over and squeezing Mia's free hand. Mia was abashed and had to shake her admirer off.

'Watch!' said Owen. 'I'll show you again.'

For a while she seemed to get the hang of it, and Owen left her to it. Then, suddenly, she gave a cry. They all jumped, engrossed as they had been in preparing the firewood. Dax immediately smelt blood and leapt to his feet. Catherine was holding her left forearm tight in her right hand and looking pale. A scarlet ditch was forming behind the web of skin between her thumb and forefinger.

Catherine closed her eyes, kneeling among her pile of twigs, and swayed slightly. And then, peculiarly, she smiled. ' 'S OK! Drama over!' She pulled her hand away, revealing a smear of blood, but no obvious wound.

Owen stood over her, frowning. 'What happened here, Catherine?'

She smiled and Dax thought she looked odd—faraway. 'I just did a little heal, Mr Hind. That's all.'

Owen snatched up her wrist and stared at the bloody but woundless skin. 'You healed *yourself*?'

Everyone looked at Mia, who shook her head in confusion. 'It wasn't me,' she said, simply.

They looked back again, like spectators of a slow-motion tennis match, at Catherine. There were twenty-two healers at Tregarren. They had varying degrees of ability; Mia was by far the best. But none of them—not even Mia—could heal *themselves*.

'Hey! Isn't that something!' laughed Catherine. Her eyes sparkled.

'She's good, isn't she?' Gideon said to Dax as they headed back. Dax nodded. 'I mean—it's really something, isn't it? To be able to heal yourself. I mean, that's—that's like a Marvel Comic thing, isn't it? Like—Captain Invincible! Maybe if she got blown up, all the bits would join up together again and she'd come back to life.'

Dax laughed. It was good to hear Gideon being ridiculous again.

'Wow!' Gideon was shaking his head again and kept turning round to look back at Catherine, who was bouncing along between Mia and Lisa now, trying to get them to sing marching songs. Mia was gamely trying to sing along and Lisa was wearing a look of amused revulsion. 'And then there's Luke,' Gideon pondered. 'Nothing going on there at all! How weird is that? Maybe it's a blood-type thing.'

'Well, you'll find out soon,' said Dax. 'We're getting tested again tomorrow and this time they are after our blood.'

'Oh yes—I saw that notice up in the hall. Yuck! I hate needles. What do they want with our blood? They know our blood groups already—it's on our medical form thingies.'

'Checking for alien DNA I expect,' said Luke, catching up with them. 'You're probably half-Martian or something. Or maybe they're going to clone you all!'

'Well, they'd better not take too much of mine,' grunted Gideon. 'I need it! I feel like someone's had a pint out of me already—I'm out of it!' He did look tired, thought Dax. In fact, they were all flagging—Mia looked half asleep and even Owen was yawning. The sea air probably, he thought. Only Catherine was pinging around like a jet-propelled tennis ball; now she was trying to do Lisa's long blonde hair in an elaborate top knot, while they were walking. Lisa wore an expression of resigned confusion.

Dax turned back to the brothers. 'Doesn't your sister ever slow down?'

'Apparently not,' yawned Gideon. Luke caught the yawn. 'I think she's a human form of perpetual motion. Don't try to stop her—she's a force of nature.'

12

'You're doing it again, Dax.'

'Oh, sorry,' said Dax, but it came out as a short bark. He shifted back again, embarrassed.

'This is a bit worrying,' said Owen, leaning back on the chair in one corner of Development 10. 'I only just started talking about the hunt and—phwip—you're all furry. Dax—I think you need to just talk it through and maybe you'll stop all this twitchy shifting business.'

Dax stared at his shoes, feeling something numb inside him. It lay like a ball of ice in the pit of his stomach. He didn't want to thaw it out. He *wanted* the hunt experience locked away in permafrost; didn't ever want even to think about it again, let alone talk about it. Most of all he didn't want to talk about it to Owen. He cringed at the very thought. Possibly because he knew how much Owen cared. It was too much.

There was a restless movement on the edge of Dax's vision. 'It would *help*,' he said, stubbornly, 'if the audience would push off.' Owen glanced across to the far wall of D10. Like all of the development rooms which ran in a network of catacombs deep in the granite rock under the college, D10, carpeted, softly lit, and painted a relaxing green, had one wall entirely made of glass. It looked a bit like a dance studio. Dax had worked out very quickly, with the help of his fox sense, that it was a two-way mirror, enabling a watcher to stand behind and follow every move in the room, undetected by most people. Owen sighed and ran his fingers through his dark, ragged hair.

'You know I can't do anything about that,' he said quietly. 'And usually Mr Eades is in here with us. It's only because I asked very nicely that he agreed to make his notes from behind the glass.'

'It's not just him, though, is it?' said Dax, also quietly. He looked hard at Owen, wondering whether he was going to be a teacher or a friend. Owen looked back and said nothing. Then, almost imperceptibly, he nodded. Then he leaned his head into his hands and his hair tumbled forward, hiding his face. He looked as if he were sighing with frustration, but the faintest whisper reached Dax's sharpened ears. 'Put on a show then, Dax. We'll do the real bit later.'

'It was terrible,' said Dax, in a monotone. 'Really awful. I thought I was going to die—but then you rescued me and I think I'm over it now. All right? That do you? Because I'm sick of all this namby-pamby, New Age, fiffy-faffy, bleh, bleh, bleh! I'm ALL RIGHT!' He pushed his voice up a pitch. 'I don't NEED to regress or get in touch with anything, or, I dunno, let my inner child out, or embrace the fear. I nearly got eaten alive by a pack of dogs—and then I got away. Nasty, nasty. All done. Can I go now?'

'Well, yes, if you're going to waste everybody's time,

you might as well,' said Owen, testily. 'But I need to get you back in that scanner, so you'd better be right about being all over it. Go on then. Go and catch some shrimps or something.' He turned away from Dax with a dismissive wave and began to make some notes at the table next to him. For a second Dax was stricken, wondering if Owen had taken his diatribe seriously, but as he walked to the door he glanced back and noticed that the man was biting his lip, for all the world as if he were trying not to laugh.

It was a warm, lovely spring day and the sea breeze was gentle on his skin as he wandered down towards the rock pools. He was out early and there seemed to be nobody else about. He sat on a rock and watched the tiny movements of sea life, see-through shrimps and faintly speckled tiny fish, performing their swift, sporadic underwater ballet.

'They let you out early too, then?' Dax didn't jump. He'd known someone was approaching for two minutes, and, for the last thirty seconds, that it was Luke. Luke, who smelt a lot like Gideon—but was not Gideon. He squinted up at the boy, shielding his eyes in the bright, late afternoon sun.

'Hi, Luke. Yeah. Underperforming as usual.'

'Yeah, right. Like *that's* possible,' said Luke wryly, and Dax felt guilty. Luke was still having to attend Development, even though he clearly had nothing to develop.

'How did it go today?' he asked, dropping a pebble

into the pool and making the shrimps and fish skitter away in alarm.

'Same as it always goes,' said Luke, sitting down beside Dax and sending his own pebble into the pool with a companionable plop. 'They ask me lots of stupid questions and I try not to give them stupid answers. They measure me with little clicky devices, meant to pick up any trace of super powers and—oh, dear—still nothing there! But look . . . ' he shifted around to face Dax and a look of deep concentration settled on his brow, 'look— I'm definitely coming on with *this*!' As Dax stared at him, the boy's ears *just about* moved, back and forth, without help.

Dax laughed and clapped Luke on the shoulder. 'You're a lot like Gideon sometimes, you know,' he said warmly. 'Family stuff will come out!'

'Not like Catherine, though, eh?' said Luke, unexpectedly. Dax paused, trying to work out Luke's meaning. The boy was looking at the water again, and scratching his fingernails abstractedly against the rock. He seemed to be waiting for something from Dax.

'Well,' Dax ventured. 'She's a one-off—that's for sure.'

'I think . . . ' Luke squinted into the sun and stopped the rock scratching. 'I think she's capable of . . . really big stuff. You know?'

Dax didn't know. All the Colas were capable of really big stuff as far as he could tell. Catherine's ad hoc bits of power didn't seem to amount to much to him. 'What do you mean?' he asked and Luke looked back down at the pool, pursing his lips and letting out a heavy sigh.

'I dunno,' he said. 'Nothing. She's—don't get me wrong—she's my new sister and that's amazing. But . . . '

'It was special with just you and Gideon for a while, wasn't it?' said Dax, aware of the irony of his words. Luke nodded, going slightly pink. That was it, concluded Dax. He was jealous too, and didn't know how to work the feeling out. It didn't help that Catherine gave much more attention to her telekinetic brother.

'Yeah! But—you know, Catherine's amazing too. I'm glad we've all found each other,' said Luke, decisively. 'Just wish I could join in a bit more.'

'Never mind,' said Dax. 'Seriously, it's good to have you around. You help us keep our feet on the ground.' He knew he was babbling, just trying to say something to make Luke feel better.

Luke was scrutinizing him with his head on one side. 'How come,' he said, 'when you turn into a fox, you don't leave all your clothes and stuff on the floor?' Dax grinned. A lot of people asked him this. 'I mean,' Luke went on, 'in like, films and stuff—you know—*The Incredible*—'

'*Hulk,*' finished Dax with a chuckle. 'Yep—I know. He always ends up starkers, except for his trousers. Blimey— I'm glad I haven't got to deal with that. I talked to Owen about it for quite a long time once, and we sort of worked it out.' Luke peered at him with fascination and nodded encouragingly and Dax went on. 'Well—when you walk down the street and you have this sort of picture in your head of who you are and how people see you and so on, you don't think of yourself as a naked human being and then start adding the clothes and the watch and the shoes and—in your case—the glasses. You just have this idea of yourself as you normally are in what you normally wear. It's a self-image thing, you see?'

Luke nodded and pushed his glasses up his nose, frowning thoughtfully.

'So when I shift, I shift into the image of a fox, and when I shift back, I shift back into the image of the boy I was before,' concluded Dax. 'What you get is a sort of projection from my mind—or my spirit, or whatever you want to call it. At least, that's what we came up with. If I'm wearing stuff when I shift, I'll still be wearing it when I shift back. If I'm just carrying something, though, I always drop it during the shift and that stays where it was dropped, as normal. But . . . if I've got a backpack on, and it's part of the image of me, that shifts too. Weird, yeah?'

Luke nodded. 'Very weird,' he said. 'But cool. Does it ever make you scared?'

'It did at first,' said Dax. 'But it was also brilliant from the first. It feels really *right* now.'

Luke was staring back into the rock pool now. 'Really right,' he repeated.

Dax stood up. 'Come on. It's pretty much teatime. Let's get in early and get the best stuff.'

They reached the refectory as the dinner ladies were bashing out fresh trays of hot vegetable curry and baked ham and chicken pie under the slanted glass of the hotplate. Jugs of water and glasses were on each table. 'What's this?' queried Dax. Normally everyone helped themselves to water at the drinks station in the corner, just getting it direct from a tap over a deep square china sink. Cartons of fruit juice were usually stacked on the shelf next to it, and there were also steaming canteens of tea or coffee and milk—also for helping yourself. Dax noticed that these were gone.

'New regime, my love,' said Mrs Polruth, stacking the cutlery trays with warm forks, fresh from the dishwasher. 'We're keeping it to just water for a while. No juices, no tea or coffee, and *definitely* no fizzy drinks.'

'Why?' asked Luke, puzzled.

Mrs P raised one eyebrow. 'Stuff and nonsense if you ask me,' she said. 'Where are we supposed to keep that lot?' She indicated, through the large serving hatch, a huge stack of giant plastic bottles, taking up half the floor space of the kitchen. 'Mineral water,' she said, sceptically. 'Like the stuff out of the tap's not good enough. They're fiddling with your diet, so they can find out why you're all so barmy,' she added, with a maternal chuckle. 'They reckon you mustn't have any stimulants. And they're even taking out the fruit juice, for good measure! I ask you!' She dropped the last bundle of forks into the tray with a flourish and marched back into the kitchen.

'What, no soda? None at all?' Catherine's pretty face crumpled with disappointment when she heard. 'Hey—I love my soda pops!' She picked up a glass and poured out some water, dispiritedly.

'I'm going to miss my cup of tea,' murmured Mia, delicately lifting a forkful of curry and rice. 'I wonder how long they'll do it for?'

' 'S bloomin' outrageous!' complained Gideon, through a mouthful of chicken and ham pie. 'They've got no right!'

'I think they probably have,' said Lisa, sceptically. 'Those forms our dads signed covered all kinds of things like this—short of poisoning us or lopping off our limbs, of course. It makes sense, I suppose. We are what we eat . . . or drink . . . as they say. Maybe they'll do another MRI scan in a couple of weeks and see if there are any differences.'

'So what have they found so far?' muttered Gideon.

'Well, obviously, nothing at all in your case,' dug Lisa, trying to load her fork with pie and peas. 'Just a bit of brain stem, maybe, so you can keep up basic bodily functions. Ow!' Abruptly, Lisa's pie and peas were spattered across her face. 'You little worm!' she bellowed, jumping angrily to her feet. 'Try that again, Reader, and you'll be wearing your dinner in the roots of your hair!'

But Gideon was looking confused. 'I didn't!' he said and then glanced in astonishment at Catherine, who had taken his hand and was smirking at Lisa.

'Hey!' she said. 'You take on one of three, you take on all!' Lisa glared at Catherine and opened her mouth to give another retort, but then snapped it shut again and instead turned and strode away, wiping peas and gravy furiously off her white T-shirt.

There was an awkward silence, and then Gideon

started to laugh. 'Blimey!' he said. 'I've never had a bodyguard before. Quick off the mark, or what?'

Catherine was also giggling, and even Mia was trying to stop herself smiling. 'Hey—but she looks great in anything,' said Catherine, finally letting go of Gideon's hand, and then sending three peas on a little pilgrimage across the tablecloth. 'Even garden vegetables!'

Dax had to laugh too—the girl was quick. The table giggled with guilty amusement. They knew Lisa hadn't really deserved it this time, but probably it made up for all the times when she *had*. Dax settled back to eating. Something nagged at him slightly, though, beyond the guilt at finding Lisa's spattering so funny. It was Luke. Luke was still stolidly working his way through his food. He hadn't laughed at all.

An hour after tea had ended the entire hundred and eleven Colas were back in the refectory, this time to queue for blood-taking with three of the staff from the school sanatorium. The dinner ladies had set out the chairs in lines, so they could sit and chat while they waited, and there were plates of biscuits and jugs of water at the serving hatch, in case anyone 'came over all funny', as Mrs P put it, and needed to up their blood sugar levels. Little groups of Colas stood around comparing puncture wounds, ghoulishly pulling up their plasters and buds of cotton wool.

Dax, Gideon, Barry, and Luke were getting to the head of their queue. Gideon was looking quite pale. 'I really hate needles,' he said again, for the twentieth time.

'Yeah, we know,' said Barry. 'You're such a wuss, Gid!'

'How much blood are they taking?' gulped the wuss, his eyes fixed as far away from the blood-taking action as possible.

'Oh, only a pint and a half—maybe two,' said Barry, with a cheery nasal whistle. 'Look, Gid, you'll be fine— you'll be . . . j-j-just like me . . . ' At this Barry faded himself out, leaving a deathly grimace floating in the air for the last few seconds before he totally vanished. Gideon stamped on his toe. Barry, being Barry, hadn't had the sense to get out of the way after his vanishing trick. 'OW!' He snapped back into view, hopping and glaring at Gideon. 'That's the thanks I get for trying to take your mind off it!'

'Two pints really won't be necessary,' cut in the crisp voice of matron. 'Two teaspoons will be quite enough. But you can sit down, if you like, Gideon. We did have a fainter earlier, but she was sitting down, so it wasn't a problem.'

Gideon went from pale to pink, and then back to pale again. 'I'll sit down,' he said, with a wobble in his voice. 'I'm already half asleep—it's shock!'

'You are a nutcase, Gideon. Honestly! How can it be shock, when you haven't had it done yet?' said Dax.

'He has now,' said matron, and Gideon looked around in amazement. 'What! You—you . . . '

'Yes—I just did it, while Dax was helpfully distracting you.'

'I thought that was just the wipey with antiseptic bit,

beforehand!' murmured Gideon, staring at the inside of his elbow, as matron swiftly taped some cotton wool over the red dot. He smiled wanly up at her—and then slumped forward in his seat, just the same.

'Oh dear—another fainter! Catherine! Can you bring those biscuits over here now?' Matron beckoned to Catherine, who had been making it her business, having been one of the first to have her blood taken, to pass biscuits around the post-needle Colas. She had been hovering among them and depositing biscuits like a well-meaning bumble-bee, giving everyone a comforting squeeze—even those who clearly were not remotely bothered by their experience. Now she dashed across the room, looking intensely worried, and took hold of Gideon, who had his head down between his knees.

' 'S all right,' murmured her brother, 'I'm all right. No—no biscuits, thanks. I just—I just need to have a nap.' He roused himself enough to sit back up, and he did, indeed, look exhausted. Catherine hugged him, and he slumped over her shoulder, his eyes glazed and unfocused.

Matron gently ushered Catherine to one side and sat Gideon up firmly. 'Come on, Gideon. Come back to us. Dax and Barry and Luke will take you back to the dorm as soon as they've been done.' The boys gave their blood samples without fuss, absorbed in watching poor Gideon. Then they helped to haul him to his feet.

As the party left the ref they heard matron call out

again. 'Another fainter! Someone come and help me with Mr Williams—he's a bit too tall for me to manage.'

'Hey! You're not the only one, Gid,' laughed Dax. 'Spook just went down like a skittle!'

13

The following morning was a Saturday, so there was no bell to get everyone up and down to breakfast in time for starting classes. On Saturdays a cold breakfast was left out for the students until 10.30 a.m., and they could wander in for it at any time from 8 a.m. It was a weekend when Dax and Gideon had a pass for Polgammon, along with half of the other students, and Dax was really looking forward to it—not least because Luke and Catherine *didn't* have passes, and wouldn't be able to go until next weekend. Dax wondered, briefly, whether Owen or Mrs Sartre had arranged this deliberately. They seemed to be acutely aware of his struggle to get used to sharing Gideon.

Dax was up and ready to go by nine, but when he emerged from the bathroom he found Gideon and Barry *still* asleep. Luke was reading in bed, his chin propped up on his hand and his spectacles skew-whiff as he lost himself in an adventure novel.

'Come on, Gideon!' Dax kicked the end of his friend's bed and the duvet emitted a weary groan. 'Hey! Gid! Get up! We're going into Polgammon, remember?'

Gideon rolled over and blinked up at him. He struggled to speak and when he finally did the words were thick with slumber. 'I dunnoyetDax. I need moresleep. Gisanotherfewmins . . . Just . . . ti . . . '

Dax sat down impatiently on his bed and gave his shoulder a shake. 'What's the matter with you? You must have been asleep for about fourteen hours! Remember—you came up for your nap after the terrifying needle trauma? Well, that was getting on for seven and you've only just woken up!'

Gideon groaned again and sat himself up, resting his elbows on his duvet-wrapped knees and trying to open his eyes.

'Are you all right?' Dax was starting to get worried. Gideon first shook and then nodded his head and stretched his eyes wide open with his fingers. 'Have you got a temperature or something?' persisted Dax, and poked at Gideon's furrowed forehead. It felt normal enough.

'Nah—I'm fine. I'll have a shower—that'll wake me up,' sighed Gideon and got out of bed wearily, as if he'd run a marathon the day before. He trudged back in from the shower, dressed, and began to look more normal. There was none of the usual Gideon spring in his step, though. Dax hoped a good breakfast would sort him out—after all, he hadn't eaten for fifteen hours or more. As they left the dorm, Luke was getting up.

'I may see you down there,' he said, pulling his shoes on. Barry, though, was still snoring.

The campus was strangely quiet and there were only about ten other Colas at breakfast. By 9.30 a.m. on a

Saturday there would normally be at least three times as many. Dax was confused. 'Where is everybody?' he murmured as Gideon poured out his water and slopped most of it on the tablecloth amid a percussion of glassy chinks. His hand was shaking. 'Stay there!' said Dax and went to collect his friend a huge breakfast including cold sausages and sliced tomato, three buttered bread rolls, and a bowl of his favourite cereal and milk. He was relieved to see Gideon wolfing his food down, and in a few minutes he was almost as good as new.

Lisa joined their table, with cereal and fruit. She didn't say anything to either of them, though, and Dax remembered the incident with Catherine and the pie and peas. 'You coming into Polgammon today?' he asked, carefully.

'Are the terribly funny triplets going?' she queried, waspishly.

Gideon shook his head. 'Only me,' he said. 'Sorry about yesterday.'

'Well, you needn't be,' she said, tartly. 'It wasn't you, was it?'

'No, well, no—I mean about . . . sort of . . . laughing and all that. It *was* quite funny, you have to admit.'

'No.' Lisa gathered up her breakfast and made for another table. 'I don't.'

Dax winced. It looked as if Lisa was battening down the hatches on her mood. She could be there for days. 'We'll catch up with her in the village,' he said. 'Maybe get her to come round then.'

'We can try,' sighed Gideon. 'Blimey! Just look at everyone! Did someone die?'

Dax looked around the room and saw what Gideon meant. Half of the breakfasters were leaning their heads on their hands as they ate, some yawning, some just staring absently into space. What conversation there was had no volume or flow—just the occasional tired sentence. 'Pass the salt' seemed to be the most lively interaction.

'Come on,' said Dax. 'Let's get out of here!'

Polgammon, too, was quiet. They wandered around the tourist shops, trying to find the worst souvenirs available, and saw only three other students. 'Your school gone down with the plague?' demanded the stout man behind the till in the Tin Tack Treasure Trove. Dax smiled and shrugged, and put back the serpentine ashtray with a cheap plastic mermaid stuck to it, bearing the legend 'I ❤ Cornwall'. It seemed to have gone down with *something*, that was for sure.

'I win!' said Gideon and held up a cheap barometer, attached to a pasteboard plaque showing several luridly tinted photos of Cornwall's most famous attractions framed with seashells which had been sprayed with pink and turquoise paint and daubed with glitter. A brass-coloured plastic sticker at the base read 'Cornwall—Land of Timeless Mystery'.

'Land of Timeless Tat!' amended Gideon and then they left, because the shopkeeper had folded his arms heavily and was giving them hard stares.

'I've got a living to make, y'know ... ' they heard him declare as they exited back onto the street. Outside Dax was relieved to see that more students *had* made it in to the village. In fact Lisa and Mia were outside the post office; Jessica Moorland was chatting to them, and further down the road, loitering outside the Chocolate Parlour and pooling their pocket money, were Jacob and Alex Teller, the telepathic brothers who were fantastic mimics.

'C'mon,' said Gideon, determinedly. 'Chocolate time.'

'Hang on, though, shouldn't we go over to the girls? Try and warm up Lisa, again?'

'Not until I've had chocolate. I haven't the strength without it. And look—they've got dodgy company.'

Dax paused as Gideon went on, and watched Spook approach Mia, Lisa, and Jessica. There was something odd about him. As he stared across the street, Dax realized that Spook was walking with none of his usual swagger. His shoulders were slumped forward, taking a few inches off his usual height, and there was no calculating expression on his face at all. Very odd. Spook reached the girls and leaned in to Mia, asking her something quietly. Mia looked up at him with concern on her face and broke away from the group. As Lisa and Jessica talked on, Mia nodded her head and then reached out and touched the side of Spook's face. Suddenly Lisa snapped her head round, and Dax, whose fox sense quickly moved up into top gear, heard her speak sharply. 'Oi! Spook! What are you up to? You know the rules.'

'No—no, it's all right,' Mia was saying, waving her hands in a flustered way.

Spook stepped back as Lisa stalked across to him. 'Go on! What was it?!' demanded Lisa. 'Headache? Sore throat? Rash of pimples? Don't you think one broken ankle is enough for a few years?'

Spook blinked, and hung his head in a most un-Spook-like way. But Dax knew that his enemy had an Achilles heel where Mia was concerned, and had never forgiven himself for letting her mend his broken ankle last year. To be fair to him—and to everybody else who had let Mia help them—nobody had known about Mia's inability, back then, to release the pain that she took from others.

'Look—it's nothing,' said Mia, patting Lisa's shoulder. 'It's not a pain thing, OK? And for what it's worth, Spook—I don't think I can help anyway. Iron pills, maybe? Or chocolate—go and get a load of chocolate down you. See if that helps.'

'Yeah—yeah I will,' said Spook. 'Thanks anyway.' He loped on down the road towards Dax and in fact he *was* looking a bit better. Certainly, when he saw Dax, his swagger and superior expression were back on him in a flash. 'What are you staring at, Dingo?' he sneered, without even bothering to make eye contact, and whacked his shoulder into Dax's as he passed.

'Feeling a bit needled?' laughed Dax and had the satisfaction of seeing Spook's shoulders stiffen with embarrassment.

'Feeling a bit *hounded*?' the boy spat back.

Dax let it go. It was a waste of energy. And nobody seemed to have much of that at the moment. He followed Spook into the Chocolate Parlour, where Gideon was loading up with almond crunch and assorted other treats to keep him going for the next fortnight.

'You look a bit peaky, Gideon,' Mrs Whitlock was saying. 'You been up having midnight feasts?'

Dax snorted. 'Some chance!' he said.

'Ah well, never mind,' said Mrs Whitlock. 'You'll soon perk up with a bit of almond crunch inside you!'

Gideon grinned and turned away, and then they heard Mrs Whitlock add: 'Mind you—if you eat much more of it, you're going to look like a tub of lard in trousers. What a guzzler!' Dax and Gideon blinked, and stared back at their friendly sweetshop keeper in amazement, but she had ducked down behind the counter to get some fondants for Spook. Spook, however, was creased up with laughter.

There was more giggling and a scuffling noise behind the Cornish fudge display and then Gideon gave a shout. '*You* two!' Jacob suddenly shot into view, shoved by his younger brother, and then pulled Alex after him. They were both pink in the face with mirth.

Dax shook his head in amazement. The brothers' main reason for being at Tregarren was their ability to communicate with each other telepathically, but they also had this incredible 'sideshow', as Gideon called it. Their mimicry was so good it was hard to believe.

'Sorry, Gid,' gurgled Jacob, who was a cheerful-looking boy with wide blue eyes and nut-brown hair. 'Just couldn't help it!'

'I'm not getting lardy, am I?' said Gideon, staring down at his midriff with concern.

'No!' said Alex, who was slighter and fairer than his big brother, but had the same blue eyes. 'You are a guzzler, though. Perhaps you should give half of that bag to us—for the sake of your health.'

'You want to look out for your own health!' warned Gideon, darkly, but he was amused. As the brothers skidded out of the shop he said to Dax, 'What a talent! They could be on telly.'

'That's just a kids' thing,' scorned Spook, who had bought his own supplies and was heading for the door. 'Now *this*,' he raised one hand and left a shower of glitter in its arc as the air flexed around him, 'is talent.'

Gideon gasped and shoved Spook hard against the doorway, glancing around him in agitation. 'You stupid idiot!' he hissed. 'Anyone could have seen that!'

Dax, of course, had seen only the wavering in the air around Spook along with the glitter, which was real. Spook smirked at Gideon. 'It's just an illusion, Gideon. Sleight of hand. Clever tricks. Everyone thinks that. They can keep on thinking that, and I'll do very nicely out of it. You wait until *I* get out there. You wait until the cameras start rolling for *me*. I'm going to be the most famous illusionist on the planet, while you're still trying to shift fridges.' He turned and left the shop, leaving the doorbell chiming agitatedly on its coiled spring.

'I'll shift a fridge right onto his head, one day!' threatened Gideon.

'What did he glamour up this time?' prodded Dax.

'Oh—a load of parrots. All colours. One of them did a toilet on you,' he added, gravely.

Dax laughed. 'So what *is* it with that glitter thing?' he persisted, hoping to get Gideon into a brighter mood. 'I mean—that *is* real, isn't it? Or am I losing my resistance?'

'No, it's real,' said Gideon. 'He keeps these little bags of it up his sleeves, with this drawstring trigger type thing. It's for faking people that he's faking, when he's not—if you know what I mean . . . ' Dax nodded. They set off back up the main street of Polgammon, which wove between picturesque thatched cottages and shop fronts with quaint bottle-glass windows.

'Fancy some fish and chips, then, Gid?' suggested Dax, still trying to lighten the atmosphere.

'Nah,' said Gideon, and Dax felt his own mood dip. 'I promised Catherine and Luke I'd be back for lunch with them. Sorry, mate.'

'Yeah,' said Dax. 'Well—you go on then. I'll stop for some on my own.'

Gideon stopped and turned. 'Look—don't be like that! Come back with me. It'll be a laugh.'

Dax felt himself smiling tightly. He didn't want to do this, but he couldn't seem to help it. 'I'll be fine here. I might catch up with Mia and Lisa. You go on back.'

'You're not going all funny on me, are you?' accused Gideon. 'I mean—you're my best mate, you know that.'

'Of course I am. But you've got a brother and a sister now, too, haven't you?' Dax said, briskly, hating the flat tone of his voice but unable to change it. 'And there's only so much of you to go round. I've had a whole hour—so off you go.'

Gideon looked angry and miserable. He turned away from Dax and then Dax did a really mean thing. He just shifted and left. The small packet of chocolate he'd been carrying was the only thing on the pavement when Gideon turned back. Dax heard his hurt shout. 'Hey! Dax! Oh, come *on*!' But by then he was high up in one of the cobbled alleys behind the main street, crouched behind a bin and seething with anger. At himself as much as at Gideon. How stupid was that? He'd just shifted in full public view, just because he was having a sulk with Gideon. He was pretty sure he hadn't been seen, but still . . . stupid, *stupid* behaviour.

Several minutes later, Dax checked the coast was clear and then emerged from the alleyway as a boy. There was no sign of Gideon. He went to the café where the best fish and chips on the south-west peninsular could be bought and got himself a plateful. Without Gideon scoffing *his* on the other side of the table, it didn't seem so good, and he ate only half of it. He was just about to get up and go when the chair in front of him was drawn out and a figure dropped heavily into it. It was Lisa, and she was still in her own sulk. That made at least three of them now, Dax reckoned.

'Look, Lisa, I'm really not in the mood for—'

'Oh, just shut up and listen,' she said, tetchily. 'This is as much for me as for you. Your wolf friend is back and he's annoying me.'

Dax sat up. He'd hardly had a chance to think about the wolf in the past few days, or work out what message it had been trying to give him up in the woods that night. So it *had* made contact with Lisa, as he'd suggested.

'How long?' he asked, guardedly, knowing that Lisa sometimes made little effort to hurry through her messages. He suspected that she thought the more she gave out, the thicker and faster they would come: dead people in a queue, speeding up and up like those old black-and-white cine films from the early 1900s.

'Yesterday, actually,' she said, with a challenging glare. 'I *would* have told you last night, only I had to go and wash my tea off!'

'OK,' said Dax, trying to sound patient. 'What does it say?'

'It says "Mind the third" and "Take it to the wind or wing or something." Usual nonsense. Don't ask *me* what it means. I wish you could do your canine get-togethers without my help!'

'Don't be nasty,' said Dax, wearily, and to his surprise, Lisa seemed to sag onto the table in front of him. She took a long breath and looked tired.

'I know I'm being nasty. I don't know why. It wasn't *you* that wound me up. I'm just—you know—narked. Rattled. Something's . . . oh, I don't know. It hasn't been the same since that girl showed up.'

Dax smiled, in spite of himself. Someone *else* with a bit of jealousy going on then.

'I thought you liked Catherine. Everyone likes Catherine. She's fun, you have to admit.'

'Yeah—she is. Hmmm. Fun.' Lisa lapsed into a mock American accent. 'And she just *so* loves the way I dress, and the way I talk and how I do my hair and, oh—my *amazing* talent. Naturally, she can do it too, you know.'

'What—the medium thing?'

'Not sure about that—but she's got the dowsing thing right. She made me test her with some hidden stuff, and I'm telling you, I *really* hid stuff. And she found it. Cute, pretty, great clothes—*and* multi-talented. Why wouldn't we all just *love* her?'

Lisa seemed to make an effort. She sat up and made a calm, sweeping gesture, with her palms to the table. 'I am going to go back now. And I am *not* sulking, Dax, thank you.' Dax grinned, realizing she must have picked this up from his mind when she arrived at the table.

'See you later, Hardman,' he said warmly and she waved over her shoulder at him and left. He thought about the message. 'Mind the third' and—what was it? 'Take it to—the wind? Wing?' He sighed. The third might be a date. They were in late April now, so it would have to be May the third. Still a few days away. But maybe something was going to happen then. Then—take it to the wing or wind? What wing? A wing of Tregarren? The only other place he could think of with an east and west wing was Lisa's mansion house. Or maybe it was wind?

That made even less sense. Dax shook his head and thought about the other clues . . . the three scrapes on the tree. The wolf had marked three scrapes—so maybe that was about 'the third'? But it kept looking up into the branches, too, didn't it?

Dax decided to go back to the college through the wood and have a look at the tree again. He found it with no difficulty, but was just as puzzled. This time he hauled himself up the gnarled trunk and had a good look around. The tree was in bud and a few pale pink blossoms were already out. Dax squinted up to its higher boughs and thought he saw some old dark leaves there, in a sort of ball. Maybe a kind of nest? No—just leaves, blowing in the wind and looking a bit the worse for wear. He gave up and slid back down through the tree. Maybe the wolf would come to him in a dream again and clear it all up.

'It would be a *help*!' shouted Dax, peering up into the sky, encouragingly. But all he dreamed about that night was flying. In and out through little squares. Then one of Alice's dolls was ice skating around the lido with Gideon and Gideon wouldn't lend Dax his spare skates. Then there was a thing about fish and Celine Dion was singing . . .

14

He tried hard to think about pizza. A slice of pizza in a pizza oven. A slice of pizza with a panic button. He felt the lozenge-shaped piece of plastic on a flex in his palm, and knew that all he had to do was squeeze the button in its centre and they'd whip him out again in no time.

'You all right, Dax?' came Owen's voice, through his headphones. No music at all today; just Owen, talking him through.

'Yeah—I'm sure I'll be fine this time,' said Dax, working on keeping his breathing steady. Being in the confined space wasn't really the problem, as long as he had a clear way out. It was second nature to him as a fox to take to tunnels. It was the horrible metallic thudding which had freaked him out before, so like the hunters' spades. His stomach gurgled musically. He had taken Owen up on the offer of doing the MRI scan again early, while the other Colas were still at breakfast. He wanted to get it over and done with and he was *determined* to keep control.

'Good—I'm sure you will be too.' Owen's voice was tinny through the headphones, but still reassuring. 'Best not talk though, now. You know you have to keep your head absolutely still, so they can get the images. I can see your feet. Wiggle your toes if you're still hearing me OK.'

Dax smiled, and then ordered his face back to neutral; he'd wondered why Owen insisted he take his shoes and socks off before getting into the scanner. He wiggled his toes obediently.

'Excellent,' chuckled Owen. 'Now, hang in there and I'll just keep talking. We're ready to go.'

With the first thud, Dax felt his insides clench and he worked hard on his breathing—slow and steady, slow and steady—don't think about . . . don't think about . . . the thing.

'You're the last one in now,' said Owen, conversationally. 'We should have some results back soon, so we'll know whether there are any obvious differences in any part of your Cola brains. It's amazing science this—just amazing. Like whipping your brain out and putting it through a ham slicer and looking at all the wafer-thin sections in turn. But less sticky! Fantastic. They'll be checking your blood samples this week, too, to see if there are any abnormalities . . . well, you know, differences.'

Dax listened hard to Owen through the crashes and thuds and it definitely helped. 'Wiggle the toes on your right foot if you're still with me, Dax.' He did. A flash of the dark hole and the foxhound, slavering, pushed abruptly into his head, like a knife through a low ceiling. His heart pounded and the panic button was slippery in his hand, but Owen was still talking. 'Stay with me, Dax, stay with me. I want you to think about smokeless fires. What did you learn last week?'

Dax feverishly turned his mind to dry sticks; stripping bark off sticks; steepling them in just the right way to funnel up the heat, not letting the burnt ones slop back into the fire. He thought of the wood, of Catherine cutting herself and healing herself, of the apple tree giving him no answers, the dark ball of leaves that might have been a nest, but wasn't, of Gideon. Gideon. He hadn't even spoken to Gideon since yesterday and that made a sourness spread through his belly. It was wrong, all wrong. The darkness lapped at him again: slavering jaws; old meat smell . . .

'Dax! Stay with me! Wriggle the toes on your left foot!' Owen had to know. Had to have *some* empathetic powers, thought Dax again. Unless he was being monitored in some other way, but there was nothing attached to his chest or pulse points.

It's OK, I'm still here, said Dax, in his head.

And Owen said, 'Good. Good.' But he may have just been responding to the wiggling toes.

'Think about your fungi now,' ordered Owen. 'I want a list of the good ones and the bad ones—and most importantly, the ones you can get confused.' Chanterelles, mused Dax, picturing the little apricot-coloured parasols, field mushrooms, death's cap—*not* a good idea. *Slavering*. Beefsteak! That nut-brown one which grew off the side of trees and you could slice it up and cook it and it tasted like meat. They'd all had that last autumn, he and Gideon, Mia and Lisa, sitting cross-legged under an oak tree with the fire going and Owen showing them how to boil the slices in the billycan, on a slanted green stick over the fire. *Spades*. Dax longed for the scan to be over. He was managing, with Owen's help, but he felt he might shift at any time. Shift and run. Like he did yesterday, dumping Gideon. The sour feeling was back. He and Gideon hadn't spoken, not because they'd been deliberately ignoring each other, but because they hadn't really made the effort to.

At supper, Gideon was sitting with Catherine, Luke, Barry, and Mia, and Dax was going to join them, but after his lacklustre fish and chips meal, he still didn't have much appetite. Not enough to sit down at the table and deal with his guilt over leaving Gideon. He'd wandered along the food hatch, eyeing the soup and bread, and then just gave up and went back to the common room.

He'd joined two or three other Colas watching a film and didn't even notice Gideon coming through and heading straight to bed. By the time he too went up, his friend (he still hoped) was already asleep—again. So was Barry, whistling rhythmically under the duvet. Only Luke was awake, reading as usual. He took Dax by surprise when he said, 'You'd better make it up with him in the morning.' Dax had stared at Gideon's carbon copy. 'He misses you too,' added Luke, turning a page. 'Sorry I came and weirded everything out for you both.'

Dax shook his head. 'No,' he said. 'I'm sorry. You're all right, Luke. This isn't about you.' Luke shrugged and said nothing more.

The next morning, Dax was again up before Gideon,

as it was a Sunday and there was no bell. He'd met Owen at the scanner room and now here he was, panic pizza, and Gideon still estranged from him. He *must* sort it out.

Magically, the noise ceased. 'All done!' said Owen. 'You did great!'

Dax wiggled both sets of toes in relief and Owen laughed. They slid him back out again and he jumped up and grabbed his shoes and socks. 'I've got to see Gideon,' he told Owen, and left the room at a run. He found them all at breakfast—there was a small flight path of cutlery stacking up above the table and Dax grinned. Flying cutlery was *so* Gideon. He would go and ask to talk to him; take him to one side and apologize. Gideon would laugh and call him names and they'd be all right. Everything would be all right.

But as he drew towards the breakfast table, everything was *not* all right. Gideon was slumped in his seat, leaning his head into one hand and shovelling scrambled egg on toast into his mouth with the other. His eyes were half shut. Mia was quietly engrossed in her muesli and not even looking at the cutlery display. Barry was eating sausages and staring ahead of him, dull eyed. Luke was the only one paying attention to the aerial fork flights and controlling them, quite clearly, was Catherine. Her green eyes were sparkling with excitement, and she was clutching Gideon's shoulder.

'Look! Look, Gideon! Am I as good as you, now? Look!'

Gideon nodded and said, 'Yeah, Cath . . . brilliant!'

but he barely opened his eyes. Dax stood and watched the scene with a sinking feeling in his heart. Something *was* wrong. Very wrong.

'Gideon,' he said, but only Catherine and Luke looked up. 'Gid! Can I have a word?'

Catherine shot him a look and nudged Gideon. 'I think Dax wants to apologize,' she said, and the cutlery all landed neatly across the tablecloth. She sounded protective. Dax was irritated; had Gideon told her everything? Gideon still didn't look up, but went on mechanically eating his scrambled egg. Could he be deliberately ignoring me? thought Dax, with a stab of misery. This would be so out of character, he couldn't believe it.

'I think maybe you should go,' said Catherine, in a very reasonable, pacifying tone, and she linked her arm through Gideon's and slid closer to him, possessively. 'You really hurt his feelings yesterday, y'know? I'll talk to him—he'll probably be ready to speak with you later.'

Dax stared at her, appalled. 'I think my best friend can speak for himself, don't you?' he said, and walked over to Gideon and shook his free shoulder. 'Gideon! Wake up, you idiot! Come outside! We've got to talk.' Gideon's eyes opened fully and he regarded Dax with a look of bad-tempered confusion.

'I'm eating!' he said.

Dax stooped and looked levelly into Gideon's face. 'It's really important, Gideon! I mean it!' Gideon sighed and dropped his fork onto his nearly empty plate with a clatter. He got up and followed Dax outside where the wind whipped into their faces.

'First of all, I'm sorry about yesterday,' said Dax, quickly. 'I shouldn't have done that—I was just really . . . '

'Jealous, yeah, I know,' mumbled Gideon, and folded his arms. 'Is that what you wanted to say? Because I had kind of worked it out, you know.'

Dax stared at him, stung. 'OK, yes, I've been feeling a bit left out. I'm dealing with it, but you have to see it from my side . . . '

'I do see it from your side, and I'm sorry too,' said Gideon, and Dax felt a small surge of relief. 'Sorry that we can't all just get along. I can't just dump Catherine and Luke every time you want me. I've only just got them. They—they're important. Don't you see? Especially Catherine. I think there's something important about the way we've been brought together. We're important . . . and you . . . you . . . '

'I'm not,' said Dax, sourly. Gideon looked unhappy, but he didn't say anything. 'You're not yourself, Gid,' said Dax. 'You know that, don't you? You're all . . . all messed up these days. And the others, too—you're all dozy all the time. Done in by teatime. This isn't normal.'

'Whatever makes you feel better, Dax,' said Gideon, with a sad shrug.

'No! No, listen to me.' Dax felt a real fear now. Suddenly all his fox instincts were rearing up, like they had on the day of the hunt. He was certain of them. 'There is something going *wrong* around here! Can't you see it? Everyone's getting weird! I think—I think maybe it's something to do with the tests! The brain scans and the blood tests and—I don't know—the food maybe. The water! Gideon—mate! Believe me, there is something *not right*!'

Gideon flapped a hand at Dax and turned back in to the refectory. 'Sure—fine, Dax. It's the water.' He went back in and Dax stood, speechless, looking after him. Only his hands moved; fists clenching and unclenching helplessly. He closed his eyes, desperate to make sense of the last two minutes. He was losing his best friend and the world was turning grey.

When he opened his eyes, two green ones were staring back at him. Gideon's sister smiled at him sadly. 'Hey—he'll come round, Dax,' she said. Her eyes looked moist, as if she were on the point of tears. 'I think it's all just been a bit overwhelming for him—Luke and me,' she said, surprising Dax with her sympathy. 'He'll get used to us and then you'll have him back again, I'm sure. I'll talk to him.'

'I feel fine—really!' Mia sat down on the warm grass of the playing field next to Dax and shook her head. 'I think Gideon is too. I mean—yes—Gideon's been a bit sleepy, but I think that's probably a natural reaction to all the emotional stuff he's dealing with. It's the body's way of handling stress.'

Dax tugged angrily at the grass under his crossed legs. 'But it's not just Gideon! Everyone's getting like it! *You* are too! You're all . . . calm. *Too* calm!'

Mia smiled. 'I do try to be, you know. All healers do. We channel much better when we're calm and we're always working on self-hypnosis in Development. That's probably why I seem that way. And yes, I suppose I have been feeling a bit tired too, but you know, with all the stuff we do, it's not really surprising. I think maybe we're being encouraged to push ourselves a bit too hard. Maybe we should ask the teachers to give us some time off. Maybe we could get our SATS delayed or something. It's not really fair to expect us all to keep up with the national curriculum when we've got all this *stuff* going on.'

'Did you call?' Lisa arrived, in her new running shoes. She'd been out looping around the campus for the last hour. At least *she* wasn't dropping into a coma, thought Dax.

'Yeah—thanks for coming,' said Dax, feeling as if he were chairing a meeting. He'd 'sent' a message to her, asking her to find him and Mia. 'I need to talk about Gideon—and why we're all getting so sleepy.'

'Sleepy?' echoed Lisa. 'Do I *look* sleepy?'

'No—I suppose you don't, really.'

'How about them?' asked Mia gently and Dax looked across the field to where the Tregarren Terrors were training on the pitch, warming up for their match against the Tigers. At this distance they all looked normal enough, if not brimming with energy.

Dax sighed and tugged up more grass. 'Look—is it just me? Or is Gideon going weird? Mia—you were there at breakfast! You saw what happened!'

Mia nodded. 'Yes—he was a bit hard on you, I thought. He'll come round, though, Dax. You're his best friend.'

'*Was* his best friend.'

Lisa flopped down on the grass next to them and began stretching her legs. 'You'll always be his best friend, you idiot!' she said, warmly. 'But I know what you mean about him—he is a bit dopey at the moment. I reckon he's just a bit overwhelmed with all the triplet stuff.'

'That's what Mia said. So . . . so neither of you are picking anything else up? Lisa? You getting anything else from the wolf . . . or . . . anything . . . ?'

Lisa was flexing both feet with great concentration. 'Of course I'm getting stuff. I'm always getting stuff. Right now a very irritating old Music Hall star keeps warbling in my ear about not dilly-dallying on the way. Silly tart! She hasn't even told me *who* mustn't dilly-dally. Time waster! Push off! Get back in the queue when you're ready to make sense!'

Dax had to laugh. Lisa really was the world's most unlikely medium.

'Trouble is, Dax,' she said, more seriously. 'Even when I do get important stuff, I don't always know. Sometimes really silly things seem heavy and significant, and the *real* messages are all light and fluffy. Nobody's given me a manual yet.'

Dax nodded. 'So you feel OK?'

'Yeah, mostly.' Lisa stood up and began to lean over and touch her toes, stretching out her hamstrings. 'But you know, I do the running and keep myself to myself a lot of the time. Keeps me from going barmy. You should come out with me again—as a boy, I mean; you're getting way too foxy at the moment. It clears your mind. I sometimes think—'

Dax felt the air punch in at him at the exact moment Lisa stopped talking. She dropped to her knees as if she'd been hit. Dax and Mia both stared at her in alarm. Lisa's face was a mask of distress; her eyes fixed in the middle distance and her pupils contracting, as if trying to shut out something she couldn't bear to see.

She raised a shaky hand to her mouth and then breathed, 'Dad!'

15

For a few seconds Dax and Mia just stood, aghast, watching as Lisa raced back across the field towards the college building. Then Dax flicked into fox form so fast there was an audible click in the air around him, and he was running to catch up with his friend.

Lisa was pelting up the steps towards Owen's cottage as Dax caught up with her. *Lisa! Lisa! What is it?* he shouted, in his head. But the thoughts that came back to him were incoherent with panic. *Dad! Dad! Oh no! Not Dad! Not*—She hurled herself against Owen's door and pummelled it for all she was worth. When Owen opened it she almost fell over. He caught her and tried to steady her. She was nearly screaming. 'Dad! It's my dad, oh no, oh no, oh no . . . Owen—please—please—you've got to take me back! I have to go! I have to go! He's—oh no, oh no . . . '

Dax was appalled. He had never seen Lisa like this. Tears were running down her face and she was leaning into the wall as though she had been struck. Owen glanced at Dax and said, 'Go and get Mrs Sartre, Dax. Now.' Dax shot away down the path, cutting down the steep rocky slopes in places where nobody could as a human. Within seconds he was streaking across the quad and into the main building through an open window.

Paulina Sartre was already coming out of her office, her face pale and worried. She saw Dax and said, 'Where is she? With Mr Hind?' Dax nodded as he skidded to a halt and turned back with her. Did she already know what had happened to Maurice Hardman? Had it even happened *yet*? Both Mrs Sartre and Lisa sometimes got information before an event occurred. Maybe they could stop whatever it was.

When they got back to Owen's cottage Lisa was still babbling hysterically, and Owen was trying to calm her and keep her still. 'Slow down!' he was saying. 'You can't channel it properly like this. Get a hold, Lisa. Then you might find out more.'

As soon as she stepped inside, Paulina Sartre rested both hands on Lisa's quaking shoulders and in an instant the girl became still, as if hit by a tranquillizer dart. Her wet eyes turned a darker blue, her ragged breathing hitched once and then evened out, and she stared at the older woman, as if hypnotized. In fact, Dax was sure she *was* hypnotized.

'Where?' said Mrs Sartre, her voice like cool grey silk. Even Dax felt calmed, and he slipped, heedlessly, back into boy form beside Owen. Lisa blinked slowly, and Mrs Sartre nodded. 'Yes. Yes—it is so. I see it too, now. And is it now, or ahead?' Lisa blinked slowly again and her lips moved as if she were in prayer, but no words came out. 'Then yes— you must go. Mr Hind will take you right away.' Lisa's eyes closed. She was very still. Dax stared, fascinated. 'You will walk to the car, *cherie*,' said Mrs Sartre, gently. 'You will get in and you will sleep until you get there. You will take no messages but for yourself, *tu comprends*?' Lisa nodded, her eyes still closed, swaying a little.

'Good, wake now,' said Mrs Sartre and let go of Lisa's shoulders. Lisa's eyes opened and she looked around her calmly, although her mouth puckered and she bit her lip.

Owen looked from Lisa to Mrs Sartre. 'Where are we going? What's happened?'

'Mr Hardman has been in a car accident,' said Mrs Sartre. 'He is still with us. He needs Lisa now. Go now, please, Owen.'

And Owen did. He grabbed his jacket and his car keys and a tartan rug from the old leather chair beside his open fire, which he wrapped around Lisa's shoulders. Then he guided her outside, up the path to the gatehouse and out. Dax watched it all in silence. He felt awful for Lisa. He really liked her dad and hoped desperately that he would be OK.

'Go and tell Mia and Gideon,' said Paulina Sartre. 'Perhaps Mia can send some help for Lisa.'

'Shouldn't Mia go with her?' asked Dax, urgently. 'She might be able to help.'

Paulina Sartre shook her head. 'No, Dax. Mia is not ready. It would be dangerous, in many ways.'

At least this might help to put aside his terrible rift with Gideon, thought Dax, as he and Mia and Gideon walked around the quad in silence. He had called them together quickly, finding Mia already looking for him, needing to know about Lisa. She had fetched Gideon from the common room. Dax didn't look at him as he delivered the information on Lisa's dad.

'Blimey,' murmured Gideon. 'Poor Lees. Poor Maurice. I hope they'll be OK.' Then he shook his head, sighed, and headed back to the common room.

Mia looked at Dax and smiled wanly. 'I'm sending good vibes and stuff,' she said.

'Can Lisa get them at a distance?'

'Oh yes—I did her straight away, but I meant for you and Gideon.'

It was dark and windy by the time news came. Just after tea, Dax got a message from the principal, handed to him in the common room by Jacob Teller. *Owen has called*, it read. *Maurice Hardman was in a two-car collision near his home this morning and had to be cut from his car. He has a broken leg and pelvis and three cracked ribs, but he is now out of danger. Lisa will stay with him for a few days. Thanks for your help. Please let everyone know.*

Dax sighed with relief and passed the note to Mia, who read it, sighed too, and passed it to Gideon. 'Phew! Close call then,' said Gideon to Mia, then went to pass on the news to Catherine and Luke. Dax perched on the arm of the sofa near the fire, next to Mia, and watched the triplets talking earnestly. Mia sent him a little warm pulse of comfort, but it didn't really help. He felt utterly shut out. Catherine was leaning in to her brothers and making worried noises. She extracted herself and came over to Dax and Mia.

'What a day!' she breathed, wiping her shiny dark fringe out of her eyes. 'Are you two OK?' They nodded and she reached out and squeezed their shoulders. 'It's all such a rollercoaster ride around here, isn't it?' said Catherine. 'Look—let's do something fun together soon! How about a midnight feast?'

Dax stared at her, stunned. She was like a character from an Enid Blyton book.

'No, look—I'm sorry if that sounds mean, with what poor Lisa's going through,' she said, as if she'd read his mind. 'It's just, Dax, I'm worried about you and Gideon. We need to work this out. He's being really silly, because I know he thinks the world of you. So how about it? Tomorrow night? If the weather's good? We could all slip out and have a moonlit picnic. What do you say?'

'I think it's a great idea,' said Mia.

Dax wasn't so sure, but he nodded anyway and Catherine clapped her hands with delight. 'Great! I'll sort out everything! Just you wait—we'll have a ball!'

Bedtime was awkward. Gideon was still not talking to him, but he was normal enough with Barry and Luke. Dax got washed and into bed and under his covers as soon as possible. An Atlantic wind dashed a volley of raindrops against the slanted window above him; maybe Catherine's plans would be rained off tomorrow night. He thought briefly of going out alone tonight, for a fox walk in the woods, but the rain was setting in and he didn't fancy getting drenched—and he was also unsure about eating from the kitchen. At tea he had stuck to some pre-packed crackers and cheese spread and some milk from a sealed carton. He was getting more and more bothered about what might be happening with the food—and water. Part of him wanted to laugh it all off; he sounded like a mad conspiracy theorist, with all these dark suspicions, but *something* had to be making the students so groggy.

He turned over with his back to the others and thought about his journalist friend, Caroline Fisher. Caroline was possibly the only reporter in the world who knew about Cola Club and Tregarren, and she had nearly brought the world's press to their gate tower last autumn when she tracked Dax down from his home town. He had hated her, with her smart suits and too-clever ways. But Patrick Wood, the first principal, had invited her in, like a deadly spider in its funnel web, and then thrown an illusion so that she unwittingly walked into the bogs above the wood to drown. As it was Dax who had saved her life (with help from Gideon, Lisa, and Mia), Caroline's relationship with him had changed dramatically. She agreed to keep the Colas safely out of the media and had been allowed, following a government debriefing, to return to her life.

But she had stayed in touch with Dax, and soon after the bog incident sent him a letter, warning him about the people in charge of the Cola Club—that some might not be what they seemed. Dax eased open the drawer in his bedside cabinet and felt up, under the wooden top, where a small paper packet was firmly taped, out of sight and touch of anyone who happened to look casually. In it was a key to a place called The Owl Box, somewhere on Exmoor. It was Caroline's bolt-hole and—as she had made clear—*his* bolt-hole too, should he ever need it. Dax had never really thought he would. Now he wasn't so sure.

More and more, he could see the sense in her warning. The Colas could really only *hope* that the establishment was on their side—and even if it was, they were here to be studied, weren't they? And what better way to test their responses than tampering with what they ate or drank? Maybe it was all perfectly safe, but he didn't like it. He didn't like it at all. He planned to stick to a ready-sealed yoghurt for breakfast. Maybe . . . maybe he would even hunt. He would have liked to say that the thought of catching prey totally repulsed him, but he knew that wasn't true. As a boy he had no urge to hurt any living thing, but as a fox he had a more practical approach to wildlife. There was a food chain, and he was at the top of it. Nature made it so.

He settled into an uneasy sleep; the flying through squares dream was back. In it he heard Lisa calling. Then she was repeating everything he said, like an irritating five year old. At last the dream receded and Dax slipped into deeper sleep, aware, on a fox-sense level, of the even breathing of slumber around him.

The crash, when it came, was so loud that Dax shouted and struck out, as if someone had boxed his ears. There were prickles across his face and a sharp rattle of something hitting the floor. Barry sat bolt upright and

Gideon rolled over in his quilt and fell off the bed; Luke, bizarrely, shot from sleep shouting 'Sorry!' and then looked around him in bewilderment. The Atlantic wind was in their room now, whistling darkly around and making the pages of his book rise up like a fan.

'What the hell was *that*?' shouted Barry. Dax switched on his bedside lamp and a thousand tiny chunks of glass glittered wetly in its light. They lay all across the floor and the bedclothes and were cascading out of his hair. He looked up in awe and saw a raggedly outlined night sky above him. The three slanting windows across the dorm had all shattered.

Dax wanted to think the wind had hurled a branch or shard of granite at the glass, but he knew better. Not all *three* windows. Not all at the same moment. Gideon had emerged from his quilt, looking confused and scared. 'I—I—I thought it was a dream,' he said.

'Was it you?' demanded Barry. 'Are you mucking around with glass now, Gideon? Because that is *not* funny, mate!'

'No!' protested Gideon. 'It wasn't me . . . at least. I don't *think* it was. I mean—that's never happened before.'

'Always a first time,' muttered Barry, irritably, shaking shattered glass off his duvet. Like Dax, he had a speckling of blood over his cheeks and brow and nose, where several sharp chunks had struck him. Luke, at the far end, was less affected, as his bed was not directly under a window. He still looked shocked and confused, though.

'Oi, Dax—do us a favour and fox-trot off to the

teachers, will you?' said Barry, gruffly, seeming to take charge. 'We'll have to move out of here.'

Dax went and brought back Mrs Dann and Mr Pengalleon within five minutes. Happily the rain and wind had stopped, so they agreed to ship the boys out and down to the lounge area, where they could camp the rest of the night on the sofas, leaving the clear-up until later. Doors opened along the corridor and other boys wandered out to find out what the noise was about.

'Back to bed, all of you!' said Mrs Dann, firmly. 'Just a little broken glass, that's all. Now, scoot!' She found some spare bedding and loaded up the refugees with it while Mr Pengalleon inspected the mess, scratching his beard.

'We'll sort this out in the morning,' he said. 'Watch where you tread and make sure you've got all that glass off you.'

'You all right, Luke?' said Mrs Dann, as they traipsed down and each found a sofa. Luke did look a bit ill.

'Just got a bit of a headache, miss,' he said. 'I had it before I went to bed and it just got worse. Didn't help it, having an exploding glass experience.'

'No, well, I should think not. I'll find you some paracetamol.' She found the pills and some water for Luke, with a biscuit to help him digest it, and then headed back to her own bed. She hadn't asked if they knew what caused the shattered glass. Like most of the teachers, Mrs Dann took Cola weirdness in her stride and it *was* very late.

Mr Pengalleon had sealed off their door with some tape, to stop other Colas from going inside in bare feet. 'I'll be in to clear up first thing, before you wake,' he said. 'So you can go in and get what you need.'

He left them all in an uneasy silence.

'Gideon,' said Dax, quietly. '*Was* that you?'

'I tell you, I don't *know*,' snapped Gideon. 'If it was, I don't know how—and I certainly didn't mean it.' He looked shaken and bundled the blankets around his head before shutting his eyes determinedly.

Barry snorted and turned over; before long he was whistling again under his blanket. Gideon too seemed to be asleep. Dax looked across at Luke, who was lying on his back, still and silent. He squinted through the dark, trying to make out if the boy was still awake, and then fluidly shifted, for a few seconds, to watch through fox eyes. Instantly Luke's features sharpened. His eyes were fixed on the ceiling, pupils wide and dark. *Can't be easy*, thought Dax, *for a non-Cola*.

16

The following morning the dormitory windows were taped up with thick, see-through polythene sheeting and the floor swept and the bedding changed. Mr Pengalleon had got the cleaning staff to work at dawn, and had sorted the windows out himself.

'We'll have a glazier in soon,' he told Dax when he edged into the room to get his clothes. 'Of course, it takes time. Have to get 'em vetted before we let 'em in,' he sighed. Dax nodded, and thought, not for the first time, that it was amazing that the college's incredible secrets had been kept even this long.

'Someone had a smashing time last night!' Dax looked round to see Spook peering round the door with a look of mean fascination. 'What happened, Jones? Another panic attack got you headbutting the windows?'

Dax didn't rise to it, but said, 'Loved the parrots, Spook. But the glitter's a bit much. My little sister would love your act, though. Do you do dolly parties?'

'Now then, boys . . . ' said Mr Pengalleon, as he finished the taping of the furthest window.

'You'll be laughing on the other side of your mangy little snout one day soon,' said Spook. 'So what are *you* planning for a career? Rat control?' And he swung away from the door before Dax could snap something back at him. In fact, he hadn't the energy. Last night's dramas and an uncomfortable lump in the sofa had left him tired and grouchy.

At breakfast Mia and Catherine and Jessica Moorland all wanted to know what had happened. Even Jennifer Troke, another vanishing glamourist from Barry's group, suddenly appeared at his elbow and demanded all the details. Gideon and Barry described the crash and the wind and the confusion and Barry was still accusing Gideon of 'messing around with glass'.

'You were trying to bend it or something, weren't you?' said Barry, although with less of a huff now that he was getting some bacon and eggs down him.

'I was *not*,' insisted Gideon. 'Dax—you tell him! I was asleep, wasn't I?'

Dax looked up and nodded, and his and Gideon's eyes met and then there was a weirdness, because Gideon had just remembered they had fallen out, and wasn't sure yet whether they had fallen back in. Dax knew this, as surely as the same pattern of thought had flashed through his own mind. 'He *was* asleep,' he said, hoping to mend fences. 'He was doggo!'

Gideon grinned and said 'There!'

'Mind you,' said Catherine, 'you might still have done it—*from your dreams*!' She allowed a dramatic pause. 'Well, who's to say?' She stepped behind Gideon and rested her fingers at his temples. 'You have such phenomenal power that it might be seeping out of you even when you're unconscious. Amazing! I wish I had that much power. Just think what you'll be able to do!'

Gideon smiled, slightly shakily, thought Dax. 'Yeah . . . think.' He looked around him uneasily and said the very thing that was occurring to Dax. 'Only, you know, maybe it's not so great. Maybe it would be better if it wasn't spread all over the school. They might decide I'm a public health hazard.'

'I will take it to the grave!' whispered Catherine and sat down prettily next to Gideon. Luke had to shift sideways to make room for her. The milk jug scooted across to Catherine's fingers, slopping a little white puddle onto the tablecloth as it abruptly stopped.

'You know,' said Mia, kindly. 'You should probably try not to keep doing stuff outside lessons, Catherine. Sooner or later you get seen and then you get a long lecture from Mr Eades. Store it all up for Development.'

Catherine beamed back. 'You're right!' she said, pouring milk into her cereal. 'You're always looking out for me, aren't you? I wish I had a sister as well as a brother! You'd be just the kind I wanted.'

There was a small pause, Dax thought, before the conversation drifted on. Maybe they had all picked it up, but he wasn't sure. If Luke, the brother whom Catherine had just edited out of her last sentence, had noticed, he didn't let it show.

The yoghurt didn't see Dax very well through morning lessons. His neglected stomach began to rumble during science. 'Is that another chemical experiment going on in there, Mr Jones?' said Mr Buckley, wryly, as he dished out a tiny spoonful of potassium permanganate and prepared to show the class its powerful explosive properties.

'Sorry, sir,' mumbled Dax, as the girls snickered across the room. 'Just a bit hungry.'

'Well, do try to cap Vesuvius if at all possible, until lunchtime,' added Mr Buckley. 'I gather you've had enough explosive situations already in the past twenty-four hours.'

At lunch, Dax dropped into the refectory to see if there was anything that he could safely eat. A still-shelled hard-boiled egg, perhaps—or something in a carton—or . . . but he knew he was wasting his time. Mrs P prided herself on good healthy menus of well-cooked, fresh ingredients. Today it was roasted Mediterranean vegetable loaf and poached trout and shallots. It smelt wonderful and Dax was ravenous, but he looked around the room at the students and what he saw strengthened his resolve. While nobody was actually asleep, face down in their plate, it was obvious that everyone was sagging after just a morning's lessons. Barry and Luke were seated with Gideon, already eating—and none of them were saying anything, or even looking beyond their food.

Catherine, of course, was as lively as ever—she was shimmying between two tables, carrying her fish aloft and smiling and chatting to everyone she passed. Their heads rose and fell like a Mexican wave as she swept by. Perhaps she was less affected because she was a latecomer, pondered Dax. Jessica and Jennifer were talking quietly together, sitting at a table close to him, and both were holding their forks with a droopy swing between mouthfuls. Jessica kept yawning. Dax had a sudden thought and walked over to them.

'Jess—have you had any interesting messages, recently?' he said, pulling up a chair. Jessica and Jennifer looked at each other and then back at him with an expression that told him he was interrupting some 'girl talk'.

'Nothing for you,' said Jessica, tartly.

'Well, no . . . not me, maybe, but . . . well, you know, generally,' Dax persisted.

'Dax, you know I can't tell you anything about anyone else's messages,' said Jessica, primly. 'And when I do, only with an SCN slip, signed by a teacher.'

Dax was tempted to tell her to stick her SCN slips— and her head—in a rusty bucket. But he took a deep breath. 'What I'm interested in, is whether you're having a *lot* of messages right now.'

Jessica seemed, at last, to realize that he was serious. 'Why? What's going on?' He felt her probe a little into his mind, and remembered that she too had some psychic ability. Not much, but enough to get in on a strong idea occasionally.

'Nothing really . . . I mean . . . I'm just a bit curious. About whether the MRI scan or the blood taking has affected people,' he bluffed; fairly convincingly, he thought.

'Or whether it's something *in the water*!' intoned

Jessica dramatically, and let out a giggle. 'I've heard about your theory!' Jennifer laughed too, and Dax was infuriated.

Thanks, Gid! he thought; all attempts at fence-mending now well off his To Do list. He stalked outside angrily. He *knew* he was right. About *something* being wrong. OK—it might *not* be about the water or the food, but he wasn't going to take any chances until he was sure. Why did nobody else see it? Surely it was obvious!

There was a rattle of footsteps behind him, as he stomped across the quad. By the time he'd sat down heavily on the edge of the fountain pool, Jessica had reached him and perched beside him.

'Want more of a laugh, then?' he muttered.

Jessica smiled, but then she leaned in towards him and said, quietly, 'Actually . . . I . . . I don't know if it means anything, and until you just came over to us, I hadn't really given it much thought, but . . . '

'What?' prompted Dax, still suspicious that she might be working up to a joke.

'I haven't, in fact, been getting much at all.'

Dax peered at her, and now there was genuine worry on her face. 'What—nothing coming through?'

'Well . . . yeah . . . *some* stuff. But, sort of fainter, and harder to understand. Only for the last few days though. And sometimes it's better—and then it goes again. Like bad reception on the telly. It's probably just a phase. Catherine says it's probably hormones.' Dax winced. 'Well, you know girls develop more quickly than boys,' she added, defensively. 'And Catherine—well, she's American— they all talk about *everything* over there. She thinks it's that. Maybe. I don't know.'

'Are you tired?' asked Dax, choosing to steer clear of female hormones, American or otherwise.

'Sometimes. Same thing probably,' she said. 'Anyway—sorry about laughing at you, Dax. You're all right, really. We don't mean it.' She got up and went back into the refectory, where Jennifer was staring dully out of the window.

A wave of weariness stole over Dax. He was tired of wandering around without his friend; tired of feeling suspicious of something he couldn't name—tired and hungry. Even if he didn't want to admit it to himself in formed thoughts, Dax knew where he was going next and what he would do. It had been a long time coming, but he'd always known it would happen sooner or later. Today, as it turned out, was the day.

The wood was still and sleepy in the afternoon sun. Unsuspecting. His paws made virtually no sound as he stole through the undergrowth, sliding under patches of holly and nettle, slinking behind fallen logs, following his snout. His busy mind was cleared, the complicated human thoughts put aside, and a basic channel of logic leading him on, along with the ribbon of scent that gave away his prey.

On the outer edges of the western side of the wood, the trees became more sparse and heather and moss ran into the soft carpet of leaf and bark litter like eager fingers. The land sloped gently towards the sea to his left and up to a rock-topped hill on the right, where only a handful of low gorse bushes cringed away from the relentless coastal breeze. A shingle path wound through the shallow valley, crossing the warning green crust of the treacherous bogs which had nearly drowned Caroline Fisher last year. Closer to the cover of the trees were the mounds of heather and moss and fine high grass, scattered in clumps. The higher levels of this landscape were riddled with neat round rabbit holes. And neat round rabbits.

Dax lay low in the heather and watched. For several minutes there was no movement, his stealthy arrival still registering with some of the sharper rabbits, who had dived for cover. But with memories as fluffy as their tails, soon they began to bob back up and before long perhaps seven or eight were nibbling at the turf. He moved his snout like a gunsight, and rested his eyes on one of the creatures closest to him. His haunches were tense, his muscles filled with unspent energy, and his heart began to speed up like the engine of an aircraft before take off, powering his limbs with high octane hunting fuel. Excitement coursed through him; he could taste it on his tongue. The world outside the fifteen centimetres around the rabbit paled to grey and the only colour left surged vividly in the centre of his target. Dax sprang.

The creature jumped, tried to flee, but he was on it before it made contact with the earth again. He felt fur and bone and the urgent surging vibration of life and then a snap and sudden metallic warmth—and it was over for his prey. Later, when he was DaxBoy again, he would choose not to dwell upon his first proper fox meal. With pure instinct, he found flesh and fat among fur and bone, and left what was no good to him for the scavengers. Afterwards he walked slowly back to the wood, in a trance of horrified satisfaction, and curled up under a fallen oak, where the scent spoke of badgers foraging the night before. He was asleep inside a minute, wrapped in his tail and the numbness of his shock.

17

'Go on—get your teeth into *that*!' said Owen, with a grin, and handed Dax a heavy package wrapped in greaseproof paper. Inside it was a giant pasty, its curves of smooth thick pastry gleaming with a glaze of baked egg and knotted along the top into a spine of neat finger tucks. Dax laughed and remembered. He and Gideon had been teasing Marguerite about Cornish pasties, and how much they missed them while they were staying at Lisa's mansion. She had taken it personally, and informed them all that no Cornishwoman could knock up a pasty to equal *hers*.

'Do I share this with Gideon?' he asked, more delighted than Owen could know with another food option outside college catering.

'No, he's got one too,' said Owen. 'I think Marguerite bakes like most people pray, when someone's ill or in danger. I don't think she left the kitchen for more than half an hour while I was there.'

'How is Maurice?' asked Dax as Owen closed the door on his bungalow and they both walked down the rocky path towards the quad. Owen had only been back an hour when Dax ran up to find out what was happening, just as the man was emerging with his home-baked gifts.

'Maurice is back at home now, in plaster and dosed up with painkillers—but he's going to be OK. He collided with a small lorry on one of those winding narrow roads near the big house. He would probably have died, but, happily for him, he heard Lisa shouting his name about three seconds before he turned the corner and got hit. He reckons if he hadn't turned the wheel left just before he realized what was happening, he'd have been crunched. Lorry driver was over the limit and on a mobile. Got out with a bruised knee, apparently.'

'So, Lisa saved him?' said Dax, awestruck.

'Seems like it. Handy thing, this premonition business.'

Dax shook his head in amazement. He felt the hairs on the back of his neck rise up with the spookiness of it all. He missed Lisa already. She was probably the only one who would listen to him now, about the water and the food—and she was gone.

'When do we get Lisa back, then?' he asked and noticed that Owen was looking at him, curiously, as they crossed the low stone bridge over the shallow waterfall stream.

'By the end of the week. Dax—what's that in your hair?'

Dax patted the area Owen was staring at and felt some hard clumps among his fine dark hair, just behind his left ear. He knew instantly what it was and wondered if anyone else had noticed in the two hours that had passed since he returned from the wood. He had gone to geography and then maths without anyone passing comment.

'It's blood, isn't it?' said Owen. 'Did you bash your head on one of the overhangs?'

'Yeah, probably,' said Dax, feeling his face growing hot. He examined his pasty intently and walked on, struggling for an idea to change the subject with. Owen was still watching him and then suddenly, as they reached the grassy rectangle of the quad, he stood still and regarded his pupil, head on one side, for a long, speculative moment.

'When you're ready, Dax,' he said at length, and then moved away to find Gideon. Dax stood and looked at his feet. Owen knew. He was absolutely sure of it. Maybe he had been expecting it to happen one day, but hey, it wasn't the kind of thing you ran up to tell teacher in any kind of hurry, was it? *'Hey, sir! Sir! I've just bitten the head off my first rabbit, sir!'*

Dax was glad he had the pasty.

Tea was as dull and lacklustre as lunch had been, and breakfast before it. Dax wanted to jump up on a table and shout out to all the students, 'Wake UP! Listen to me! Don't you think this is even a teeny bit strange?' But knowing that people were already laughing at him, he didn't. He needed to be sure, and after all, everyone was still going to class and doing all the stuff they usually did. They were just a bit . . . damped down, mostly. Only Gideon and, increasingly, Mia, seemed *really* tired. Dax took a deep breath as he joined them at the table. Luke was still getting his food, with Catherine, and there was no sign of Barry. *Really* no sign. Dax could tell with his nose and ears that he wasn't just lurking nearby in a vanish.

'So! Happy campers, how are we?' he said, briskly. Mia smiled faintly, toying with her soup, and Gideon nodded and grunted over his ham salad sandwich. 'Everyone ready for our midnight feast with Catherine?' went on Dax, in a stage whisper. 'Reckon you'll be able to get out of bed, Gid?'

Gideon sat up, slightly huffily, and looked a bit more alert. 'Of course I will! Long as we don't get any more surprises like last night. How about you, Mia?'

Mia yawned and stretched gracefully. 'I'll go to bed early, so I can be fresh,' she said, although, looking at her, thought Dax, it would take about three *days* sleep to sort her out. Mia was paler, even, than usual and there were shadows under her eyes.

'You're tired, aren't you?' said Dax, seriously. 'You're tired too! Don't you—'

Mia put her hand on Dax's arm. 'Yes! I am tired, Dax. I've been sending a lot of healing to Maurice and worrying about Lisa—and about you two,' she gave Gideon a hard stare, 'so it's not surprising, really, is it? I've also been helping Catherine with her maths since the end of lessons and that *really* wipes me out!' She gave a wry chuckle and Catherine, arriving with her food, looked stricken.

'Hey, look! I'm sorry. I shouldn't take advantage of

you like that,' she said, earnestly taking Mia's hand. 'You *must* say when you've had enough of me! *All* of you!' She looked around the table, her face awash with guilt. 'I know I'm really high energy and I just *exhaust* people sometimes. My last adoptive mom said I'd be the death of her!' There was an uneasy pause—at least two of them at the table knew that her last adoptive 'mom' *had* died. 'Anyway,' swept on Catherine, 'I'm a non-stop yackity-yack-machine and I know it and I really won't mind if you tell me to cool it and leave you be awhile. They used to do that *all* the time back at the homes. Hey, Luke!' she turned to her brother, as he pulled out a chair. 'Promise me you'll tell me to shut up if I keep going on!'

'Yeah, right,' mumbled Luke. 'Shut up, Catherine.'

She bit her lip, dropped her eyes to her plate and then began to eat in silence. Nobody spoke.

At length Luke said, 'Look—I was, kind of, *joking*, you know. How's the . . . ' he dropped to another stage whisper, ' . . . midnight feast thing going?'

'Oh! It'll be amazing,' gasped Catherine, dropping her spoon with a clatter so she could clap her hands together in delighted anticipation. 'I've lined up some real good picnic and a blanket for sitting on, some cordial, and Gideon's given me a . . . a patty?'

'Pasty,' amended Gideon. 'Dax can bring his too, can't you, Dax?'

Dax nodded. He had been intending to eat his, or some of it, now, but in fact was still quite full from his lunch on the edge of the woods. He glanced across at Gideon and felt a swell of sadness. He really, badly, wanted to talk about his hunting experience that afternoon with his best friend, but Gideon seemed to be hardly there. Dax unwrapped some cream cheese and crackers again, and undid another carton of milk. He'd be getting plenty of calcium to go with the raw protein, that was for sure.

'Oh, *what*? What's *he* doing here?' spluttered Gideon, and ahead of them, down the moonlit path, Dax could make out Spook, walking arm in arm with Catherine.

'Look—don't be nasty,' said Mia, shivering a little inside her thick robe, pyjamas, and trainers. 'Catherine invited him this afternoon. I don't think she realizes you don't really get on.'

'Don't get *on*? That's the understatement of the week!' huffed Gideon.

'Oh, Spook's good for a laugh, sometimes,' said Barry, who was coming up behind them with a basket containing their feast. Somehow Catherine had induced Mrs Polruth to give her a load of cakes and some illicit cans of lemonade from the pantry. Dax's and Gideon's huge pasties were also in the basket, with a knife for cutting up and sharing and paper napkins for handing the chunks around. 'He did a brilliant show last Bonfire Night,' Barry told Luke. 'Mega firework display, with some of the other illusionists. Really cool—even if he does think he's God's gift to glamour. Of course,' he puffed his chest out a little and then stumbled sideways on a loose bit of granite, which undermined the effect slightly, 'it's not *real* glamour, like vanishing is. I bet he'd give twenty-five firework displays for *that*.'

They found a sheltered spot on the edge of the playing field, where the sea wind was held off by wooden fencing and Catherine laid out the tartan rug and a couple of rolled-up beach mats. Everyone, still in their pyjamas and robes, sat down around the basket and looked at each other in the moonlight, slightly embarrassed. It was a warm night for late April and Catherine was in her element, undoing the basket in the centre of them all and lifting out a glinting glass bottle of cherry cordial. 'It's mine!' she said, happily, as she slopped a small amount into a plastic cup for each of them. 'I brought it over from the States. It's amazing. You can really taste the cherries. Let's do a toast. To Cola Club! Power to us!'

They mumbled 'Power to us!' self-consciously, and then drank the cordial. Mia gasped and coughed and Spook let out a cackle of amusement. 'Catherine!' Mia stared at her. 'This is *alcoholic*!'

Catherine pouted and then smiled wickedly. 'Well, there might be a *little* alcohol in it,' she admitted. 'Just to keep it from going off. Seconds, anyone?'

They all looked at each other, then Spook thrust out his empty cup. 'Fill me up, Cath! I can handle it even if your brothers can't.' Gideon and Luke immediately held out theirs too and Dax, shaking his head and laughing, also decided a little more wouldn't hurt. It was surely only about as strong as lemonade shandy. Barry and Mia finished what they had and then allowed Catherine to top them up again too.

The pasties, sliced and handed round in heavy, meaty chunks, were delicious. Dax was so hungry by now he had to stop himself groaning aloud with relief. It was extremely hard for him to turn down the cakes, but because he couldn't be sure of them, he had to. The food and drink put everyone in a good mood and Catherine was an excellent hostess, drawing lots of chatter and silly stories out of everyone.

'Remember when you nearly got caught with that floating frog by the old village horse trough?' gurgled Barry, through a mouthful of banana cake. 'Mate! I thought I was gonna die!' He leaned over to Catherine and filled in: 'We were outside the fish and chip place and then Dax goes, look—there's a frog in the water trough and so we went over for a look and Dax, you know, had to try not to eat it—'

'Barry!' protested Dax, but he was laughing too. 'I've never eaten a frog! Only spiders and beetles and . . . and . . . ' He petered out, remembering his lunch, but Catherine was already holding her hands over her mouth and stretching her eyes wide in an agony of revulsion.

'You are kidding me! You *are*!' she was gasping, but she was laughing too.

'Only when I'm a fox,' grinned Dax, embarrassed. 'It's instinct, you know. Like the way Gid eats chocolate buttons without even remembering.'

'Anyway!' Barry wrestled the story back. 'We're at the

trough and looking at this frog, and Dax *isn't* trying to eat it, and it just bobs under the water where we can't see it properly, so Gideon just, casually like, lifts it back up again.'

'Just so we could get a better look at it,' butted in Gideon. 'And only a couple of inches over the water.'

'And this frog,' Barry was guffawing with laughter now, 'this frog looks *so* surprised! I didn't know a frog *could* look surprised, but this one did. And we all start laughing . . . and . . . and . . .'

Gideon picked up: 'Well, you know, it just seemed to want to go for a little ride, so I started gently spinning it round, quite slowly, and then it sort of got a bit higher, and Dax and Barry are on the floor laughing by now, and you know I can't resist that.'

'So,' Barry jumped in again, between wheezes of laughter, 'so this frog is just, like, spinning in the air, looking, well, a bit concerned by now when there's this voice behind us saying "It's not kind to do that to an amphibian". And there's this kid, about six or seven, standing there with an ice cream and a stern look.'

'So it was *plop*,' said Gideon, 'back in the water and we're all turning round looking all innocent and this kid runs over to his mum and says, "Mummy, those boys are floating frogs in the air!" And she—' Gideon lost himself in fits of laughter again, 'she . . . she just whacks him round the head and says, "I've had enough of your nonsense, Jimmy! No TV today!" and hoiks him away down the road. Poor little kid!'

They all fell into gales of laughter, Barry thumping the ground, Mia almost choking on her cake, and even Spook wiping away tears of mirth. 'You were *so* out of line, Gideon,' Mia giggled. 'You'd have been in such trouble if that got out!'

Catherine pulled another bottle of cherry cordial out of the basket and they all cheered rousingly. Dax felt good for the first time in many days. *Look at everybody!* he thought. *We're all fine. You've just been getting overwrought for no reason*, he told himself. They all downed another glass and Spook performed a bit of glamour for the party; Dax did his best to look as if he could see it and Gideon, just as he always had, muttered a few words to help him out: 'Dancing frogs. In pink tutus.' Dax clapped loudly with the others when Spook finished with a flourish and Spook shot him a look of surprise.

Dax shrugged back at him and said, 'Don't panic— I'm just being sociable!'

More stories were told, some funny, some dramatic. Dax and Gideon even told Catherine a little bit about what had happened in Dax's first term: the rescuing of the journalist and the death of Patrick Wood.

'You've all been having such amazing adventures,' sighed Catherine, putting her arms around Gideon and Mia, who were on either side of her. 'While I was just hanging around junior high and going to the mall. I can't believe I'm here now! I want adventures too! I'm going to catch up with you all, I am! Hey—c'mon—Dax, Luke, Barry—you too, Spook! It's so great to see you all getting on so well. I *hate* it when people fight. C'mon—for me—group hug!'

Dax and Gideon exchanged appalled looks, but Barry was already heavily ambling over to Catherine on his knees and leaning into them in a gentle rugby scrum manoeuvre. Spook shrugged and rested one elbow on Barry and the other on Mia. Dax went to lean on Gideon and Mia, but then found himself holding back. He felt odd and embarrassed, but fortunately the group hug was bundling inward and he didn't think Catherine had noticed him not joining in. Luke was looking extremely self-conscious, but he took part anyway, his glasses getting knocked slightly askew. The group hug paused for a few seconds of self-conscious silence and then Gideon gave a snort and they all began laughing again, falling back down onto the dewy dark grass.

'More stories! More stories!' laughed Catherine. 'Or—I know—Dax, shift for me! Go on! *Please!*' She was holding on to him—her arm round his neck. 'Go on!' she begged. 'For me!' He nodded, feeling slightly uneasy, probably because Spook was there, and tried to move away from her before he shifted, but she clung on to him. 'No! Don't! I want to *feel* how it is that your skin turns to fur!' Dax was shocked. He stared at her.

'I—I'm not sure if I can, when someone's hanging on to me,' he said. This wasn't strictly true, but the only time it had happened *had* been a matter of life and death.

Spook gave an unkind shout of laughter. 'No—you need your space, don't you, Jones?' Dax shot him a startled look. After the warmth and fun of the last few minutes, the sudden antagonism back in Spook's voice was like a jug of cold water in the face.

'How so?' prompted Catherine, quite oblivious to the sudden drop in the atmosphere.

'Well, it's another quite funny story, really, isn't it, Dax?' said Spook, grinning. 'You tell it—or shall I?'

Barry looked troubled. Mia was getting to her feet and briskly wrapping up the picnic remains and glaring at Spook, but the illusionist was staring hard at Dax with a look of huge enjoyment on his face.

'No—this is a great one, Cath! Dax goes out on a little furry run one day—and guess what?! Ends up in a fox hunt! It's *so* funny! He's totally *wetting* himself, going like the clappers, and he's too scared to stop and change back, so he just has to keep running.' Spook was chortling, but it sounded forced; mean.

Catherine was now looking from Dax to Spook, fascination on her face. Dax was frozen to the spot with anger and embarrassment. He could not believe this was happening. Gideon was getting up too, now. His fists were clenched.

'So,' went on Spook, 'he runs down this foxhole! And, of course, all the hounds run in after him, and he's all squashed up inside and now he *can't* shift back, because there's no space, and he's going to be doggie dinner! Ow!' Spook flinched as a small shard of rock struck him hard on the temple.

'Cut it out, Spook, or you'll get a chunk of cliff

next,' warned Gideon, but Spook just raised his arms protectively around his head and stood up, determined to finish his story while Catherine stared at him, totally gripped.

'Anyway, he'd be doggie droppings by now, if he hadn't been rescued.'

'Who rescued him?' gasped Catherine. The others now seemed as frozen as Dax, as the story was unfolded.

'Good old Mr Hind! Who happened to be passing with a spade and dug him out—and—well, I suppose you could say *me*, too.'

'You!' spat Gideon. 'What are you talking about?'

'Well, how do you think I know all this?' jeered Spook. 'I was *there*, you idiot. And it was me who got the hounds off him. I got all the hunt running off after another fox—a *glamour* fox—so poor fwightened Dax could climb down from where he was hiding, crying, in a tree. You never did say thank you, Dax.'

If Dax still had any doubts about Gideon being his friend, the next second squashed them flat. Gideon leapt across the picnic basket and decked Spook with one blow to the chin.

18

'Ow, ow, *ow*!' Gideon sucked the air in through his teeth and screwed up his face as Dax did his best to wrap a wet, cold flannel around his friend's rapidly swelling fingers. He laughed and patted Gideon on the head.

'I don't know why you didn't tele-whack him!' he said. 'You could've done just as much damage with your mind and an empty cordial bottle.'

'Sometimes,' said Gideon, grimly, 'it has to be done the old-fashioned way. You need the satisfaction of fist hitting face.' He grinned as he laid his injured hand carefully in his lap. 'It was good, wasn't it? Did you hear the crack? And the thud when he hit the ground?'

'It was brilliant,' said Dax, warmly. 'It should've been me really.' He paused and thought about the consequences of the nasty end to the midnight feast. 'He's going to spread it all over the college now, isn't he?'

'Doesn't matter. Nobody will believe him.'

'But why wouldn't they? He was right.' Dax bit on his lip and looked up at the newly installed dorm window above him. Something flew past it in the glow of the sinking moon, and he felt a small shift inside his ribcage, as though he, too, should be in flight. He'd never run away from anything though—until the hunt.

'What—that you were scared to death of being eaten alive? Cod's trousers, Dax! Who wouldn't be? *I* wouldn't just have cried—I'd've wet myself!'

Dax smiled. Gideon was back—no question of it. But he shook his head. 'It's not just that, though. Although, for the record, I *didn't* cry. I just couldn't walk and then I threw up in a bush. It's not just that, though,' he repeated. Then he told Gideon about Spook bringing the foxhound into Tregarren and how he had reacted.

Gideon was aghast. 'How did he get a *dog* past Mr Pengalleon and Barber?'

'I think he must have thrown an illusion or something, and maybe Barber wasn't there. He does go off on his own for a run sometimes. Anyway—I was a mess. I couldn't *do* anything except sit there. I was so scared I thought I was going to faint.' Dax buried his face in his hands, acutely ashamed even in front of Gideon, but Gideon was quite matter of fact in his response.

'It's just a panic attack, Dax,' he said, simply. 'Like the one in the scanner. I mean—' he hastily amended, 'it's not *just* a panic attack. I don't mean it's nothing—it's just . . . you know, *normal*, when you think about it. A reaction thing. My aunt Mary used to get them about buses. Her bag got caught on something while she tried to get off and she got dragged along quite a way before they saw her. She was quite calm when it happened. She did the panic bit later. For *years*. She got worse and worse until all you had to do was go "Ding-ding—any fares please?" and she'd go cross-eyed and shuffle backwards into the nearest corner. Really embarrassing once, at my school sports day.' He shook his head. 'I shouldn't have done it . . .'

Dax stared at him, aghast. 'Years?' he echoed. 'It lasted for *years*?'

Gideon shrugged. 'She might still be like it, for all I know. Haven't seen her since I was nine.' At this point Luke and Barry came in. They'd helped Catherine take back the picnic stuff before coming back to bed. They both sat down and made Gideon unwind his cold flannel, so they could see his messed-up hand.

'That was so cool,' said Barry. 'He went down so fast he blurred.' He shot Gideon a look of admiration. 'But he's going to get you back, Gid, you know that. And, Dax—he's really got it in for you now.'

Gideon began to re-wrap his hand tenderly. 'You're not telling me he can still talk, are you? I thought I'd shut him up for the night.'

'Mia helped him,' said Luke, and Dax and Gideon snorted with disgust.

'Well,' said Luke, 'he was rolling around and groaning and she just couldn't help it. She told him what she thought of him though. And anyway, Gid, it's better for you that she did. If Spook goes off to a teacher and reports you, he's not going to have much evidence now.'

Gideon sank back onto his pillows with a degree of contentment. 'Brilliant time though, eh?' he said, through a yawn. He giggled and they all grinned. Luke and Barry got into bed and Dax pulled up his own duvet.

Tiredness poured over him like an incoming wave and he sank willingly under it. He felt happy and worried in equal measure. Happy that everything was OK with Gideon again—but so, *so* worried about panic attacks. Years. Was it possible they could last for *years*? Another wave came in and Dax let it wash him away to sleep.

The next morning was how the end began. When Dax looked back later, he remembered this. It was as if a pebble was kicked off the side of a mountain. Inconspicuously. No hope of stopping it. Or the rocks it would unsettle as it fell, and the chaos that would follow.

Gideon wouldn't wake up.

Nor would Luke or Barry.

By the time he'd been round and vigorously shaken them *all*, Dax was shaking himself and a cold slick of fearful sweat was across his skin. Something was so wrong here.

'Gideon!' he tried again, shoving his friend's shoulder hard and pulling his duvet off. Gideon just curled up in a ball, with an incoherent mumble, and would not open his eyes. 'Gideon! Mate! Look—I'm getting worried here. Please say something to me . . . even "go away". Just *speak*!'

Gideon did say something, but it was like sleep talking and Dax couldn't make it out. What was wrong with him? Dax stood still and tried to think. They'd been up very late, but *he* had woken up as usual, so why not the others? Maybe . . . maybe . . . He thought back to the midnight feast. Was it that cordial? There was alcohol in it, so perhaps they were all sort of . . . hung over? But no—he had drunk the cordial too. He'd felt heavy and clumsy, getting up, but he was not hung over. Dax sank down on his bed and stared at his feet. Had he been right all along about the food? That was the only difference he could see. He had to be right. He hadn't eaten any of the school food—and he was the only one awake.

In an instant he had shifted into DaxFox and he shot out of the dorm and down the corridor, where other Colas were beginning to emerge, trolling across to the bathroom or downstairs for a hot drink. 'Hey, Dax,' called Alex Teller, as Dax fled past, but he didn't ask what was happening. The Colas were quite used to the fox in their midst by now.

It was a different story when he found the girls' dormitory building and shot in as Jessica Moorland opened the door. 'Oi!' she called after him. 'You can't go in there, Dax! This is girls only!'

Dax shifted impatiently and swivelled round to Jessica. 'I have to see Mia—NOW!' he said.

Jessica blinked and then led him straight upstairs. 'Boy coming through,' she bellowed. 'Urgent. No nuddies!'

'Hey, Dax! What's up?!' Catherine bounded out of the doorway as he reached their room. She looked astonishingly bright and energetic for a girl who'd been up half the night. Her green eyes sparkled and her skin looked flushed—as if she'd been running.

'I need to see Mia,' he said, grimly. 'Can I come in?'

'Yeah—sure. Everyone else has gone to breakfast. Mia's still asleep though. Go wake her!'

Dax felt a further stab of fear. Even as he stepped inside the room and saw Mia comatose in her bundle of bedclothes, he was grappling with his theories. If it had been the food, how come Catherine wasn't affected? Maybe . . . maybe that was her main talent—superhuman energy or resistance . . . that could be it. Jessica Moorland hovered behind him as he gave Mia's shoulder a shake.

'Wake up, Mia! Please!' She rolled over and groaned and seemed to shake her head.

'Is she all right?' asked Jessica, her voice low with concern.

'I don't know,' said Dax, miserably. 'Mia! Mia! Wake *up*!'

Jessica pushed him aside and put her hand on Mia's forehead. 'She hasn't got a fever or anything,' she observed. She gave her dorm-mate a shake but still Mia's eyes remained closed. Jessica snapped up and strode out of the room. 'Wait!' she called back and then, seconds later, returned with a large glass jug. 'This should do it,' she said and before Dax's amazed eyes she upended the jug and tipped a torrent of cold water over Mia's head.

'WHAT?' Mia shot up to a sitting position with a shriek and stared wildly around her, her soaking hair slapping wetly across her cheeks and forehead. 'What? What?' she asked again, staring at Dax. He grinned wryly and nudged Jessica. 'Why did you do that?' Mia whimpered at the girl.

'Foxboy needs you,' shrugged Jessica. 'And you were in a coma. Had to be done.'

'Mia,' said Dax, urgently, sitting down on the opposite bed. 'You have to come with me. I can't wake Gideon, Barry, or Luke. Not at all. They're like you were just a moment ago. I *can't* wake them up. Something's wrong.'

'Well, you woke *me* up,' grumbled Mia, surveying her wringing wet pyjama jacket. 'Go back and try the cold water technique! I'll follow on when I'm dry.'

By the time she arrived, marching through the boys' dorm building and wearily calling, 'Girl coming through . . . no nuddies!' Dax had soaked Gideon and Barry and was just about to do Luke. His first two victims were sitting up in bed, bedraggled and dazed.

'Whydyawanndothatfor?' burbled Gideon, shaking his head and sending droplets scattering left and right.

'No other way,' said Dax and let the third jugful plummet onto Luke. Luke shouted and flailed his hands around with a shocked gasp. 'Sorry, mate,' said Dax.

He then sat down on his bed. Mia stepped in and sat next to him and they watched as the soggy trio gradually came to. When they were all able to speak normally, Dax said, 'We have to talk.'

They were very quiet as he concluded his theory. He waited for just one of them to say, 'So *that's* what it is! I've been wondering why I've been feeling like this!'

It was Luke that spoke first. 'So if we're all being poisoned by the government, how come Catherine's all right?'

Dax shook his head. 'I don't know. I haven't worked that bit out yet. She might just be resistant . . . like I'm resistant to glamour.'

Luke looked sceptical. Gideon seemed even less convinced. 'Dax—mate—think about it! What about the teachers? They all eat and drink the same food, and they're all right, aren't they?'

'Well . . . well, we don't know that, do we? We don't see what they're like when the alarm goes off,' said Dax, beginning to flounder. 'Or maybe they're getting different stuff . . . from . . . from different tins or something . . . I don't know!' he finished sulkily. 'But don't you agree that *something* is weird here?'

'A lot of things are weird here, Dax,' said Mia, kindly. 'That's the whole point of this place.'

'You don't believe me, do you?' mumbled Dax, a cold needle of panic beginning to thread deep inside him.

'It's not about that,' said Mia. 'You're probably right in some sort of way—yes—we *are* all a bit groggy. But it could be just as much our . . . our *age*—you know? I mean, we're all meant to be at *that age* now, aren't we? And maybe, when you're a Cola, it just takes a lot more out of you.'

Dax looked around at them all. 'Aren't any of you even a bit worried?' he asked, faintly.

'I'm always worried,' sighed Luke, flopping back on his pillow. He shot up again, sharpish, when he realized it was sopping wet. 'Shattered glass, freezing cold water—I don't know what's going to wake me up *next*!'

Dax sighed and got up. 'I'll see you all at breakfast then,' he said. Nobody spoke as he left.

He badly wished he could talk to Lisa, but she wouldn't be back until teatime. Then he had a thought. Perhaps he *could* talk to her. He shifted, climbed a little way up the cliff face and perched himself on a comfortable outcrop of moss-covered rock. Wrapping his tail around his paws he steadied himself in the stiff sea breeze and closed his eyes. First he just called her name, over and over again. He felt faintly foolish. This was silly. She was hundreds of miles away.

Just as he was about to give up he felt a push in the air around him. The fur rose up on the back of his neck and a shiver rolled across him. Then Lisa snapped, *All right! All right! What is it?*

You can hear me! marvelled Dax. He felt, rather than heard, Lisa's impatience.

Yesss! But only just and you're giving me a headache. What is it?

He grinned, delighted. He really hadn't thought it would work. Quickly, he gathered his thoughts. *Lisa— when your train comes in today* . . . He paused . . . he had thought she was coming by train, but now he wondered whether Owen was collecting her again.

Yes! What? she prompted, testily.

Is Owen meeting you? Dax asked.

Yes. Why?

He tried to work out the best thing to say. It was impossible to explain it all like this. She'd end up with

a migraine. *Just don't get off the train until you've seen me.*
Silence. *Lisa! Did you get that? Don't get off—and don't be
seen—not until I get on and talk to you! It's VERY important.*
Silence. And then …

OK, Dax. OK. I'll see you later. On the train.

She was gone. The tingling sensation of their telepathy
faded abruptly and Dax realized he was ravenous. He was
just about to dash down to the refectory for breakfast
when he remembered. No food here. No water, either.
Dax eyed the clifftop and the wood that peered over it, on
its gnarly rooted tiptoes. He heard the throaty crooning
of a wood pigeon and made up his mind.

19

Dax worked out his route to the station while eating his packet of crisps (hopefully untampered with) at teatime. Aware of the occasional glance of concern from Gideon and Luke, as they tucked into fresh breadcrumbed haddock, chips, and peas and a smile of sympathy from Mia as she ate her vegetable chilli, he said nothing more about his 'conspiracy theory'. It made him feel sad though, because it was making things awkward again, and he had felt so good the night before when Gideon thumped Spook and proved he was still his best friend. If things were 'normal' he would have been talking to Gideon about his hunting. It was terrible that such an amazing thing was going on and he hadn't found a way to tell Gideon. The kill of the pigeon was still fresh in his mind—both horrifying and exhilarating—and Dax badly wanted to talk about it with someone. He knew Gideon would *love* to know about it—every detail—but here they were again, Luke on one side, Catherine on the other. Gideon seemed fairly normal now, having shaken off the torpor of that morning. Not that Dax would describe him as sparkling, exactly. Mia, too, was quiet, while Barry was picking at his food and propping his head up with one hand.

Catherine, of course, was still upbeat and fizzing with energy. She had a rounders ball with her at the table and, despite Mia's earlier kind warning, was intent on floating it across the ceiling and making it circle slowly around the lights. 'Look, Gideon! Look!' she whispered, squeezing her brother's arm.

Gideon smiled up blearily and Luke looked up too. 'Mia said not to, remember?' he said drily and Catherine pouted.

'I know—but it's such *fun*—and I'm not doing any harm.'

To Dax's surprise Luke shot her an angry look and muttered, 'No! But you said you wouldn't! It might—' and at that point there was a loud crack and the small hard ball suddenly dropped—Luke shot out his hand and caught it neatly. One of the topmost windows was now dissected in its frame.

Catherine put her hands over her mouth, her pretty eyes widening in horror. 'But I didn't . . . ' she whispered. Luckily for her, the catering staff had been crashing out some more steel tins of pudding at that point and hadn't noticed the noise.

'Just pretend not to notice,' muttered Barry. Nobody else seemed that bothered either, thought Dax, except Luke, who had gone extremely pink. He obviously felt responsible for his sister.

The low key drama didn't end there. Spook had been glowering at them all day and Dax wondered what kind of revenge he was cooking up. The illusionist's jaw had a mottled purple bruise on it despite Mia's healing, and much to Gideon's delight. '*I* did that!' chuckled Gideon, glancing over again at tea. 'It's a work of art!' Luke grinned in amusement, and then glanced down again to his plate and froze. The colour drained from his face.

'What's up?' asked Dax and Gideon looked back at his food too. The brothers eased back from their plates. 'What?' demanded Dax, screwing up his empty crisp packet.

'Fingers,' mumbled Luke, thickly. 'Severed fingers.'

Gideon shuddered. 'Spiders on mine,' he informed them. 'Big black ones, making thick funnel webs across my chips.'

Behind them, Spook was resting his chin in his hand, elbows on his table, and concentrating hard. Gideon set his mouth in an angry line and suddenly Spook's plate was dashed into his face. There was a shout of fury and laughter around him and the twins both visibly relaxed. 'All gone,' muttered Luke, but neither he nor Gideon seemed keen to pick up their knives and forks again.

Dax got up and told the others he'd see them back at the joint common room. He had spoken to Owen earlier that day and discovered that Lisa's train was due in at 5.10 p.m. He had half an hour to shift and get down to the station. Once he was clear of the wood above the cliff he would be officially breaking school bounds and could get into a lot of trouble, but it was a chance he had to take. It made him feel bad because he knew people like Owen and Paulina Sartre allowed him more freedom than other Colas, on trust. It was known that he would go to the woods in fox form quite regularly, and technically the woods too were out of bounds, even though they were owned by the school. No other student could reach them without going through the gate tower and past Mr Pengalleon, but Dax, it seemed, was a special case. Respecting his needs, no teacher had ever ruled on it. They might, though, if they discovered he was going further afield.

Luckily, Dax could reach the station easily without needing to shift back to a boy. He needed to cross only two roads and these were fairly quiet. He shot across both like a molten red arrow and arrived beside the line before Owen did. Lisa's train was early. Dax could hear the tracks singing news of its approach as he slid silently among the low scrub along the far side of the line, keeping down and eyeing the platform on the other side. As he did so, Owen wandered along it and then sat on a bench, flicking through a book. Dax tensed. He was going to have to be fast.

The train was just three coaches long and grimy from its long trek across the country as it hissed to a halt, shielding Dax from Owen's view. He hoped to spot an open window that he could spring through, but was appalled to see that they were all closed. He shifted back to boy form and then sprinted to the nearest door. Getting to it from ground level wasn't easy, but he hauled himself up and pulled the door open, thankful that it was an old slam-door type of train, and not a push button job which would have been much harder to get into. Inside he moved rapidly to his left, his fox sense picking up Lisa's scent in that direction. He found her hauling her weekend bag down from the overhead shelf.

'Go on then,' she said, before she'd even looked round. The carriage was empty, but Dax could just see Owen getting up and walking along the platform. He felt a stab of panic. He mustn't be seen. 'What's happening, Dax?' said Lisa, swinging the bag over her shoulder. She looked worried.

'Look—I can't tell you the details now.' Dax crouched into the seat, keeping his head down. 'Just this much— do NOT eat or drink *anything* at Tregarren.' She stared at him incredulously. 'I mean it, Lisa—eat and drink nothing! Not until you've talked to me. Meet me in the crying place as soon as you get back.'

Lisa nodded and then smiled. 'Hi, Mr Hind. I'm just coming—had to gather up all my stuff.' Owen took Lisa's bag and asked after her dad as they got off the train and Dax, his heart thudding with anxiety, pulled the window down to his left and then ducked to the floor as Owen and Lisa walked past the window. A second later, as the train pulled away, a passenger in the third carriage was convinced that she'd seen a fox leap out of the train window and run into the bushes. She told everyone else in the carriage about it. Fortunately for Dax, she was two, and nobody really took her seriously.

'All right. It's late, I'm hungry, I'm sitting in a freezing cold hollow and my bum is getting damp,' stated Lisa, shortly. 'What is all this about?'

Dax shuffled in next to Lisa. There wasn't much room in the Crying Place. Last year this had been the spot where Dax and Lisa had first met properly. It was a sort of baby cave, a hollow just big enough for two children to fit into, at a push, which lay hidden by rocky outcrops and wiry seagrass, just a few feet down from the outer edge of the school field's perimeter fence. On the first occasion Dax had found Lisa here she had been having a good cry about having to be at Tregarren. She'd hated it to start with. Ever since then, they'd both known it as the Crying Place even though neither of them had ever gone and cried there since.

'How have you been feeling, Lisa? While you've been at home?' asked Dax.

She stared at him and shrugged. 'I don't know— worried! My dad was full of tubes. What do you expect?'

'No—no. I mean . . . physically.' Dax struggled to explain. 'Compare it to how you were here, before you heard about your dad. How was it different—physically?'

She peered at him, trying to work out what he meant. 'I don't know . . . um . . . I felt OK at home. Pretty good, I suppose, considering. I mean, once I knew Dad was out of danger I felt fine—physically. Got to go out riding a couple of times, which was brilliant. I *still* want my pony down here.'

'OK—now—remember how tired and groggy you were last week?' asked Dax.

'Um . . . yes. What's all this about, Dax?'

Dax took a deep breath, hoping feverishly that Lisa would take him seriously, and then told her about the events of the past few days; how tired and vague everyone was; how he could barely wake Gideon, Luke, and Mia after the midnight feast, and finally, how he suspected that their food and drink was being tampered with. 'So I've not been eating any of it for the last few days—and I think I'm OK now,' he concluded. Lisa was silent for a while and he began to fear she was going to pour scorn on his ideas, but then she pursed her lips, fiddled with her neatly manicured nails, and peered out to the darkening sea.

'I don't want to believe you Dax,' she said, finally. 'But I think there might be something in it.' Dax sighed with relief.

'I saw what you're talking about as soon as I got back. There's a kind of—fog—almost, over this place. I don't think I would have seen it if I'd stayed here because it's probably come in so slowly. People's minds are a bit blunt. I'm not picking up stuff so easily, not because anyone's putting up barriers . . . they're just . . . sleepy. And I don't think it's *me* because I'm still getting all the usual yak from the hereafter. But . . . the food? Do you really think they'd put stuff in our food? Why would they do that?'

'I don't know,' said Dax, miserably. Strangely, having Lisa agree with him had made him feel better and worse at once. The idea that they were really being poisoned in some way was awful. He loved Tregarren and couldn't stand the thought that Caroline Fisher's warnings were going to be fulfilled.

'Of course, we're being watched and studied and stuff, all the time,' went on Lisa. 'What about that two-way mirror thing, eh? Like we wouldn't work *that* out. You know, once, there were *six* people jammed in behind it. All watching and taking notes. Trouble is, you see, Dax, they don't know what we are. Or what we might do, eventually. Sometimes, in development, I pick up real fear. Not from people like Owen Hind or Mrs Sartre, but some of the others. The ones behind the glass—they're wetting their pants. And that's just us mediums. Imagine what they're like watching the telekinesis group. Gideon's the one I'm most worried about.'

Dax nodded. He felt the same way. Most of the powers at Tregarren were pretty harmless, as far as he could tell. What danger did *he* represent, being able to turn into a fox? The healers and the mediums, psychics and dowsers were intriguing and useful. But what about kids who could shift stuff with their minds? Maybe from miles away, eventually. What about kids who could make you see a firework display in your bathroom or turn a plate of chips into a pile of bloody severed fingers? Kids who could disappear and reappear at will. Yes. Lisa was right. Fear was their biggest threat.

'So you think I'm right then,' he said, dully, picking some grass out from the rock and twisting it unhappily between his fingers.

'Well, you're right that something is wrong—and it

is a bit of a coincidence about the food and drink being changed around. But what about you? Have you been feeling better since you stopped eating and drinking here?'

'I feel OK. Not great. Worried all the time and nobody wants to know. But not all sleepy and dull like everyone else. Well—nearly everyone else. It would take a mallet to keep Catherine under,' he added.

'She's probably ten times worse when she's not being secretly drugged,' said Lisa, acidly. 'What about the teachers, though? Are they eating the food? Are they going all funny too? Owen seemed normal enough.'

'I know,' said Dax, dismally, and Lisa read his thoughts. She sighed too.

'No,' she said, quietly. 'I can't believe Owen's in on it. He wouldn't let them.'

'Well . . . ' Dax fumbled for an explanation. 'You know—it might be that it's another test, and it doesn't do any damage, and they just need to see . . . how we react.' He felt a wave of grief wash over him. It was too much. If they had only said to everyone that they were experimenting, and not to worry, but they might feel a bit tired and . . .

'Dax?' Lisa suddenly sat up, grazing her head on the top of the hollow. 'You say you haven't been eating or drinking anything. So—so what are you doing? How are you getting by?' She narrowed her eyes at him and then breathed out . . . 'Oh—my—God!'

20

'OK—here's what we do,' Dax said quietly, as they made their way to the dorms. The lights strung along the zigzag paths of Tregarren had come on, and the campus had its fairy-lit quality again. It was hard to believe anything sinister could happen somewhere so pretty.

'You can drink the cartons of milk—they're packaged and delivered in direct, so I don't think they can be messed with. Same with some of the pre-packed biscuits and crisps, when you can get them.'

'Oh yum,' said Lisa.

'But for proper food you'll have to let me hunt for us both.'

'Oh, yuck! What—dead rabbits? Mouldy old pigeon?'

'There's nothing *mouldy* about pigeons. And anyway, you won't have to eat them *raw*. We'll build a fire and cook them—like Owen showed us.'

'Where? Where are we going to build a fire? I can't get up to the woods like you, remember? Only when I can get a pass—and I don't think I'll manage *that* every day. Oh—sorry, Mr Eades! I just need another permission slip so I can go and butcher a bunny and have my tea!'

Dax laughed—it was so good to have Lisa and her catty

comments back. 'Don't worry. I've found somewhere. I'll show you tomorrow.'

'So—are you going to talk to Owen?'

'Yes. But not yet. I want to be sure. We'll wait a few days and see how you are, and then we'll know. Then I can tackle him about it.'

'OK. I'll talk to Mia, too, but I won't say anything about not eating the food. Just try to find out what's going on with her. I'll see you at the breakfast we won't be eating,' she finished smartly and disappeared into the girls' dorm.

Dax moved slowly back to the boys' building. Gideon would probably wonder where he'd been for the past two hours. He *hoped* Gideon would wonder. As he passed under the rocky outcrop along the path, Dax scented and heard Spook Williams close behind him. He turned and saw the boy gaining on him, holding his hands out in a weird way, as if he were carrying a tray before him. There was a nasty look on his face and Dax sighed. He was too tired for more Spook nonsense.

'What is it now?' He folded his arms across his chest and stood squarely in the middle of the path. It was probably about time he hit Spook for himself. Spook's eyes glittered and there was a wavering in the air around him. Dax suddenly realized the boy was doing a glamour on him. A fairly major effort too, judging by the look on his face and the beads of sweat on his upper lip. Dax opened his mouth to speak, but then faltered. This was a problem. Spook's eyes were narrowing at him now.

What was the illusion? Dax needed a hint—but there was no handy Gideon, Barry, or Luke nearby to tell him. Finally, Dax muttered, 'Very funny, Spook,' hoping he'd not missed the mark.

'You think so, mongrel?' said Spook and dropped his arms. A look of hostile curiosity swept across his face and then—oh no—then a cold realization. Spook stared and stared at Dax, as if trying to see inside his skull. 'You . . . ' he whispered. 'You . . . you're not . . . you don't. Oh yeah . . . I get it now.' Suddenly, Spook snapped towards him and grabbed Dax by the shoulders. He smacked him up against the wall of rock so hard that Dax yelped in pain. Crags of hard granite cracked into his head and spine. 'You don't see it, do you?' breathed Spook, his face close and his teeth gritted. 'You can't see any of it? What's wrong with you, Dax Jones? You're not like the rest of us, are you?' Dax shoved back against Spook hard and raised his fists. But the boy pulled back easily, stepping away from him, his hands hanging at his sides. For a moment he looked almost as if he were about to cry. *He's scared*, thought Dax, wildly. *He's really, really scared*.

'I see that you're trying,' he said. 'I can see the effort you're putting in and I know every time you try. I can *smell* it.'

Spook bit on his lip and looked at Dax as if he would like to throw him into the sea.

'But no—you can't dupe me, Spook. I'm resistant to glamour. To me, you're just an ordinary kid with no powers. Get over it.' Dax turned and walked away, heading for the common room building. He knew his words were far, far worse than anything he could have done to Spook physically. He felt the boy standing, watching, until he closed the door behind him.

It was quiet in the common room. Most of the Colas seemed to be in the television area, watching some kind of game show, but Barry was sitting on the couch by the fire, playing a hand-held computer game. 'You've got one that works?!' murmured Dax, as he sat down next to Barry. Most gadgets broke down or froze at Tregarren. Gideon said it was because of all the supernatural activity.

'Yeah, seems all right at the moment,' grunted Barry, lost in his fight with a tiny pixellated dragon. 'Won't last though.'

'How long have you managed to keep it going?' asked Dax, casually.

'All day, on and off,' said Barry, still not taking his eyes off the tiny screen.

Dax sighed. Much less supernatural stuff going on. It was obvious if only Barry could see it. 'Barry—can you vanish for me?' asked Dax. Barry shot him a quick glance before fixating back on his game. 'What for? Doesn't work properly for you anyway, does it?'

'No—no, it does. You do vanish. It's just that I can always smell and hear you . . . and see the wavy lines. But you do vanish. Go on—I just want to test something.' Barry sighed heavily and then snapped his game off, shrugged, and vanished. Only, he didn't really vanish.

Not by anyone's standards. He just went a bit dim. See through. Dax gulped and felt a little sick. It was definitely getting worse.

'Well?' said Barry, rather irritably, coming back into full, dense, colour.

'Brilliant!' said Dax. 'By the way, Barry, just so's you know, Spook knows. About my resistance to glamour. Should've seen the look on his face when I told him.'

'Why'd you tell him?' Barry frowned at Dax. 'I thought you wanted to keep it a secret.'

'I did. But he worked it out. It took the smirk off his face for a bit, anyway.'

Barry looked into the fire for a few seconds and when he looked back at Dax his face was unusually grave. 'You want to be careful, Dax. Of Spook. I mean, I know he's a stupid git, but he's getting meaner about you. And about Gideon. Don't wind him up.'

Having Lisa at the table at breakfast was a huge relief for Dax. Mealtimes had become almost unbearable over the last week, but as they both ate their pre-packed yoghurts and opened sealed cartons of milk, watching the others was at least something he could now share with her.

Gideon and Luke weren't as tired as the day before, and they wanted to know how Lisa's week had been, so they were far more lively than they had been. Mia, too, was looking more awake as Lisa related what had happened to her dad. As they left the refectory Dax muttered to Lisa that he would meet her at lunchtime, at the Crying

Place, for some real food. She pulled a disgusted face, but nodded.

In class, Dax found himself watching Mrs Dann closely that morning. Her students, while not exactly a bunch of zombies, were so low on concentration she surely *had* to notice something. And to his relief, she *did* seem to be noticing. Several times she stood, vexed, her hands on her hips, sighing and shaking her head as her pupils stumbled over their answers or gazed away into the middle distance.

'What *is* the matter with you all?' she demanded, as the lesson drew to a lacklustre close. 'Far be it from me to complain, but nobody's even tried to sneak in a bit of glamour and I've had my back turned for *ages*! Barry! Jennifer! Indulge me! Vanish, will you?'

Barry and Jennifer glanced at each other in confusion. They'd been caught out in class by Mrs Dann before, and sprayed liberally with her 'anti-glamour' aerosol, which covered them in bright green pigment ink, so they could be seen, even when vanished.

'Go on!' prodded Mrs Dann. Barry shrugged and Jennifer nodded and both faded out—only slightly to Dax's eyes, but obviously more effectively to everyone else's.

'Good!' said Mrs Dann. 'That's more like it!' She looked at her watch. 'Right—there's fifteen minutes until lunch. I command you all to go up to the sports field and run about a bit.' Some of the girls groaned. 'I mean it! You're all groggy and obviously not eating your greens,' concluded Mrs Dann. 'Go on—off you go. The Scottish crofting industry is obviously a lost cause to you lot today.'

The class emptied rapidly and Dax nodded to Lisa to indicate that he'd meet her as planned, but he hung back. He wanted to talk to Mrs Dann. She was resignedly stacking her books away in her desk drawer, her shiny brown bob of hair falling across her face, when the last student left and the door fell closed. Dax took a deep breath, hoping he wasn't making a big mistake, and said, 'What do you think is going on, then, Mrs D?'

The teacher paused in what she was doing, and Dax couldn't see her expression. Then she shoved the drawer back in and stood up, wiping her hair back from her face, revealing a look of—'straightness'—was how Dax thought of it. She was stepping off the teacher plinth and looking at him, one to one. For a few seconds she regarded him openly and Dax wondered, briefly, if she had any mind-reading talent. No. He picked up nothing, except a naturally insightful personality. 'I'm not sure, Dax,' she said. 'What do you think?'

Dax wasn't ready to say. He needed more from her first. 'There is something wrong, isn't there?' he said.

She sighed and sat down heavily at her desk. 'I don't know, Dax! I don't *know*! That's the trouble, you see, with us ordinary people. How are we supposed to know what's normal, surrounded by you lot? You know—in my old school, my *normal* school, I was a year counsellor for the children, and I had a really good reputation as someone who could tell, straight out, when a child was troubled, or lost or lying or bullied or being a bully. I *was* really good at it. That's how I got the job here. But with you lot . . . I'm adrift. I can teach you all, but half the time I can't read you. So . . . is there something wrong? Or is it just normal for you all to do all this way-out stuff and then get really tired . . . And don't forget you're all at *that age*.'

'Yeah, all right!' said Dax, hastily. 'I know! But it's more than that. I think . . . I think we're being messed around with, somehow. Tested.'

To his amazement, she nodded. 'Undoubtedly,' she said. 'It's why you're here. That's what the scans and the bloods were all about. We have to find out about you, because we can't just sit around wondering what's going to happen next. We have to make some effort to understand. And, Dax, even if you do feel as if you're under the microscope, remember Tregarren *is* still the safest place for you all.'

'Is it?'

She didn't answer for a long time. Then she stood up. 'I'm not part of the scientist crew, Dax. You know that. I don't actually *know* what the tests are, but I truly believe that nobody is meant to be harmed by anything that's done here. I'm going to talk to Mr Hind. See if he has any ideas about this fogginess.' Dax blinked, surprised that Mrs Dann had used the same term as Lisa. 'In the meantime, try not to worry too much. It'll probably all blow over in a few days—and *you* seem to be all right.'

Dax smiled, thinly. He didn't offer his theory on why he was all right. He turned to go, but as he did he paused and just asked one more question. 'Mrs D—do you always eat in the ref?'

She tilted her head to one side, birdlike. 'Not every meal. A lot of us have our own kitchens in our cottages. We like to get away from you lot sometimes!' she said. 'Why?'

'Ah—nothing,' said Dax.

'You have got to be kidding!' Lisa stood, hands on hips, and pulled a face of revulsion.

'Oh, don't be such a drama queen,' muttered Dax, and knelt down to pick up the soft body of the recently killed rabbit; one of three that had lain, in a furry pile, since early that morning on the floor of the cave.

Lisa folded her arms disdainfully and looked around her. 'This is brilliant, though,' she said, eyeing the low ceiling of the small cave, which undulated back into the rock in a narrowing V-shape. The floor, littered with pebbles, shards of granite, and ancient bits of sea-polished driftwood, climbed in a gentle upward slope to the high end of the V where the ceiling dipped to meet it. It was dry, but the muffled burble of the sea rang around it constantly.

Daylight flooded through the opening of the cave, but now another light grew as Dax swiftly made a fire inside a ring of larger stones. 'They're not damp, are they?' said Lisa, finally kneeling to join him. 'You know what Owen's always saying about using damp stones around the fire—they might explode.'

'No,' snapped Dax. He was hungry and it made him tetchy. 'I fetched them down from the top end, where the sea doesn't reach even at spring tide. They're bone dry.'

'When did you find this place?'

'Back in the winter,' said Dax. 'I'm surprised nobody else has yet, but you can't really see it from the college grounds. I only found it out on a fox-trot. Then I worked out a human path to it. You can't get to it at high tide, though. Anyway, stop stalling.'

He handed her a knife. It was one that Owen had given him and was flat on the underside and slightly domed on the other, its edges very sharp and true, designed to separate skin from muscle. He'd also brought his penknife, which wasn't quite so good for the task of skinning rabbits, but would do. Lisa needed the advantage—she'd only had one lesson at this with Owen, back in the winter months. She hadn't liked it one bit.

'This is disgusting,' she muttered.

'If you're not up to it, I'll do it,' murmured Dax, trying not to grin when Lisa immediately snapped her head up from the task.

'Of course I'm up to it! But I don't have to *like* it, do I!' Together they skinned and then gutted the rabbits, removing the fur and soft innards, and piling them outside behind a rock where the scavenging seabirds would make short work of them.

Dax's fire was burning steadily now, and the embers

at its base were glowing ashy red. No smoke rose from it; he'd followed Owen's lessons closely, using only dry wood, stripped of bark. Wordlessly they skewered the fresh carcasses on fine green hazel twigs and suspended them over the low flames between two stouter sticks, dug firmly into the sand and shingle at an angle. Dax then began to slide a dozen or so field mushrooms onto another twig, ready to barbecue when the meat was nearly cooked.

'You sure they're not poisonous?' said Lisa, eyeing the fungi warily. Dax fished a small, dog-eared book from his back pocket. It was a field guide to mushrooms and toadstools. He flipped it open to the right page and then invited Lisa to compare the mushrooms on the stick to the picture under his thumb. She pursed her lips and then nodded. 'Yeah. OK.'

The meal wasn't bad. The rabbit meat was tender, if odd for Lisa who had only tasted a little during the winter woodsman lesson with Owen. Dax was impressed that she ate plenty of it. She was a practical, hard-headed girl. She ate the mushrooms too, and they washed down their lunch with mineral water, which she'd brought back with her on the train.

'Are we going to have to do this every day?' she said, checking her watch. It was only a short time until afternoon lessons. 'I mean—it's really time consuming, and people are going to start to notice we're not around.'

'We'll keep it up long enough to see what happens to you,' said Dax. 'If you start to go all tired and floppy like everyone else, then we'll know it's not the food or the water.'

'And if I don't—and you're right? How long can we keep this up?'

'If I'm right,' said Dax, feeling the Owl Box key on its chain around his neck, which he had taken to wearing again, 'we won't have to keep it up. We'll be getting out of here.'

21

That night there was more commotion in Dax's dorm. The windows had been re-glazed and all traces of shattered glass removed, but this time it was something less dramatic. Barry had the most almighty sneezing fit.

Dax was wrenched out of a vivid dream, where he had run off the edge of the cliff above the campus, only to turn around in mid-air and glide slowly down and back to the dorm, unharmed. Barry's sneezing was loud and prolonged and everyone woke up as the noise rebounded off the walls and Barry began to stomp about, looking for tissues.

'What's going *on*?' moaned Gideon, snapping on his bedside light.

'Wooshhooo!!' commented Barry. Luke padded back in from the bathroom and handed him a wodge of loo roll. Barry sank back onto his bed and blew his nose like a foghorn. 'It's by allergies!' he groaned through the scrunched-up tissue. 'I'b allergic to somedig! Who's been sprayig duff?'

'No one!' said Gideon. 'Why would we want to be spraying stuff in the middle of the night?'

'Piddow fide, den!' Barry peered accusingly at them all, over his swollen nose. His eyes were also puffy and streaming. 'You *dow* I'b allergic do feadders!'

'No—we were all asleep!' said Gideon. 'Maybe it's something in the air. Pollen, or something. Dax's window is open.'

Dax glanced up. He didn't remember opening the new window, but it was ajar by several inches, the sea air winding around it. Dax sat up and looked around, suddenly filled with an eerie feeling of déjà vu. The sea air, winding around the ajar window . . . meeting his face . . .

'See! Dook!' Barry was pointing, self-righteously. There were three small, curled, yellow-white feathers on the floor. 'You've been piddow fiding!' Dax picked them up and threw them out of the window, with difficulty against the breeze. 'And don't piddow fide again!' muttered Barry, getting back under his duvet.

'Oh, get over it, Barry,' groaned Gideon, switching his lamp back off. 'Go back to sleep.'

With much sniffling and grumbling, Barry did. Dax lay back and gently touched the outer edges of his mind, trying to track the recent déjà vu feeling. What was it? It was already receding, and he was beginning to drift back to sleep when one thought, clear and calm, entered his head. Their pillows and quilts were stuffed with bits of synthentic foam. There wasn't a single feather in them.

'Feeling fine, feeling fine,' sang Lisa, in a breathy voice as she jogged past Dax on the way down to breakfast. 'Oh no!' She doubled back and ran in the opposite direction.

'I didn't see her! I didn't see her,' she sang again, as she went past Dax again. 'Oh—I've left something behind,' she said in a louder voice.

Dax peered along the path and saw Catherine jumping about further down and waving. 'Hey, Lisa! Hey!' she was calling eagerly. Dax turned and followed Lisa back up the path, running to catch up.

'Are you trying to avoid someone?' he grinned as he found her skulking about on the girls' dorm steps, waiting for Catherine to go on down to the ref.

'Look—I'm just not in the mood for Cuddles this morning!' said Lisa, tartly.

'I thought everyone liked Catherine!' said Dax, laughing.

'Hey! Yeah! She's so cool! So cute! So warm and fun-nee!' drawled Lisa in a fake Californian accent. 'What's not to like, hey?' She paused, puffed out a relieved breath when she saw the path ahead was clear again, and they retraced the route to breakfast. 'Oh, she's all right, I suppose,' she muttered, glancing at Dax. 'But she's always so . . . so . . . so yuckily cheery! So *nice*. And she's always patting or squeezing some part of you. Don't tell me you haven't noticed! She's always trying to grab a hold of *you*! She wants you to be her furry *pet*!'

'You're not jealous, are you?' dared Dax and then dropped to the path, laughing, just before Lisa could whack him round the head.

'In your *dreams*, Jones! Now then . . . Cheddar and

biscuits? Yoghurt? Milk? Euch! I'm going to turn into a cheesecake!'

Dax made to follow Lisa into the ref, but was hailed from the quad. He turned to see Owen striding across to him. 'Dax—have you got a minute?' Owen was smiling, but Dax could see something else in his face and scented the man's tension. He turned and approached his mentor, treading slowly across the grass surrounding the quad fountain. The air around him seemed thin and the image of the water splashing prettily into the pond behind Owen was very sharp. Dax was, like it or not, preparing for trouble, and he didn't know why.

Owen motioned for him to follow and they went into the college building and across to Paulina Sartre's office. The principal wasn't there, but Dax saw Mrs Dann pause at the corner of the corridor, watching uneasily as they went in, and realized she must have been talking to her colleague about their conversation. Owen closed the door and sat on the edge of the large oak desk, motioning for Dax to sit on the leather sofa in front of it.

'Dax, what's happening with you?' said Owen. It was blunt and direct, but laced with something else. Hurt? Disappointment?

Dax said nothing. He just narrowed his eyes at Owen, trying to read him.

'Stop it,' said Owen, abruptly. 'You don't need to prod around in my head. Just ask! Have we not been friends this last year? Don't you trust me? What have I done to lose your confidence, Dax?'

Dax felt bad. Nothing. Owen had done nothing.

'You haven't done anything,' he mumbled, looking at his hands. 'I do trust you. Of course I do.'

'Yeah, well, we've had issues there before, haven't we?' said Owen. He looked at the floor and Dax knew he was remembering the terrible few minutes spent in the previous principal's study last year, when he had struck Dax into semi-consciousness and seemed to be about to kill him. Owen had been bluffing Patrick Wood, hoping to pull the man back from the edge of murder and his apparent betrayal had nearly cost Dax all hope and his very life.

'So,' Owen said, 'something is happening—something serious—and you're not telling me.'

Dax spoke without further delay; it was time. 'I think the college is tampering with our food and drink to see what it does to us. I think that's why everyone's so dull and tired. I don't like it. And I don't know if you know about it, and if you did and you hadn't said, I don't know if I could . . . if I . . . ' Dax felt his throat close with emotion. He shut his eyes and breathed slowly, keeping control. He didn't want to see Owen's face because he was scared.

There was silence in the room. Then he heard Owen get to his feet and begin to pace around and, when he finally did look, the man had his arms folded over his chest, hands tucked into his armpits, in his familiar way. Owen's lips were compressed and he shot a glance at Dax which was a mixture of anger and fascination.

'You've gone a bit wild on me, Dax, haven't you?' he said, still moving around the office in his distracted way. Dax gulped and said nothing. 'You went hunting, didn't you?'

Dax dropped his eyes to his shoes and nodded, not sure whether to be ashamed or proud.

'So, rather than come to me and tell me your concerns, like you would have done last term, you say nothing, and just shift, shift, shift away from it all. Animal instinct, eh, Dax? Is that what took over when you saw the pigeon or the rabbit or whatever it was you'd just killed when I saw you with blood in your hair?'

Dax stared at him, rigid with anxiety. He simply couldn't read Owen now; he was too distressed. What did Owen think of him? That he'd gone too far?

Owen walked around the far side of the desk and then slapped both hands down on it, making Dax jump. 'What is your fox sense telling you now, Dax? What do you think I am? Friend or foe?'

Dax's mouth was dry. He closed his eyes. Owen said nothing else, but he heard him sit down heavily in the leather desk chair. Then he heard the receiver of the telephone being lifted from its cradle on the desk and Owen punching out a number quickly. His sharp ears picked up the ringing tone and a flat voice which grunted, 'Chambers.'

'It's Special Operative Hind here,' said Owen and Dax started, his eyes opening wide. He had never heard Owen use that title before. There was an acknowledgement and

Owen cut to his question. 'Chambers— the tests on the Colas. Anything showing up yet?'

Dax felt his jaw drop. They *were* testing! Owen was admitting it. 'OK—stage three. Anything on that? And are we just withdrawing stimulants? Any plans to add them? Yup. No. Nothing to report yet, but I may get back to you later in the week. No—no, it's great. You know how I like to be beside the seaside!' And he laughed— *laughed*—and put the phone down.

Dax stared and stared and Owen smiled, folding his arms and tucking his hands back into his armpits and sighing ruefully. 'Dax—you're right. We have been tampering with your food. We have withdrawn all stimulants, such as caffeine and high levels of refined sugar. And we've *added* multivitamins, zinc, calcium, and fish oils.'

'Stupid? Why should you feel stupid?' Lisa stopped running around the field (something which she very rarely did before she had finished her planned route) and turned to look at Dax, who'd been trying to catch up. He'd wanted to talk properly and couldn't do it in fox form.

Dax shrugged. 'I should have just asked him in the first place.'

'Dax—has it occurred to you that the great and good Owen Hind might *not* know everything that happens here?' Lisa bent to tighten the laces on her left running shoe. 'And besides, it doesn't make sense! If it's *not* stuff in the food and water, what is it? Did Owen have any ideas about that?'

'I didn't ask,' admitted Dax, shuffling on the grass. It was a Saturday and the Tregarren football teams—the Tigers and the Terrors—were having a 'friendly' match behind them. Although the shouting that was going on between Gideon and Spook, in opposing teams, sounded anything but friendly. 'Maybe I've just been imagining it all. Maybe it's just . . . something to do with my panic attacks.'

'Panic attacks?' Lisa was peering at him in confusion. 'What panic attacks?'

Dax realized that she hadn't heard. Grimly, he told her about the scene in the scanner, about the dog on the field. He was pink with embarrassment and wondered if she'd laugh. Lisa wasn't known for her finer feelings. But she didn't. She just looked up to the heavens and shook her head, her blonde ponytail marking a zigzag in the air.

'Are you nuts, Dax? Of *course* you're having panic attacks! Don't forget, I was right in your head for most of what happened that day—*I* was having a panic attack the whole time! You should have seen the state of *me*! Look—that's that and this is *this*. You're right. People *are* weird here and it's nothing to do with your messed-up head.'

Dax looked at the footballers and rubbed his hair distractedly. 'What about *them*? They look normal enough now, don't they?'

'Yesss!' hissed Lisa. 'But by lunchtime they'll all

be face down in their stew! You know it! Speaking of which—what are *we* having?'

'You mean you still want to go on with the wild food?' said Dax.

'Damn right!' said Lisa. 'I'm not so soppily devoted to Owen that I'm just going to nod and smile and start knocking back dodgy pie! I feel fine, right now, and I want to keep it that way—until I'm sure. So what's on the menu?'

Dax felt better. 'Pigeon? Squirrel?' She looked repulsed. 'All right—it's the poor little bunnies again.'

They met at the cave an hour later, Dax arriving in fox form, two rabbits hanging limply in his bloodied jaws. Lisa compressed her lips and sucked air in through her nose. 'What—what does it feel like?' she asked at length. Dax shifted and tried to explain, feeling disloyal to Gideon. Gideon should have been the first friend to hear this, but he was at lunch now, with Luke and Catherine, and maybe Mia and Barry, and probably hadn't even noticed Dax wasn't there.

'It's quick,' he said. 'Not drawn out and nasty. Sudden and quick.'

'You don't have to make it nice for me,' said Lisa, getting to the skinning without a murmur of disdain this time. 'How does it feel inside you?'

Dax thought. 'It's powerful . . . like the need you get to . . . to . . . probably like how you need to run. Or how some people need to climb or swim. It's physical. Exciting. But really, really fast. Everything else just zones out and your whole self is—*focused*—aimed, like an arrow, on what you need to do. If I forget about being Dax the boy it's amazing. Just—pure instinct. But if I remember, and I have a couple of times, it's also kind of horrible. Like being in my own horror film. Not for long though. It's—like I said—it's quick. I wouldn't do it if we didn't need it. Not for fun. I wouldn't.'

Lisa looked at him as if she wasn't sure. 'Handy talent,' she said. 'Wolf-boy is proud of you.'

Dax sat down with a bump. 'He's back?'

Lisa nodded, working the meat loose from the blue-veined membrane of skin and fur. 'Poke the fire a bit.'

'He's back! Why didn't you say so?'

Lisa gave him a *look*. 'Don't wet your pants! He's in and out all the time at the moment. Along with the rest of them.'

Dax squawked with frustration. 'Well, don't you think that might be *important*? Honestly, Lisa!'

'He hasn't said anything *new*,' she said, defensively. 'Just the same as before . . . you know . . . "take it to the wing" and "don't touch the third" and the bushy green stuff and all that. Didn't think there was much point in bleating on about it every five minutes. I'm not the hereafter's speaking clock, you know!'

Dax took the skinned rabbit out of Lisa's hand, rested it on the stick over the fire and then took hold of her shoulders. 'Shut *up* and listen!' She looked shocked. 'You said something *else* then! Something you *haven't* told me before. About green stuff. Lisa! What is he saying to you? What is he showing you?'

Lisa had the grace to look slightly guilty. 'Sorry—I thought I'd said!' He shook his head, glaring at her. 'Oh . . . well . . . it's just this stuff he shows me. A sort of plant—bushy and green and in a round sort of shape.'

'Where? Where is it?'

'I don't know . . . up—up a tree or something.'

'*LOOK!*'

'All right, all right!' She closed her eyes and wrinkled her brow. 'Yes . . . definitely up a tree.'

Dax immediately remembered the night in the woods, when the wolf had appeared to him and taken him to the apple tree. 'OK—OK,' he said, waving his hands in the air and thinking aloud. 'What plant is found, up a tree, in a sort of green ball? What is that?'

'Sounds like mistletoe,' said Lisa, opening her eyes again.

'Mistletoe?'

'Yes. You know—the stuff people kiss under at Christmas. Our gardener grows it for our parties. Revolting custom.'

'And it grows up in trees?'

'Well, yeah. It's a parasite. It gets rubbed into the bark of a tree—by a bird or by our gardener—and grows there, sort of drinking energy out of the tree. Well, technically, it's a partial parasite because it does photosynthesize for itself . . . we did it in biology at my last school. I think—'

'STOP!' Dax stood up and began walking around the fire. 'Back up! What did you say? About drinking out of the tree?'

Lisa frowned and backtracked. 'It saps energy out of the tree! It's a parasite. Parasites live off other beings. It's quite pretty, though, mistletoe. Deadly poison to eat, mind you.'

'And . . . don't touch the third.' Dax sank to the floor of the cave. He felt the planets slow down. A muffled sound covered his ears like water. A *knowing* rolled over him.

'Don't touch the third,' he whispered. Lisa was staring at him now, oblivious to the rabbit beginning to char over the fire.

'What? What?'

Dax steepled his fingers together and pressed them to his mouth for a moment, then raised his eyes to Lisa. 'Catherine is the third.'

'Dax—what are you *on about*?'

'Lisa,' he said, slowly. 'I want you to think carefully about this. How does Catherine make you *feel*—honestly?'

Lisa narrowed her eyes at him. 'Catherine? I dunno. Irritated. She's so cute and clingy and kissy. I just find her—I don't know—*tiring*.'

'Tiring?'

'Yes—and she's always going, "Oh, it must be so great to be like you! You're so gifted!" ' Lisa did another impression of the gushy, girly, Californian accent. 'And it's always, "I wish I could have just a tiny bit of what you've got!" It makes me feel sick, to be honest with you.'

Dax gave a wild laugh. 'That's it! That's it exactly. She's mistletoe! He's right!'

'What *are* you talking about?'

'Think about it!' Dax seized Lisa by the wrists. 'When she's around you she's always squeezing your hand, or putting an arm around you or something—yes?'

Lisa grimaced. 'Unless I can avoid it!'

'And she's the same with everyone else, too. Every student, that is. *Except* Luke. She doesn't bother at all with Luke. Now, isn't that *odd*? Given that Luke is her brother. It's only ever Gideon she's all over like a rash! Why? What's different?'

Lisa's mouth opened in a sudden 'O' of understanding. 'Luke has no powers!'

Dax nodded, feverishly. 'You see? No powers. No point. And when she's gone everyone feels exhausted! Tired out! Sapped of energy. And they're all flagging now *except* Catherine. Catherine's doing really well. Catherine's drinking everyone dry!'

Lisa stared at him, and then dropped her eyes as the sense of his words filtered through to her. 'A little bit of what *I've* got. She's been trying to leech power off me! The parasite!'

'But look! She *hasn't* got to you since you came back, has she? You were avoiding her this morning, and yesterday, so she hasn't had a chance to get hold of you ever since you've had your week away. Or me! I've just not been around any of the triplets, what with all the running around hunting and trying to get to you! And we're all right—aren't we?'

Lisa was pacing now. 'It makes sense. Remember when

she did that weird self-healing thing? Up in the woods? She'd just leeched that off Mia! And she's always doing little telly tricks at mealtimes, while she's cuddled up to Gideon.' Lisa shuddered visibly. 'No wonder he hasn't been bothering with you! She's been siphoning off everything he's got! Nasty, sneaky little tic!' Lisa ran to the entrance of the cave. 'She's getting something off me NOW!'

Dax shot across to block Lisa's path. 'NO! No, Lisa— you *can't*!'

'Oh, I *can*!' Lisa was dancing around like a boxer in the ring. Dax had never seen her so furious. 'Think about Mia! You know how sensitive she is! You know how we have to protect her! Catherine is drinking up all her energy, too—just for fun!'

'Lisa, SIT DOWN!'

Dax must have shouted louder than he'd thought because Lisa blanched and sat down with a bump. 'Your eyes went funny then,' she muttered.

Dax took a deep breath. He was shaking, too, and he wanted nothing more than to run up to the college with Lisa and disable the parasite in their midst. But he was thinking more clearly. 'Quite apart from all the amazing energy you'd be offering up to her—with two straws in!—we've got to remember Gideon. She *is* his sister— and maybe she doesn't know she's doing it.'

'Oh, she does,' said Lisa, bobbing her head in certainty. Dax believed her.

'We ought to at least give her a chance. Let me talk to her. See if we can stop this without anyone getting hurt.'

Lisa took a deep breath and let it out, flexing her fingers in and out of fists. 'All right,' she said, more calmly. 'Do it your way, Dax. For Gideon's sake. But if she starts up again, she's going to suck up something from me she won't forget in a hurry. Knuckles.'

Dax started to laugh. In a way, it was a relief. It made sense. At *last* it made sense. The 'take it to the wing' bit was still not clear, but everything else . . . Dax felt a weight begin to lift and, at the time, he wanted it so much, he decided the other bit wasn't important. In Lisa's mind, the wolf whined, but she was so pumped up with indignant rage, she didn't notice.

22

When Dax found Catherine she was sitting on the edge of the fountain pool in the quad with Spook, practising some illusion glamour. Spook was clearly hugely entertained to be her teacher. Although exactly what illusion they were creating Dax couldn't see, he could tell by the shimmer in the air that Catherine was making something. Spook inclined his coppery head like a patient old sage and then Catherine jumped up and clapped her hands in delight.

'Did I do good, Spook? Did I do good?!' she gasped and when he nodded indulgently she threw her arms around his neck and hugged him hard. Spook looked immensely pleased with himself, but as Catherine disengaged herself and he lifted up his hands to show her another trick, Dax could clearly see them trembling. He wondered how quickly the smug look on Spook's face would fall off if he knew exactly what Catherine had been doing when she'd given him that friendly hug.

'Catherine,' he called and she stopped still before turning to him, perhaps already picking something up from the tone of his voice (well, she'd been leeching off the psychics too, reasoned Dax).

'Hey! Dax Jones! You gonna do that foxy thing for me now?' She beamed at him while Spook curled his lip.

'Been marking your territory, mongrel?' he sneered. 'It stinks around here.'

Dax ignored him. 'Catherine, I need to talk to you,' he said, gravely. 'Alone.'

'Sooo serious!' she teased, with mock gravity, before turning back to Spook. 'Thank you, Mr Teacher! I have to go now,' she simpered, reaching to give him a goodbye hug and Dax, although he wasn't quite sure why (this was *Spook* after all), called out, 'No! Stop it! Right now!'

Spook was too startled even to come up with a jibe and Catherine's hands dropped to her side abruptly. She looked hard at Dax with no attempt at a smile. In fact, he caught the faintest scent of fear from her.

'We talk now,' said Dax more quietly and walked away, knowing she would follow. They went to the top end of the college grounds, where soft hedging hid them from view and beyond it a gentle rocky slope led down to the sea. As soon as he was sure there was nobody within hearing distance Dax turned to her and spoke.

'I know what you're doing, Catherine.'

Her pretty green eyes widened and she tilted her head to one side. 'What do you mean?'

'Your Cola talent,' said Dax. 'If you can call it a talent. I know what it is.'

She straightened up and lifted her chin. 'So, what would that be, then?'

'You sap the powers of other Colas.' She stared at him, her face like stone. 'Don't you?'

For several seconds she neither moved, nor spoke,

and then she sat down on the tussocky grass of the slope, hugged her knees, and looked out to sea.

'You're right. That's what I do. I'm a . . . a sort of . . . borrower.'

'A borrower?' Dax said, his voice thick with scorn. 'Well, maybe if you asked first. I don't remember *that* ever happening.'

'Look, you don't have to worry, Dax,' she said lightly. 'It doesn't seem to work with you. Although I'd really like to try a bit harder,' and she actually reached up towards his hand, as if he were her greatest friend. 'C'mon! I won't hurt you!'

He dodged away from her, appalled. 'But you *do* hurt people, Catherine. You're weakening them. You must know that. You snuggle up and you suck the life out of them! Don't tell me you don't know!'

Catherine made a little regretful pout and shrugged. 'It's not permanent—they get better again. I only borrow from them. I wish I *could* make it permanent. Think how strong my powers would be!'

Dax stared at her in disdain. 'And everyone else would be lying face down in the sea!' he muttered. He was later to wish with all his heart that he'd never said that.

Catherine suddenly turned to him, her mouth trembling, and then buried her face in her hands. 'Don't tell on me, Dax!' she said, in a muffled sob. 'Please! People would hate me and I couldn't stand it. Gideon . . . he'd wish he'd never found me.'

Dax looked at her speculatively. 'I'll give you *one*

chance. I want to see everyone back to normal by the end of the week. You've got to keep your hands off them. You understand me?'

She bit her lip and nodded.

'And then I won't tell. Not even Gideon. You promise?'

'What choice do I have?' she said, sniffing. 'You win, Dax Jones.' And she got up and walked away for all the world as if she meant it.

There was no sign of Catherine at teatime that day. Or in the evening in the joint common room. Lisa found Dax at their usual spot by the fire and sat down next to him on the sofa.

'She's in bed,' she said quietly. 'Says she thinks she's coming down with something. Wouldn't let Mia check her over.'

'Good,' said Dax.

'Hmmm,' said Lisa.

'What?'

'It's just a bit too easy, don't you think?'

Dax sighed. 'Not everything has to be difficult! Sometimes things do go easily. Don't they?'

Lisa pursed her lips and stared into the fire. 'I don't trust her as far as I could kick her. I think you should tell Owen.'

But Dax shook his head. After the scene in Owen's study he really did want to tell him, but he'd given his word to Catherine. 'We made a promise. If she starts anything again, *then* we'll tell Owen. And look, she can't be all bad. Remember she is Gideon's sister. I know you think you're picking up something on her—but you're still really angry about what she did and you've never liked her anyway . . . I think it could be that you *want* to be proved right.'

Lisa stared at him coldly. 'What is *that* supposed to mean?'

Dax moved uncomfortably and dug his hands into his pockets. 'Well—she's very, you know, pretty—and has really cool clothes, and . . .'

'You think I'm *jealous*?' demanded Lisa. For a moment, Dax thought she was going to thump him. But she just glared at him and then left the room.

Even falling out with Lisa couldn't damp Dax's joy as he watched Gideon returning to his old self. Catherine kept her promise and for the first few days was barely seen at all, still pretending to be tired out by some kind of bug. When she did emerge again she was still bright and friendly but she had stopped all the physical contact. Once or twice, during mealtimes or in the common room, Dax saw her actively pull herself back from people. Once she noticed him watching and gave him a cool stare. He nodded very slightly at her, impressed that she was sticking to her promise.

The fun began to seep back into their lives. The cacophony of talking, laughing, and shrieking was once more rebounding off the walls of the refectory every mealtime and Mrs Dann was called upon at least twice a day to warn her students not to try anything in class. She was much happier. Gideon was back to being animated and naughty, endlessly concentrating on lifting the big set in the television room, despite complaints from the viewers.

Lisa and Dax resumed eating proper meals with great relief. 'Not that I didn't appreciate our little barbecues,' said Lisa, after she'd got over her earlier huff with him. 'But, oh, that Launceston pie! I've missed that so much! Hey . . . ' she leaned in to him as they edged along the hot food counter waiting to have their plates loaded up, 'I heard that Catherine's scores have gone right down in Development.' Dax smiled and nodded with relief.

'Oi! Daxyboy! You up for a chocolate mercy mission?' Gideon yelled, first thing on Saturday morning, floating a pillow across the room and then dropping it heavily on Dax's head, to wake him up. Dax was so delighted that Gideon was up before him he could have cried.

The May sunshine warmed their backs as they headed to the village through the woods. Dax took a breath and then told his friend all about the hunting. Gideon was amazed.

'You actually *ate* a rabbit? Raw?'

'Well, I didn't coat it in breadcrumbs!'

Gideon stared at him with awe. 'You've got to do it again, when I'm with you!' he breathed, going pink in the face with excitement.

'I don't stand much chance of catching anything with you clodhopping along behind me!' laughed Dax.

Gideon grinned happily, and then looked slightly more sober. 'I'm sorry I left you out a bit for a while there, mate,' he said. 'I think all the long-lost triplets stuff made me a bit weird for a while.'

Dax nodded. 'It's not surprising really. I'd be pretty freaked if it was me.'

'I'm feeling OK now, though,' said Gideon. 'And I think Cath and Luke are OK too. Cath's calmed down a bit. In fact, I think she must have made good friends with someone in her dorm, because she hasn't been hanging round with me quite so much.'

'Good,' said Dax, a little too enthusiastically, because Gideon shot him a look. 'No—I mean—it's good for her, that she's, you know, fitting in,' he added, hastily.

Suddenly a familiar French voice rang out behind them and both boys jumped. 'Gideon Reader! You have been interfering with the laws of physics outside Development! Your weekend pass is cancelled!' Dax and Gideon stared around wildly, wondering where Principal Sartre was. Gideon looked stricken.

'I only levitated the telly a few feet!' he gulped.

There was a gurgling noise off to their left, followed by a shout of high-pitched laughter, and then the Teller brothers shot past them on the woodland path. 'Had you going there, Gid!' chortled Jacob, and Alex just doubled up, cackling.

'You little . . . ' began Gideon, but Dax was already laughing. There was something so funny about the Teller brothers, and it was good to see them back on form.

'Wait,' said Dax. 'Do some more.'

The brothers slowed to a companionable walk with Dax and Gideon and treated them to a whole host of Tregarren characters. Alex was particularly good at Mr Pengalleon. 'Mind out, Barber,' he rasped, in a voice exactly like the weatherbeaten tones of the old gatekeeper. 'That'll be a rabbit poo—not a chocolate drop. Mind out there!'

Jacob began to dance about, clapping his hands and executing a perfect impression of Catherine. So perfect it sent chills up Dax's back. 'Oh, you guys! You are *so* incredible! I just love what you do! Back home we don't have anything like you! If only I was as clever as you, Gideon! Can you just jump in a box and gift wrap yourself?'

Gideon looked abashed and Dax said quickly, 'Do Spook!'

At once Jacob's gushy Catherine face rippled and became the affected, self-impressed mask of Spook Williams, while his walk slowed to a languid lope. He raised his arms and spoke in exactly the right tone: 'Twinkle, twinkle—everybody watch my glittery special effects! Oh—I am so, *so* gorgeous I think I'm going to die! Has anyone got my emergency mirror? I haven't snogged myself for at least five minutes!'

Dax and Gideon laughed so much they had to lean against a tree.

Dax had expected Catherine's new-found reserve to last for a while, and possibly even turn to sulkiness, but he was surprised to see her back on full form within a few days of their confrontation. True, she was still rigidly controlling her physical contact with the other students (oddly, nobody else seemed to notice!) but all her verbal and expressive charm had begun to flood back. It seemed she just couldn't stand not to be the centre of attention, so she had taken measures to keep herself at the top of the social tree.

Dax found her in the post room one morning, putting up an elaborately decorated poster which read:

AMERICAN SUPPER

Come to a May BBQ this Saturday
★ Californian-style! ★

Hotdogs, burgers,
and veggie sausages
on the Sports Field
at 7 p.m.

Volunteers for entertainment required!

★

*Please see Catherine Reader,
Your new Cola Club Social Secretary*

Dax read it and glanced at her. 'You're really reinventing yourself, aren't you?'

Catherine smiled at him, prettily. 'Well—I've got to have some point to my talentless life,' she said lightly. 'And I thought about what you'd said and I decided to give something *back* to all you Colas. If there's one thing I can do without any kind of borrowing, it's make a party! I've got permission from Mrs Sartre and the teachers said they'd help. So—what are you going to do? Help out with the entertainment?'

Dax shook his head, but smiled at her. 'I'm impressed. I think you've handled this really well. I'll help with the barbecue probably. Entertainment's not really my thing. Try Spook,' he added wryly.

'Already signed him up!' said Catherine. 'And some of the other illusionists. And Jennifer Troke is going to sing— and the Teller brothers are working out a whole routine!'

'Should be good,' said Dax and left her to it, marvelling at how well things had turned out.

Down in the subterranean corridors of the Development quarter, Lisa flinched as she filled out her fifteenth Spirit Communication Notice and slid it across the table for Mr Eades to read and sign. 'Stop whining,' she muttered, distractedly. 'I'll get to you!'

Barry woke up sneezing on the morning of the American Supper party. He accused Gideon of floating pillows again and held up four small yellow-white feathers that he'd collected as evidence, but Gideon denied all knowledge and then mentally flung each of the feathers into a corner of the ceiling with a cackle.

'That must have been hard work,' observed Luke, over the top of his book. He took off his glasses and wiped them with the edge of his pyjama jacket. 'It's not Gid, though, Barry. These pillows are full of fluffy foam stuff, not feathers. They must have come in through the window.'

Dax, getting his school jumper on, felt a sudden jolt. That odd déjà vu feeling again. He sat down heavily on his bed and noticed Luke staring at him.

'You all right, Dax?' he said. 'Your eyes just went funny.'

Mr Pengalleon was ambling across the lower end of the sports field watching Barber as he headed for the rock pools of the lido. The dog pounded energetically into the pools, sending up ragged plumes of sandy water, trying to catch a crab and, as usual, failing.

'Go on with yer!' Mr Pengalleon encouraged. 'We'll have crab paste for tea today! Go on, Barber.'

But Barber didn't go on. The dog suddenly stood still and lifted his shaggy snout to the horizon. Mr Pengalleon actually saw the wiry hair rise on the back of his neck. After several seconds frozen in that position Barber suddenly turned and galloped towards his master, taking a jawful of the old man's greatcoat sleeve before he'd even slowed and nearly pulling him over.

'Barber! What in heaven's name is up with you? Give over!'

Barber's teeth sank more firmly into the thick black cloth and a low whining growl began to rumble up from his chest as he tugged and tugged. Only when Mr Pengalleon had allowed himself to be led right back up the field and onto the lower rocky steps did Barber let go. And then he ran back up to the gatehouse, stopping every few steps to turn and check that his master was still following.

When man and dog were back beside the fire, the man felt his hand rest along the receiver of the gatehouse phone and felt he should call the Frenchwoman. To tell her what? That his dog was in a funny mood? Mr Pengalleon settled back to think about it some more, and in doing so, fell into a troubled sleep.

23

Everyone seemed to be in the mood for the party. Whether or not they'd been aware of how low the Catherine effect had brought them, the students now seemed to be throwing extra verve and vitality into their time at Tregarren.

Development scores had really shot up in the past few days. A chart had gone up on the noticeboard outside the assembly hall, showing marked improvements among the telekinetics, the glamourists, and the healers, according to the regular 'psy' tests that they all underwent. The mediums, too, were experiencing much more spirit communication, while the dowsers' abilities to find hidden test objects were, in some cases, measured to pinpoint accuracy. The teachers said it was the improvement in their diet and the minerals and fish oils they'd been consuming.

But it was hard work, however natural to them, along with all their school work, so the Colas were pleased to be doing something just for fun and had wholeheartedly taken to the American theme of the barbecue. Some of the girls had even made up some stars and stripes outfits to wear, while others had agreed to help Mrs Polruth bake some apple pies.

At teatime, having left some sandwiches to see the students through until the supper, Mrs P and her staff wheeled four steel trolleys, containing gas-powered barbecues, up to the sports field. Later, in the warm May sunset, the Colas helped lay out trestle tables and unrolled two dozen rush beach mats around the grass, facing towards a makeshift decking stage where the entertainment would take place. Stout sticks were driven into the ground around the party area, and thick, lemon scented candles mounted on them to light the supper and keep away the midges.

Lisa, Mia, and Gideon worked together at a trestle table, splitting dozens of hotdog rolls and cutting up salad vegetables. 'This is really nice,' sighed Mia, happily. She looked so much better, it was hard to imagine that just a few days ago she had seemed so tired and frail, thought Dax.

He glanced along the table to where Catherine was unwrapping napkins and talking to the Teller brothers about their act. He saw her go to squeeze Alex's shoulder, and then finish with just a light tap before stepping away from him. Good. As long as that was the worst of it, things were still OK. Sooner or later, though, he thought, Gideon would have to know. He was already worried about his sister's development scores and Luke had suggested, with some satisfaction, that maybe he *wasn't* the only dud triplet after all. No—Gideon would have to know. Perhaps Dax could persuade Catherine to tell him herself.

The American Supper BBQ might have gone down as one of the most successful events at Tregarren, if it hadn't been utterly eclipsed by what followed. Catherine did have talent, certainly, even if it was of a more earthly kind. Her way with a crowd was remarkable. She had managed, almost effortlessly it seemed, to pluck the most entertaining Colas out of any reluctance and marshal them into a spirited programme of entertainment.

First the telekinetics worked together on a weird kind of juggling act, each floating a kitchen utensil in carefully choreographed moves, like a bizarre kind of synchronized swimming, only without the water . . . or the swimming. It was amazing to watch and hilarious too, when Gideon shouted '*en garde*' to Peter Foster—one of the others in his group—and the pair began to joust with their mind-powered utensils (Gideon's an egg whisk and Peter's a ladle) in mid-air. The cutlery clashed and clinked and eventually spiralled high into the air like a pair of stainless steel dancers, before landing, upright, on the top of the gym roof. Here the whisk and the ladle bowed, until, released from the grip of the two telekinetics' minds, they fell over sideways.

Everyone roared with laughter and cheered and those without a handful of burger or hotdog to juggle clapped loudly. Next up was Jennifer Troke, who bashfully sat on the edge of the shallow stage with her guitar and began to sing. Her choice of songs was haunting and folky and her voice was mellow and true; it made Mia and the healers shiver as one and Dax felt his throat thicken at the pulse of emotion in the air. Healers simply couldn't contain it.

The Teller brothers followed with a hilarious routine of mimicry which ranged from Paulina Sartre (who smiled and laughed indulgently from the folding chairs where the teachers and staff were watching, behind the Cola's rush mat seating) to Spook, Gideon, Mr Eades, and even Barber the dog.

'Where is Barber?' Dax asked Lisa as she laughed long and hard next to him. 'And Mr Pengalleon. I would have thought they'd be here.'

Lisa clapped wildly as the brothers finished their act with silly, scraping bows. 'Don't know,' she said, vaguely. Then her fevered clapping slowed and then halted, although everyone else was still applauding around her, and shouting 'More!' while Jacob and Alex backed off the stage, still bowing to their feet. Dax felt, rather than saw, the coolness rush into her. When he looked round, Lisa was rubbing her left shoulder and staring into the middle distance.

'Blimey, can't you tell them you've got a night off!' sympathized Dax, realizing that the spirits were tapping on the little sliding window hatch he often pictured Lisa hiding behind, demanding she take their messages like a postmistress on their payroll. Lisa shook her head, as if trying to clear it. Then she stood up.

'Make them wait!' said Dax. 'The illusionists are starting! I need you to tell me what I'm missing.'

But Lisa was moving away. 'I won't be long,' she said, lightly. 'I just want to check something.'

Dax felt frustrated but not bothered. It happened all the time. He didn't envy Lisa or the other mediums. He couldn't imagine anything worse than having anyone and everyone from the hereafter queuing up to use your head as a kind of inter-world portal. He shifted over to Gideon, back from his act, and leaned an elbow on his best friend's shoulder, so that he might get a faint echo of the show the illusionists were starting. He had managed to get a vague idea of their firework display last November by doing this. Gideon would usually give him a quiet running commentary.

Despite the fact that Spook was once again leading the show (Dax had to admit, reluctantly, that the boy clearly *must* be the most talented of the illusionists) Gideon seemed to enjoy it hugely. In deference to the American theme that Catherine had set, the illusionists had staged a Mardi Gras style parade, featuring all kinds of American film stars, cartoon heroes, and historical figures. Catherine screamed with delight and jumped up and down as she watched and everyone applauded and laughed still more. Glancing around, Dax could see the enjoyment on the Colas' flushed faces; the teachers, too, looked relaxed and tickled.

As the show wound up and the performers all trooped onto the stage, Spook gallantly stepped forward and held out his hand. 'Ladies and gentleman,' he called, in his best showbusiness voice, 'a hand please, for our Cola Club Social Secretary and director of tonight's event— Catherine Reader!'

The applause continued warmly as Catherine took his hand and stepped up on to the stage. *Let it go now*, thought Dax, with a twinge of concern. But it didn't trouble him too much that Catherine didn't, right then. It would probably have looked very odd if she'd shaken Spook off as he led her into a bow.

'Everyone! I want you to join me in a song!' called out Catherine, her voice bubbling with fun. 'You know Beatles stuff—right?' The teachers guffawed behind them and several Colas yelled out 'Ye-ess!' in mock sarcasm. 'OK—I guessed you probably *would*!' giggled Catherine, inclining her head prettily. 'Jennifer! Would you mind . . . ?'

Jennifer smiled, brought out her guitar again, and then began to loudly strum the opening bars of 'All You Need Is Love'. At any other time, thought Dax, most of the Colas would have groaned and made sick-making noises at something like that—even if it *was* a Beatles hit. But not tonight. They were well and full of humour and the warmth of being in what was possibly the world's most exclusive gang. They started singing 'Love—love—love . . . ' with gusto—even Owen and Mrs Dann were joining in, raising their plastic tumblers and swaying them in the air.

Dax grinned and decided to join in, but before he got past the 'Nothing you can do' line he was silenced by a call—a sharp and frightened call—slicing through his mind like a cold blade. It was Lisa. And she was scared. Very, very scared. Dax shifted to a fox before he'd even formed the thought and he shot through the crowd and lost himself behind the light of the candles and the dim glow from the cooling barbecues.

Lisa! What is it? Where are you? He sniffed the air, trying for her scent, but couldn't pick it up. Either she was too far away or all the scents swirling around him from the barbecue and the excited crowd of Colas was making it impossible. Dax listened hard—he was picking up something, but he couldn't tell *what*. Fear—panic even. Something about—*Barber*? Maybe . . . maybe not. He was about to turn and run up to the gatehouse to check when he was distracted by something he saw back on the school field. In the time it had taken him to shift, run, crouch down and try to connect with Lisa, the singing had advanced only a few bars and the crowd was now on its collective feet, swaying and laughing as it sang. It was the *shape* of the crowd that bothered Dax. It was widening into an arc—no—a circle. The Colas, swept along on good feeling, were following instructions from the stage and linking hands. Low down now and half hidden in the wiry grass at the edge of the field, Dax couldn't see who was inducing them to form the circle, but the knowledge fell upon him like a block of cold concrete. Suddenly, sickeningly, he knew. Catherine had given something back to the Colas. Now she was on the take again.

He crouched and readied himself, preparing to shoot through a gap in the ring and bring the triplet down with his teeth if necessary. She couldn't be allowed to take advantage like this! It was—it was—*indecent*!

Dax!!! He froze, checking his leap. *Dax!!! Take it to the wing! Oh, now, Dax. Now!!!*

He shook his snout in panicked frustration. He *still* didn't know what that meant! He could feel the fear from Lisa coursing through his own veins, but it was running parallel with his own fear now—and his own fear was the only one he could act on.

He crouched again, seeking the gap—but even as he found it there was a hot paranormal punch in the air; a silent crash that made his sensitive inner ear machinery spasm. Dax could hardly believe what he was seeing. All around him, Colas were falling senseless to the ground.

24

Gideon's brow struck a small lump of granite as he keeled into the earth, his eyes filmy and half closed and his mouth working slightly, as if he were trying to speak. Dax was at his side in less than two seconds, instinctively remaining a fox because he realized the brutal reaping of energy wouldn't reach him that way. He could smell the mistletoe sister at the far end of the field, moving away fast, but he couldn't give chase until he knew how his friend was.

Urgently he pushed at Gideon's cheek with his snout and pawed at his chest, but the boy did not rouse. In an eerie, but much worse, reprise of that morning in the dorm, Gideon seemed to be pinned down beneath a sea of unconsciousness. But he was breathing! He was alive! Dax leapt over Gideon's chest, treading lightly on Alex Teller's back—the boy was face down and holding his big brother's ankle. Jacob was curled up like a baby, his eyes closed. Dax sniffed quickly, caught his exhalation and felt a tiny lift of relief. They were not dead. Mia, too, breathed shallowly, and murmured as if sleeptalking, and her eyes, narrowed to a slit, looked white.

Dax became aware that the teachers, perhaps less stunned, were coming to. Most of them had not been part of the linked chain enjoying the song about love being all you needed. Wasn't enough for *her*! his mind spat, while fury began to scream in his animal mind. Dax shot across the field, following the scent of her, which was all adrenalin and sweat and triumph and . . . an almost singed electric smell of *power*. He groaned. How long could she hold on to it? Long enough to do him some serious damage, he guessed, as he leapt the fence on the edge of the field. Once again Dax reminded himself that he was *not* a superhero. Unlike Gideon, Barry, even Spook, he didn't have the kind of power that offered much protection in the face of someone as well-armed as Catherine must now be. He caught the top of the fence, paused, swaying, on the wooden support strut and tried to work out what to do. Getting himself swatted like a fly wouldn't help anyone. Perhaps he should run to Owen, who was even now turning over Colas, checking their breathing and barking orders to the rest of the dazed staff.

Then he heard Lisa. *Actually* heard her—through his sharp fox ears. 'Dax! Dax! Help! Oh, help me! I'm in our cave—help me!' She sounded weak, desperate—completely unlike her normal self and that shocked him badly. He didn't waste one more second weighing up his odds. His friend was in danger.

He skidded down the craggy slope and along the dark ribbon of shingle that wound between the rocks, thankful that the tide was only halfway in and he could take the flatter route. The mouth of the cave glowed with firelight. What was Lisa doing down here? He thought she'd gone to the gatehouse.

Lisa! he called in his mind. *What's happening?* Her reply was odd—far away. *Oh no, Dax! It's* . . . there was a roaring sound and then something he couldn't make out . . . it sounded like *incoming!*

The second his forepaws landed on the sandy carpet of the cave the smell hit him like a hammer. Catherine was here, reeking with triumph and excitement. But not Lisa. He couldn't smell Lisa. The fox turned in a wary circle, its tail flat and its snout high.

Then Lisa called, loudly, from the very far end of the cave. 'Help me, Dax! I'm stuck back here! Oh please! I'm scared—help me!'

He fled through the cave and ran up over the boulder pathway to its deepest recess. Confusion and fear hummed in his head. His senses would not agree. He could hear her but nothing else spoke of her. It was just the *sound* . . . Realization hit him too late. An image of Jacob and Alex Teller flashed in his mind—then Catherine, reaching and touching Alex's shoulder. The fox gave a feral scream of frustration at its own stupidity and then there was a thrumming whine, like a jet passing low overhead and something metallic struck the rock behind him, before he'd had a chance to curl around in the tight turning space of the cave's end. A thick metal grille, still warm from the barbecue, was rammed up against him; his right flank flared with pain where the grille's lower end had struck.

Glancing urgently around it, Dax realized that it

wasn't just *propped* against the rock, blocking his path—it was *embedded in it*. The metal corners of the grille had been driven three or four inches deep inside the granite and a fine powder of displaced rock was turning in the air in front of it. He flung his fox body against it, but the grille didn't even rattle. Not that he could get much of a run up to it; he barely had the space to turn around and a sick dread was rising in his stomach as he realized how carefully planned this had been.

Through the falling powder of granite dust, between the criss-cross weave of his metal prison, Dax saw her. She appeared to be dancing. She was twirling and skipping and raising her arms above her head like a ballet dancer. Then she stopped and turned her head over her shoulder to look at him. She was smiling like a naughty child and her green eyes glittered between the swinging dark gloss of her hair.

'Oh, that was so *easy*, Dax!' she giggled. 'I can't believe how easy that was!'

Dax realized he was growling. He wanted to ask her why she was doing this—to try to shame her into stopping—but, of course, he couldn't unless he shifted back into a boy, and once again, there just wasn't space to. He hurled himself at the grille a second time, but it didn't shift even slightly.

'Don't get yourself so worked up, Dax!' sighed Catherine, coming closer with a truly lovely smile. 'It won't make any difference! The sea will come in soon, anyway, so it'll all be over!'

Clearly she wasn't aware that the tide didn't come up this far, thought Dax, but he felt sick with the realization that Catherine had turned out to be so callous—so—*evil*. Was this her revenge on him, for stopping her 'borrowing'?

'I bet you're wondering what all this is about, huh?' asked the triplet, kneeling down in front of his cage, so she could peer in at him.

'Well—you know we had our little chat about me borrowing powers from the other Colas—and you said I had to stop. It wasn't nice of you, Daxy boy, to make me do that. It made little Cathy real sad! I went all sad and droopy for a while,' she said, in a nauseating little girl voice. 'But then I had a think. You know, when I was borrowing Spook's power, or Gideon's or Mia's, I could keep it for quite a long time. It was only when I *saw* them again, that it all left me. It wants to go back, you see, Dax. It knows it doesn't belong to me, so it's always trying to go back.

'But!' She pressed her face even closer to the grille and he could see her eyes sparkling malevolently. 'But! But! But! What if it *couldn't* go back—because it had no little Colas to go back to? *Then* I'd get to keep it for ever. All of it!'

Dax crouched back on the floor, hoping that he wasn't really getting this. Hoping that the horrible, cold understanding in him was all wrong.

'You don't have to look at me like *that*!' she suddenly snapped. Then she took a little deep breath, sucked her thumb, and hummed a few notes of 'All You Need Is Love'. *She's mad*, thought Dax. *She is really mad.*

Catherine stopped humming, withdrew her thumb, and took a deep breath, straightening her back and lifting her chin proudly. 'So—I fixed it all up! A way to get as much from everybody as I could—and then—and then—get *rid* of them and their selfishness. Y'know, Dax, it's all "I wannit back! I wannit back!" ' she chanted. 'Well, what about ME?' She jumped up, her nostrils flaring with rage. 'What about ME? Why should *I* be the only one to miss out? Well? Why should I? I deserve to be a proper Cola just like the rest of you! It's not *fair* that I get left out! Don't you see?! I DEE—ZERVE IT!'

At this a few rocks shot violently across the cave floor and smashed into each other, shattering and blasting shards of granite and serpentine in all directions. It seemed to calm Catherine slightly. She smiled and raised one eyebrow. 'Good, aren't I?' she murmured.

'Anyway—I got everyone's power. And I must say, Jacob's and Alex's was brilliant for getting you down here!' She dropped perfectly into Lisa's voice: ' "Dax! Oh, Dax! *Save* me!" Oh yeah, I knew *you* wouldn't play my game—you never do! Shame. I wanted to turn into a cat. I would've liked that. I could try to get some of it now, but—no—you're too dangerous to let out, and . . .' she pointed her fingers towards the grille as if to poke through, and then withdrew them with a giggle, ' . . . I have this feeling you would *bite*! So I guess I won't get to be a shapeshifter, but, hey . . . I'm a healer, a medium, a psychic, a mimic, a telekinetic, a dowser ... um ... oh, and a glamourist and an illusionist.' She chuckled. 'Mustn't be greedy!'

She began to walk away down the cave, humming. Dax threw himself against the grille again, with another feral shriek.

'You can't get out, Dax, forget it,' she called back. 'I worked it all out, y'know! You underestimated me, little fox. There's nobody to run and warn those poor Colas. Lisa's locked in the gatehouse, Mia's a total wipe-out, and Gideon—well, he's a dried-up husk now. Shame, but it can't be helped. He got our dad, didn't he? While I got kids' homes. Now it's his turn to lose out. He'll be gone soon. They all will. They're all just empty containers now anyway. No good to anyone now. So I'll clean them up. I'll wash them away, then I'll be the only Cola left on earth. And everyone will know me! Bye bye, Dax.'

She stepped around the fire, and then skipped out of the cave.

A panic attack tried for him. It smacked into the base of his spine and tried to climb to his heart and throat but Dax swatted it down with barely a thought and it kicked once and subsided. This was no time for self-indulgence. He had to think—he had to *send* to Lisa. She might be locked in the gatehouse, but her mind was still accessible. Dax sent *LISA! LISA! LISA! It's Catherine— she's mad! She's going to try to kill everyone! Tell Owen! Get to Owen!* But all that came back to him was a roar. A huge, deafening, rumbling roar and a terrible, desperate cry from Lisa. One word: *INCOMING!* He felt something of her struggle too—she was beating at something, hacking atsomething. The door of the gatehouse? He thought so.

He had never felt so helpless and so angry with himself. He should have done what Lisa said. He should have told Owen. If everyone died it would be his fault.

The fire flickered. Dax lifted his shaking snout and saw the wolf, moving like a shadow towards him. It seemed to be in no hurry but its eyes, silver discs of intelligence, connected with his firmly. As if for the last time. *Take*, it said, clearly, *it—to—the—wing!*

Dax felt his fur melt away. He was amazed that he could feel foolish and elated at the same time, but he didn't have even a second to dwell on it. With a sound like taps turned on to their fullest in his ears, he shifted, not back to a boy, trapped and dying in the earth, but to a bird. As the wolf faded away DaxFalcon compressed his unused feathers and slid through the nearest square between the metal bars. He was free. He spread his new wings for the first time, trying to contain his wonder at the width of his vision and the grander scale of the cave—the luxurious pull of brand-new avian muscles—later! If there was a later. Dax made a new sound: *Screeeee-screeeee-screeee!* Then he shot out through the mouth of the cave and soared high into the turbulent sea air, his talons flexing.

25

Confusion filled the field. Teachers and kitchen staff were stumbling among the Colas, desperately trying to rouse them, and one or two of the students were being lifted onto makeshift stretchers. Mrs Dann was crying and shaking Jessica Moorland. But a handful of Colas were beginning to wake up, Dax saw, high above them as he wheeled in the air, seeking out Owen below. Luke was on his feet, staring around in bewilderment and Spook Williams was up on his knees, rubbing his head.

Dax saw Owen, crouched over Gideon, and he flipped himself into the shape of a downward arrow and plummeted towards him. He turned talon-down in a split second before impact and felt his sharp feet bite into Owen's shoulder.

'God alive!' shouted Owen, and made to slap at his avian attacker, but something just stayed his hand and Dax flapped up and away to the ground in front of him. He was at such screaming pitch urgency he found he *couldn't* shift again—like the day of the foxhunt. Instead he rose up into the air in front of Owen's startled face and let out a high-pitched falcon cry: *Screee! Screee! Screee!*

'Dax?!' gasped Owen and at the sound of his name, something clicked and Dax found himself staggering, heavy and human, on the grass, his heart still clattering in his chest at birdspeed.

'Catherine! It's Catherine! She's going to get them all!' he shouted. 'Where is she?'

Owen stared at him for a second and then looked wildly around. 'I don't *know*, Dax! What do you know about all this? What's going to happen?'

Dax felt helpless again. All he could think to say was 'Incoming! Something is incoming! Lisa knows—but she's trapped in the gatehouse!'

Dax felt a hand pull urgently at his shoulder and turned to face Luke, whose spectacles were reflecting the pale moonlight. 'Look!' Luke pointed up. High on the cliff above them, crouched on a little rocky shelf, was Catherine. Her arms were wrapped around her knees and she seemed to be rocking and singing and her eyes were fixed, staring out to sea.

'Catherine!' shouted Owen, but she didn't break her gaze for a moment. Dax jumped high into the air, and was in flight before he could think about it. He knew he had to break her stare. She was bringing something awful to them. Something *incoming*. He curved around and up in flight, careful not to come at her head-on, where she would have a better chance to attack him. To drop from above would be best. Dax rose and rose, beyond the top of the cliffs, higher than his wood, and then inverted his incredible new body into that downward arrow and fell, locking his sight on the crown of Catherine's head. The world around him became a streaked blur of colour and with less than a second before impact he brought round his razor sharp talons.

He struck her hard; a satisfying shockwave juddering through him and the scent of her blood in the air in an instant—but she had raised her arm in that last second and managed to offset his strike just enough to keep her hold on the shelf of rock. She screamed with frustration as she was forced to break her stare for a second and then swiped at him with telekinetic energy, smacking his light body hard into the rocks. For a second his world tipped and his head hung over the edge of a clump of cliff-clinging moss, several feet below her. As his vision cleared he could see more Colas waking up, getting unsteadily to their feet. Some crying, some groaning; all weak and vulnerable. He rolled and found his wings and feet—bruised but not broken—and saw Catherine still rocking and staring. A strange sucking wind seemed to be pulling down over the cliff and out to sea, dragging her hair over her face. It was warm and eerie. Dax followed her line of sight and almost lost his footing with shock.

Out at sea, the horizon was no longer flat. It was puckering and pinching upwards, like a fold of dark cloth. The sea was being twisted into the air in a huge, curling, agonizing funnel. It seemed unsteady at first, weaving and buckling and almost falling back into itself, as if only reluctantly manipulated by the all-powerful New Cola on the cliff. *She means to wash us away . . . like she said . . .* thought Dax. He now understood what Lisa meant by *Incoming*.

With another screech, Dax threw himself up into the air and tried again to attack Catherine. His fury screamed for more blood; he would drag her scalp off her head if he had to—he would take out her eyes without a second's thought. But he was less than a foot from her this time before she blasted him high up into the air again, leaving him spinning out of control and then plummeting, wings wild and lost, towards the ground.

DAX! INCOMING! YOU'VE GOT TO GET THEM UP!!! Lisa bellowed in his head, breaking his stupor and giving him three seconds' start on the ground as it hurtled to meet him. Dax landed heavily and had shifted before he stopped rolling. He stumbled to Owen and shook his shoulder. 'LOOK!' he screamed, pointing out to sea. 'LOOK! *INCOMING!* GET THEM UP!!!'

Owen's mouth dropped open and then he began to shout at the top of his voice and the panic—the vital panic—tore around the confused crowd like a gunpowder flame. At once there were screams—healthy *awake* screams—and the Colas began to run, the staff with them, looking with horror over their shoulders and pushing each other on.

Dax shifted again and shot back up into the sky. The weird toppling and buckling of the seaspout had steadied and now it was bearing down on them with much more purpose. Dax thought they had maybe ten seconds. He scanned below; saw Gideon staring out to sea in disbelief and then plummeted down, striking his friend across the cheek with one talon. Gideon shouted with pain, clapping his hand to the line of dark red, but it seemed to work because he turned and fled with the others.

It's not enough! It's not enough! Dax's ten seconds were now five and the water was rumbling and thundering towards them like something set free from hell. Catherine was standing now and her arms were outstretched and she was laughing, the wind whipping the hair around her head. Dax could hardly bear to look down. In three seconds everyone he loved would be dashed away like driftwood. He shot for Catherine's eyes this time, but even as he did so her face crumpled and her stare shifted down and she let out a piercing scream of fury.

Dax turned in the air, inches before impact, and swiftly surveyed the ground. Maybe Paulina Sartre had been able to beat her. But no, the principal was propelling Mia and Jennifer up the path ahead of her and then turning to run back and pull up more of the terrified children. Dax thought she might not even be able to see Catherine.

Just one student remained back on the field, motionless and staring out to sea. There was no shock in his face and as Dax swooped down to see, he realized how totally, totally wrong they had all been about this one. The dud.

The sea hung over him, a huge tornado of saltwater, rock, and weed, more than two hundred feet high and spinning in the air. It did not drop and it did not recede. It paused.

Luke's eyes were opaque with the strain. His mouth

hung open and his breathing was shallow. His fists were clenched at his sides, fractured spectacles clamped inside one, and a trickle of blood ran from one nostril. Dax felt a wave of guilt and misery. He had never given Luke credit. He had never even guessed there might be more going on with him. Now he remembered Luke staring into the dark, down on the couch after the windows had shattered in the dorm. He had thought poor, ordinary Luke was bothered by all the weird stuff going on around him, but now he knew that hadn't been it. Luke hadn't been bothered—he'd been terrified. He must have known what was in him, so powerful it escaped from him even— and only—in dreams. He was intelligent enough to know how dangerous it was if he couldn't keep it inside and how he must have fought, in every Development session, to keep it hidden. That he had managed that, in the face of every other Cola's intuition and all their tests, demonstrated how incredibly strong he must be.

But now . . . ? What was it doing to him now? Luke continued to stare at the towering shelf of water and the blood continued to trickle down his lip, following its slackened curve and dripping from his chin. *What is that doing to his head?* Dax thought, hovering over the boy and wishing desperately that he could help. Behind him the Colas were gaining the higher ground and Dax thought that maybe Luke could stop now. But . . . but if he did . . .

Luke's head suddenly jerked back and his eyes snapped back to full clarity. Catherine was behind him and had him by the hair, her fingers knotted viciously into it, yanking his head back again and again. She was shrieking with every yank. 'You cheat! You cheat! You dirty little cheat!' Luke reached behind him and weakly tried to push her away, keeping his face up to the threat above them, but she pulled him backwards, and down on top of her, still viciously tearing at his hair and bellowing at his audacity. Luke only looked a little puzzled and then his eyes shifted focus, first to the falcon hovering above him and then to something behind the falcon.

'Go on now, Dax,' he said, with the faintest wry smile, and Dax shot up through what felt like heavy rain. How he managed to avoid it, he never really knew. But in three seconds he was eighty metres up and had a bird's-eye view of the worst thing he had ever seen. For a moment Tregarren College lay below him in perfect clarity; all well-designed, straight-lined buildings, winking glass, formal pond and fountain, grassy slopes and fairy-lit walkways. It seemed to smile sadly up at him; this place where he'd found such happiness.

A moment later it was gone. Endless torrents of plummeting green-black water and plumes of white foam were thundering in all directions and only ragged chunks of glass, steel, and masonry occasionally thrown up by its assault gave any clue to what had existed beneath. The roaring and rumbling drowned everything and then a funnel of cold, displaced air shot up, turning Dax over and over in its passage until he could no longer know which was sky and which was sea and which was cliff and which was soil and, now, no longer wished to try.

26

IN and out the dusty windows, in and out the dusty windows, in and out the dusty windows of my lady's chamber.

The low, slightly breathy, girl's voice paused, before taking a light inhalation and then singing the nursery rhyme line again. Dax saw himself, going in and out, in and out of little square windows. The dream again—but clearer this time. The windows weren't windows at all, but the gaps between the grille in the cave, and he wasn't 'going' so much as flying. Awful dream, though, this latest one. Dax rolled over, reaching for his quilt which must have fallen off, leaving him shivering and aching. His hand met only something dry and twiggy and now he could smell it, too. Dax's eyes sprang open and he saw dark crumbling wood inches from his nose. He glanced sideways and realized quickly where he was—in a hollow under a fallen tree in his favourite part of the wood above the college. The morning sun was warming his right shoulder, which lay beyond the shade of his shelter and he could hear the low crooning of wood pigeons and the distant sigh of the sea.

There was no sudden crack of realization. The knowledge of what was real rose up gradually around him like damp. He didn't try to jump to his feet and run to the gatehouse to find out who had lived and who had died. For one thing, he had nothing left for that journey, and for another, as long as he lay here and didn't *know*, all might be well. They might all have been saved. Then he remembered Luke as he lay, surprised, on his back, smiling gently and saying, 'Go on now, Dax,' before allowing a million gallons of seawater to fall.

Dax closed his eyes. The girl began singing again. *In and out the dusty . . . oh, hang on. I'm getting it now. Sorry about the singing, it was the only thing I could think of when I saw it. Yeeesh! I'll be acting like a healer next!* Lisa! It was Lisa. She was dowsing for him, he was quite certain. And up until now all she'd found was his weird dreamscape, which didn't give her much hope of finding him. In spite of everything, Dax smiled and laughed, even though it hurt his ribs a little. *I'm in the wood, Lisa,* he sent. *I know!* she said. *You don't have to give me any clues. Let me show off a bit. Owen and Gideon are coming. Don't move, in case you're all busted up or something.* Dax grinned again. She had a great bedside manner. *Are you all right? Is . . . everyone else?* he sent, scared though he was of her answer.

The college is a war zone. Hardly anything left. Government types arriving. The Colas are gibbering wrecks and I'm sure I saw Spook pat Gideon's shoulder a while ago—and that was scary. We all thought he was dead, you see, for a while. My fault. Picked up something that wasn't actually true. Well, not exactly . . . Look—I have to go. Loads of sending for loads of people and—and a bit more finding. They're nearly there with you. I'll see you soon.

Even as she cut off from him, he heard footfalls thudding through the trees. Gideon and Owen doubled their speed with a shout when they saw him and skidded to their knees in the leaf litter, anxiously peering at him. Dax waved a tired hand and Gideon grabbed hold of it and squeezed it hard. He said nothing, but his eyes were wet and his shoulders hitched once.

'Anything broken, d'you think, Dax?' asked Owen, who was pulling open his backpack.

Dax shook his head. 'No,' he said. 'I'm just . . . so . . . tired.'

Owen pulled a carton of juice out of the bag and pierced it quickly with a straw. 'Drink,' he said and Dax did so, gulping down the sweet blackcurrant drink. It poured through him like liquid healing and almost immediately he was able to slide out from under the log and sit up.

'How many dead?' he asked, dragging the twigs and leaves out of his hair and not able to look at either of them.

'We don't know for sure,' said Owen, checking him over for any injuries. 'At least two missing though. We did think we might have lost *you*—but Lisa insisted you were just having a bit of kip somewhere. Lazing around.'

Dax laughed mirthlessly and looked at Gideon. 'And the missing?' he asked.

Gideon gave a sort of shaky smile. 'Luke,' he said. 'And Catherine.'

* * *

Lisa, it turned out, had gone straight up to the gatehouse and found Mr Pengalleon asleep in his chair, while Barber was going almost crazy, trying to wake him. He seemed to have been emptied of all energy and consciousness. She had realized immediately that it was Catherine's work but as soon as she had turned back to the inner door to get help it had slammed shut with supernatural force and held fast—as had the windows. She had urgently tried to get into the girl's head—but all she could get was the deafening noise and that word 'incoming'. The only other thing that pounded through from the hereafter at that point was the wolf and his strange command 'Take it to the wing'.

It had taken Lisa sixty seconds to find an axe in Mr Pengalleon's old store cellar under the floor (she had dowsed it quite quickly), but hacking through the barricaded door had taken longer. In fact she only broke it ten seconds before the sea fell.

The Colas had made it far enough up the cliff to escape the violent wash, which had mostly hit the lower campus, destroying everything. The surging mass of water had lapped within three feet of Owen as he'd shoved the Teller brothers to safety and many of them got drenched with spray and peppered with shingle. Amazingly, the staff cottages in the cliffside were left bone dry and undamaged and were now hosting a few remaining dazed Colas; those that could walk and talk had already been helped out into the large turning area in front of the gatehouse, where two luxury coaches were parked. Inside they sat or lay, wrapped in blankets, some silent and some talking quietly. At least twenty people Dax didn't recognize, but whom he guessed must be government agents, were interviewing the Colas one by one, using three sleek-looking vans, with mirrored windows, as makeshift offices, while the catering staff, shaken but determined, had fetched food and flasks of hot tea from the village. Further down the lane towards the village Dax noticed the road had been closed off and local police and ambulances were stationed there. A helicopter flew overhead—army, not media.

Dax himself was interviewed by Owen and the agent known as Chambers, an athletically built man with close-cropped dark hair and expensive rimless glasses who continually clicked his ballpoint pen in and out while they talked. Owen indicated that he could speak freely. 'Chambers here has seen some pretty weird stuff in his time, too, Dax,' he told him. 'He knows about you—although not about your latest incarnation.'

He told them everything, beginning with his realization that Catherine was the mistletoe among them. He told it flat; no dramas, no frills, and no excuses. 'Lisa said I should tell you,' he said, looking sadly at Owen. 'I should have. If I *had*, Luke might still be alive.'

'We don't know that he's dead,' said Owen, gently, but Dax saw Luke's faint smile again, heard his last words, and he put his hand over his eyes. 'Besides,' said Owen, 'the Catherine you've described to me would never have stopped until she'd found a way to get what she wanted.

If she managed to get past you—and Lisa—with what she was planning, she would have got past me too. Maybe even Mrs Sartre. Dax,' he leaned across and touched his shoulder, 'if you hadn't done what you did—got us all moving and attacked Catherine when you did, we might never have survived, even *with* Luke's sudden . . . amazing . . . ' He tailed off. 'If it helps,' he said, 'I feel pretty shabby that I didn't spend more time with him; didn't try to work out what was happening in his head.'

Chambers suddenly stopped clicking, laid down his pen and sat on the third chair in the little interview room. 'When you two have stopped beating yourselves up,' he said, drily, 'I'd like to know a bit more about what it's like to fly.' He peered intently at Dax and, inexplicably, they all burst out laughing.

The Government's best moved fast. Preparations to return the Colas home that very day were already being made and plans for a new base for their education were being discussed at Whitehall level while Gideon and Dax were wandering back into the woods, given a nod from Owen as they approached the security perimeter. 'They'll be back,' he told the anxious-looking soldier patrolling it.

In the late afternoon, shafts of green gold sun hung in the air and the birds and insects cheeped and buzzed as if everything was normal. Quietly, slowly, Dax told Gideon everything he'd told Owen. How his pretty, funny, cuddly sister from America had planned so carefully to kill them all. And how his quiet, unassuming, slightly dull brother from the Isle of Wight had struggled so incredibly to save them all. Gideon nodded when Dax finished his story. 'I'm so sorry, Gid,' he said and the look on his friend's face made him cry.

'Don't be,' said Gideon, getting up and pulling Dax up beside him. 'We don't know how it ends.'

And we don't. Anything can change an ending. For example, at the end of that shocked, quiet day, with their files filled in and their security lines unbroken, and everybody that could be vouched for, Owen and his team of agents expected to load the Colas on the coach and send them all home.

He expected no resistance. No belongings had been found; they and any other remains would probably drift to shore in the coming weeks, so there was nothing to pack. Dax and Gideon were the last to get on to the second coach. Each Cola carried a letter to their families and a note for themselves on how they were expected to behave and what they were meant to do for the next few weeks while the new college was found. Dax folded his, tucked it into his back pocket, roughly mussed Gideon's hair, and pushed him down in his seat.

'Are you really going to do it?' asked Gideon, his eyes shining with fascination for the first time that day. It did Dax good to see it.

'Yep,' he grinned. 'You might have to cause a distraction—but I reckon you won't. I'll come to see you soon. I want to know you'll be OK.'

Gideon flicked his bit of paper. 'Not if you stick to these rules,' he said, but a slow grin was breaking over his pale face. Dax grinned back and turned round.

'Where are you going, Dax? The coach is just about to leave!' said Owen, as Dax hopped off the step by the driver and back onto the road.

'I forgot something,' said Dax, with a smile.

'What?' said Owen.

'It's quicker by air.'

And he shifted and soared up into the clouds before Owen could say another word. As he rose and rose, torn air pummelling the grey, white, and yellow feathers on his aerodynamic frame, Dax felt the most extraordinary elation. The sky was blue and teased with cloud, and the curve of the earth fell away below him, releasing him.

He flew a wide circle around the rocky jut of wasteland which had once been Tregarren College, setting his internal compass. Then he directed his curved beak to the north-east and flew, while the world below him turned and people tried to guess the ending.

ACKNOWLEDGEMENTS

With thanks to Andy Hinton and Mike Riley at the Hawk Conservancy Trust in Weyhill, Hampshire, for invaluable information. Also to Highcliffe Beach, Steephill Cove, and The Lizard—for being there.

ALI SPARKES

Ali Sparkes was a journalist and BBC broadcaster until she chucked in the safe job to go dangerously freelance and try her hand at writing comedy scripts. Her first venture was as a comedy columnist on *Woman's Hour* and later on *Home Truths*. Not long after, she discovered her real love was writing children's fiction.

Ali grew up adoring adventure stories about kids who mess about in the woods and still likes to mess about in the woods herself whenever possible. She lives with her husband and two sons in Southampton, England.

READY FOR MORE?

GOING TO GROUND,

OUT NOW!

THE SHAPESHIFTER

GOING TO GROUND

Dax Jones is on the run

WINNER OF THE BLUE PETER BOOK OF THE YEAR

ALI SPARKES

HAVE YOU READ THEM ALL?

THE SHAPESHIFTER